PUFFIN

DUNGEONS
OF DARKNESS

V. M. Jones lives in Christchurch, New Zealand, with her husband and two sons. Her previous novels are *Buddy*, which won the Junior Fiction and Best First Book Awards in the 2003 New Zealand Post Children's Book Awards, *Juggling with Mandarins*, winner of the 2004 Junior Fiction Award, and *The Serpents of Arakesh*, the first book in The Karazan Quartet, shortlisted for both the 2004 New Zealand Post Junior Fiction Award and the 2004 LIANZA Esther Glen Medal. *Dungeons of Darkness* is the second book in The Karazan Quartet.

karazan.co.uk

Books by V. M. Jones

THE SERPENTS OF ARAKESH
DUNGEONS OF DARKNESS

Coming in September 2006

THE LOST PRINCE
QUEST FOR THE SUN

DUNGEONS OF DARKNESS

KARAZAN
The Second

V. M. JONES

PUFFIN

PUFFIN BOOKS

Published by the Penguin Group
Penguin Books Ltd, 80 Strand, London WC2R 0RL, England
Penguin Group (USA) Inc., 375 Hudson Street, New York, New York 10014, USA
Penguin Group (Canada), 90 Eglinton Avenue East, Suite 700, Toronto, Ontario, Canada M4P 2Y3
(a division of Pearson Penguin Canada Inc.)
Penguin Ireland, 25 St Stephen's Green, Dublin 2, Ireland (a division of Penguin Books Ltd)
Penguin Group (Australia), 250 Camberwell Road, Camberwell, Victoria 3124, Australia
(a division of Pearson Australia Group Pty Ltd)
Penguin Books India Pvt Ltd, 11 Community Centre, Panchsheel Park, New Delhi – 110 017, India
Penguin Group (NZ), cnr Airborne and Rosedale Roads, Albany, Auckland 1310, New Zealand
(a division of Pearson New Zealand Ltd)
Penguin Books (South Africa) (Pty) Ltd, 24 Sturdee Avenue, Rosebank, Johannesburg 2196, South Africa

Penguin Books Ltd, Registered Offices: 80 Strand, London WC2R 0RL, England

www.penguin.com

First published in New Zealand by HarperCollins Publishers (New Zealand) Ltd 2004
First published in Great Britain in Puffin Books 2006
1

Set in 11.5/15 pt Monotype Plantin
Typeset by Rowland Phototypesetting Ltd, Bury St Edmunds, Suffolk
Made and printed in England by Clays Ltd, St Ives plc

British Library Cataloguing in Publication Data
A CIP catalogue record for this book is available from the British Library

ISBN-13: 978-0-141-31943-8
ISBN-10: 0-141-31943-7

To Tiger Lily, my companion and inspiration, with me on the journey every step of the way

CONTENTS

PROLOGUE

The little cream cat crouched in the warm sunshine, her golden eyes fixed unblinkingly on the bare stone floor in front of her. She was absolutely still except for the very tip of her tail, which gave an occasional twitch.

Suddenly, as if in response to some signal only she could hear, she sat up, blinked, yawned and stretched luxuriously. She looked round the circular chamber, almost as if she was looking for something, or someone; but it was empty and utterly silent.

She trotted purposefully over to a doorway in the curved wall. It gave on to a steep stairway, leading upwards. She hopped nimbly up the steps until she reached the top. It was almost dark here, but in the dim light even a human could have made out the blank wall: a wall with no suggestion of a doorway, or an opening of any kind.

To the little cat, it was light as day. Delicately, she put out one velvet paw and patted the wall. She stretched up, in much the same way as she might have reached up a tree trunk to sharpen her claws, and scratched at the stone with both front paws.

1

Then she sat down, very tidily, with her tail curled neatly round her, and looked up at the wall, unblinkingly, her eyes very wide and dark . . . almost as if she was waiting for something, or someone.

At last, her mouth opened in a little *mew*. It wasn't a loud miaow; it had never needed to be. It was followed by another; then another, more insistent.

Without warning, an explosion of sound crashed through the stone like a battering ram, sending her streaking back down the steps, every hair of her body on end, her tail like a bottlebrush. In the room below, she pressed herself into the deepest shadow, heart hammering like a tiny drum, every sense raw.

Gradually, the echoes died away.

But something about the little cat was different. It was as if the barrage of sound had stripped away her tameness . . . as if some deep instinct had warned her that somehow – between the silence that went before and the echoing emptiness that came after – everything had changed.

Slowly the sleek fur between her shoulder blades began to rise. She sensed it long before any human could have, ears straining to catch the tiniest whisper of sound, whiskers sensitive as radar, tuned to detect the faintest tremble of air. She could hear them clearly now. Voices below . . . and footsteps. Coming closer.

More clearly than the voices – more distinctly than the footsteps – the little cat could sense something else. A greyness; a shadow; an eclipse of light, like darkness falling over the face of the sun. The wild instincts of her ancestors knew it instantly, in a chilling second of recognition.

Evil. It swelled up from below like a tide. Adrenaline surged through her blood. Her pupils dilated. In absolute silence, she crept away from it, her terror of the gong forgotten. Softly as a shadow she drifted back to the doorway and melted up the stairs.

She reached the top. The dead end. Her heightened senses told her instantly there was nothing for her beyond the wall – not now. She turned her back to it and waited in the darkness, eyes gleaming: a wildcat at bay.

They were coming.

Night blanketed the city like soft velvet, unbroken by the sound of cars or the barking of dogs, by electric lights or the cosy murmur of television sets behind curtained windows. The only light came from the stars.

It was that time of night when sleep is deepest and daybreak seems most distant. The little loft above the stable was warm and snug. The uneven pane of glass over the single small window was thick enough to keep out the chill of pre-dawn; the heavy wooden door held in the warmth that rose through the floor from the slumbering beasts below.

On the low pallet in the corner of the room the boy muttered in his sleep and rolled onto his back. His rough brown hair was damp and tousled from a night of disturbed, fragmented dreams, a cow's-lick standing up at a comical angle. Something glinted in his curled fist – something smooth and metallic-looking, gleaming red as blood in the darkness.

A light sheen of sweat filmed his skin. His eyelids flickered. He tossed and moaned, then muttered again, a single word: *friends*, perhaps, or *fiends*. But there was no one to hear him. Not yet.

Below, the animals were restless. Their horny hooves scraped on the stone floor; their ears twitched. One by one, they woke. Their eyes rolled, the whites luminous in the darkness. The foals pressed closer to their mothers.

Outside, a shadow separated itself from the deeper shadow of the stable wall and drifted to the foot of the rough stairway leading to the attic door. It was joined by another, and another. No words passed between them. The only sound was the faintest sniffing of an indrawn breath, questing, seeking . . . catching with a rattling snuffle on something loose or rotten deep within the dark hood.

The leader reached the attic door – a sturdy door studded with rusty rivets. On the inside, where the boy lay sleeping, a stout bar rested on heavy brackets. The door was latched . . . from the inside.

What had once been two hands emerged from the folds of the cloak and groped their way across the pitted surface of the door. At last they felt what they were seeking, and were still. Long moments passed.

On the other side, in the darkness, the heavy latch twitched. Slowly, it lifted and the door swung open. There was the faintest hiss as the hands pulled away, leaving fragments of rotten skin on the rough wood.

4

The three dark shapes loomed over the bed, their shadows falling on the sleeping boy. His next breath breathed them in: the sweet, cloying odour of the open grave. His blood turned to ice and his heart froze, lurching in his chest like a stone. His eyes flew open. He flung up his bare arms in an instinctive attempt to shield himself; his mouth opened like a dark wound in one single, hopeless cry. Then the boy's eyes rolled back in their sockets, his head lolling uselessly against the bolster. His face was grey as death.

The three shadows melted together over the bed; groped; snuffled. The faintest gurgle; then they floated back to the open doorway and were gone.

The bed was empty.

Somewhere far away, a rooster crowed.

Somewhere far away, a rooster crowed.

The four poster bed floated like an island on a sea of golden light, drifting towards morning on a tide of dreams. The little girl stirred and smiled in her sleep. One arm, thin and fragile under her pyjama sleeve, reached blindly for something . . . but all it found was the emptiness of the cotton sheets.

The man in the armchair beside the bed bent down and picked up a battered, one-eyed teddy from the floor. Gently, taking care not to wake her, he placed the teddy within easy reach. He considered, then repositioned it closer still, to rest against her hand.

The faintest dimple dented the pale cheek. The hand groped; the arm curled round the teddy and pulled it close. The cheek snuggled against it, the hand stroking the nubbly, threadbare fur. The stroking stopped abruptly. The man watched intently, as he had watched all night, pain and love etched on his face.

The little girl's eyes opened and flew straight to the teddy. A curiously adult expression settled over her face. Her voice, when she spoke, was the thread of a whisper. 'Oh, Teddy – it's you.'

Her eyes moved to the man. She reached out a hand.

'Hello there, Chatterbot.'

'Open the curtains, Q. I want to see the morning.'

Obediently, he crossed to the bay window and drew the curtains wide. Rose-coloured light flooded the room. The sky was streaked with indigo and copper, magenta and gold, and the child's face was lit with a rosy glow. Her eyes feasted on the lustrous sky, and for a moment her thin face reflected its radiance. She sighed, and scrunched down again into the pillows. The teddy lay on the rumpled sheet beside her, forlorn and forgotten.

The man crossed to the bed and took her hand. 'How does breakfast sound, sweetheart? Nanny could make you a boiled egg, perhaps . . . with soldiers. Would you like that?'

Her eyes, shadowed and sunken from gazing so closely into the face of death, looked beyond his words into his heart. The words that neither could speak hung between them like a sword. Her lip trembled. 'Q . . .'

Instantly, he was beside her on the bed, cradling her

frail body in his arms. 'Sweetheart – don't think about it now – you need to rest, to gather your strength . . .'

Her eyes burnt into him, anguished, remorseless. 'Q – *I need to know.*'

He looked down. Then, with a colossal effort of will, he told her. 'She didn't come home, Chatterbot. She's still there – in Karazan.'

'Is she . . . dead?'

'No, not dead. She stayed with them, almost to the very end. She was brave – she was a hero. Adam will tell you later, if you feel strong enough. But then, at the very end, they were . . . separated. There was no way Adam could get to her. The children came home – they had to. There was no other way.'

He bent his head close to hear her. 'Where . . . where was she?'

'They were in the Temple – the Temple of Arakesh.'

'Are there priests there, like in the game?'

'Yes, there are priests.'

'Do you think one of them will find her? And take care of her?'

'Perhaps, Chatterbot. Yes, I'm sure they will.' He couldn't meet her eyes. 'Don't worry about her. I'm sure she'll be safe. And maybe . . . maybe one day soon, when you're better . . . we'll go and choose you a little kitten – not to take her place – no one could ever do that, I know – but to . . . well, to fill the space. Maybe. What do you think?'

She tilted her head and looked her father full in the face. Though she was only five, she read all that was written there with an accuracy that sent a bolt like an arrow into her heart. Her face didn't change, but tears filled her eyes, brimmed over, and rolled slowly in twin tracks down her thin cheeks.

Her lips moved, but no sound came out. 'Maybe.'

THE NEW BOY

I took one look and knew he was trouble.

I could tell from the way he hopped down from the unmarked welfare van and smirked at us all – standing on the red concrete porch in a silent, watchful huddle – as if he owned the place.

His mouth stretched into a thin slit of a smile, his lips disappearing like a toad's as his eyes darted from one face to the next, clever and calculating. They were a strangely dark, opaque brown, like mud.

He twitched the welfare lady's hand – a hand you could tell was meant to be kind – off his arm as if she had some kind of infectious disease. Shouldered his grubby bag and walked over to the bottom of the steps. Stood there waiting as if he had all the time in the world – like already he knew he'd be calling all the shots.

He looked about my age, I guess, but shorter than me and runtier, with a pale, ratty-looking face. Looking at that face, you knew right off that here was a person who'd been kicked in the teeth once too often . . . and who'd decided the only way to handle that was to kick back – harder, sneakier, and preferably below the belt.

I recognised that look because I'd seen it before, once or twice, when I looked in the mirror. Not that I was proud of that now.

Matron, brisk and businesslike as ever, signed the papers, handed them back to the welfare lady with a terse nod, and joined the new boy at the foot of the steps. Behind me, I heard Cookie make a little *tut-tut*-ing sound. She'd seen enough trouble walk through the door of Highgate to recognise it up front, no problem.

'Children, I'd like you to join me in welcoming Willie Weaver to our little family,' said Matron.

An uncertain chorus of *Good morning, Willie*, along with a couple of ragged *Welcome, Willie*s, went up from some of the little ones. There was a snicker and a mocking *Willie Weaver!* from Geoffrey – too soft for Matron to hear, of course.

The boy looked up at us. It didn't seem like the welcome had made much of an impression. 'Weevil,' he said flatly. Just that. *Weevil*.

He walked up the steps, past us all without so much as another glance, and disappeared into the shadows of the hallway as if he'd lived at Highgate – or some-where exactly like it – all his life.

My heart sank. Cookie wasn't the only one who could recognise trouble when she saw it – and it was the last thing I wanted.

Things had changed for me in the two months since

I came back from Quested Court – since I came back from Karazan. Not so much changed *for* me, as changed *in* me. Highgate was still the same – always would be, I reckoned. Matron was the same – nothing would ever change *her*, worse luck.

But me . . . I was different. Before, I'd thought of myself as this dumb, hopeless waste of space – bad at school work, stupid at spelling, always in trouble, angry with everyone. Especially myself. I'd felt trapped – not just by where I was, but *who* I was. And there'd been no way out that I could see.

Then along came the little reply-paid card that changed everything. More than just an entry form to a competition: a passport to a truckload of things I'd never dreamed existed for someone like me.

My first real friend: Cameron Harrow.

Luck – that went *my* way, for the first time in my life.

Quentin Quested – Q – and his feisty little daughter Hannah . . . people who actually liked me, and believed in me. And, in Hannah's case, *needed* me, more than I'd ever been needed before.

More friends. Rich, Jamie, Kenta, Gen.

An adventure so bizarre – so impossible – that I struggled to believe it had actually happened.

Tiger Lily. But I couldn't bear to think about that.

I'd come back from Quested Court feeling like a conquering hero. Suddenly, here was Adam Equinox – same guy who'd never brought back anything more exciting than a dud report or a detention slip – breezing in decked out in designer clothes, with

Quentin Quested's personal bodyguard staggering along behind him under a mountain of boxes full of state-of-the-art computer equipment that would be my escape route from Highgate – in my imagination, at any rate – any time I wanted.

Here was Matron, sweet as sugar, offering Shaw a cup of tea and a squashed-fly biscuit, and asking me whether I'd *had a good time, dear*!

Then the door slammed behind Shaw, and reality slugged me in the gut. The computer was hedged around with more rules and regulations than Fort Knox. The *Collector's Set of Quest Fantasy Adventure Software* was advertised in the *Buy and Sell*, and disappeared without a trace. A new DVD player appeared in Matron's private sitting room (though of course we weren't supposed to know about that), along with a super-flash flat-screen TV with digital stereo sound.

One afternoon when we arrived back from school there was a brand new shiny red car parked in the garage, and the rusted-up old Highgate mini-van had shifted to a bare patch of garden off to the side.

As for Q's 'strategic donation' to Highgate . . . well, that was simply never mentioned again.

A new look appeared on Matron's face when she looked at me, and a new note in her voice when she spoke to me. It was as if she'd thought she had me all figured out and pretty much pegged down . . . and now she wasn't so sure. I needed to be watched.

It came from the knowledge that once – just once – I'd gotten the better of her. That was one thing I knew

Matron would never forgive, never mind forget. I'd started something that wouldn't be over until the balance had tipped the other way, with Matron back on top and me squirming helplessly on the ground, waiting for the heel of her shoe to squish me like a bug.

I didn't follow Weevil into the house. Instead, I drifted over behind the garage and round the back of the woodshed, where the garden was scrubby and overgrown; it was where the little kids made huts and Geoffrey and a couple of the others went for a sneaky cigarette. Me too, to be honest, once or twice. OK, maybe more. Not now, though – all that was in the past.

But right now I had something just as off limits in mind – something I knew would make me feel a whole lot better, instead of dizzy and sick like the cigarettes. It was the perfect time, with everyone's attention on the new boy.

I shoved my way through the scrub behind the shed until I came to the fence. The ground was littered with dented old cans and crumpled sweet papers. It was no one's idea of a perfect picnic spot, but it was private, so it was a place most of us ended up at one time or another.

The mesh fence was higher than my head, rusty and warped, although the double strand of razor wire at the top was still sharp enough to slice your hands to ribbons if you tried to climb it. The mesh was dented and kind of collapsed here and there where branches had fallen onto it. Over the years holes had appeared, at ground level mostly, tucked away out of sight. Every now and again they'd be wired shut or patched up by the part-time caretaker, but then they'd pop open again, sometimes in the same place, sometimes in a new one.

My most recent hole was still there. I wriggled through, stood up on the other side, and dusted myself off. Heaved a huge sigh and headed up and away into the hills behind the house, following the almost invisible paths I knew well enough to have followed in my sleep, leaving Matron and Highgate and the other kids far behind.

Five minutes later I was perched on my special flat rock, looking out over the patched roof of Highgate far below. My rock caught the late afternoon sun, warm and comforting under the palms of my hands. With a deep sigh of utter contentment I lay back with my hands behind my head and gazed up into the blue sky.

They say you can't see stars in the daytime, but I could sometimes glimpse them – almost invisible pinpricks of white in the blueness – if I looked long enough. I lay and searched the sky, drank in the silence and soaked up the solitude like sunshine.

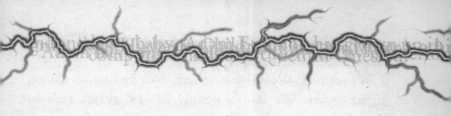

MATRON

The next day – Monday – Matron was waiting on the porch when I mooched up the drive from school. My spirits were already at an all-time low, but they clicked down another notch.

'I want to see you in my office, Adam. Your hands and face are filthy – wash them first, and put your lunchbox away – for goodness' sake stop dragging your bag over the gravel, and pick up your feet when you walk.'

In the boys' cloakroom I washed my hands and splashed some water on my face. As usual, I didn't bother to do anything about my untidy thatch of hair, other than shove it out of my eyes. Back it flopped. I glowered at my reflection, and it glowered back. My pale eyes peered out warily from under my dark brows, worry about whatever lay ahead making my mouth turn down. Even to me, I looked like a surly, bad-tempered loser. I sighed. What could Matron want now? For once I hadn't done anything wrong. Hadn't the day been bad enough?

Weevil was in my class. Even worse, he had the desk next to mine – at the very front, where I'd been

15

moved at the beginning of term to be right up under Miss McCracken's nose.

Worse still: Weevil was smart. Not just so-so smart: super-smart. We had a couple of real smart kids in the class – goody-goody Nicole, who always got top marks and never once had her name up on the board, in all the years she'd been at school. And there was Cameron Harrow, the rich kid with thick specs who worked hard, kept on the right side of the teachers, and always kept me at arm's length . . . until we'd got to know each other properly last term, and started to be friends. Turned out neither of them was a patch on Weevil.

Miss McCracken liked to start the week with a hiss and a roar, so first up, it was maths-test time. 'A quick revision of the things you already know – or *should* know,' she goes, with a steely glance at me. 'Basic facts, and a quick flip through twenty simple long multiplication and long division sums – nothing tricky, just a warm-up to get the week underway. The questions are up on the board – away you go. No talking . . . and keep your eyes on your own work, Adam.'

Well, I meant to. But it wasn't long before I got totally bogged down – my columns had a life of their own, and I was constantly times-ing the wrong thing, and getting muddled about which numbers I was supposed to add together. After a few crossings-out, and rubbing out a couple of things even I could tell were wrong, the page looked like a battlefield and I was totally confused. I scraped my chair away from the desk, tilted onto the back legs, and had a stretch.

I shot a lightning glance over to Weevil's desk, in the hope that he was making even more of a dog's breakfast of it all than I was.

He wasn't. Head down, pen poised – so I was still the only one in the class using pencil like a little kid – he was neatly writing down the answer to the last long division question. But the weird thing was, there was no working-out at all – just the sum, with that brackety thing with the line on top, and the answer written up above it, tidy as you like.

'*Adam!*' snapped the McCracken.

Thump! Down went my chair. Looking at the battlefield, I decided I'd better start again. Dug in my desk for my special rubber – the one on the end of my pencil left pink smudges. Found it. Started rubbing the whole mess out. But when I'd finished the page was more of a disaster than ever – the pattern I'd decorated the rubber with had somehow smeared itself over the paper, which was all crumpled from the scrubbing back and forth.

Sighing, I picked up my pencil for another go. It was blunt. I had another dig in my desk and unearthed my sharpener. Sharpened the pencil up real good; tested it on my finger. Wicked! Put pencil to paper – and out pops the lead, and rolls away on the floor.

Next to me, McCracken was bent over Weevil's desk. 'Now, William, you've been very quick. Let's have a look at your answers. *Adam* – what are you doing on the floor?'

'Looking for my pencil lead, Miss McCracken,' I mumbled from under the desk.

'Well, get *up*, sit *down*, and start *work*,' she snapped. 'You should have two pencils: use the other one, or sharpen the one you've got. Now, William . . . hmmm . . . yes, yes, yes, yes . . . and . . . yes! But where's your working? You didn't use a calculator, did you?' she asked suspiciously.

'No, Miss. I did them in my head.'

'You . . . oh!' For once, Miss McCracken didn't have a comeback . . . not for a second or two, anyhow. 'In your *head*? Well, William . . . that's very clever, I'm sure. But you do need to show your working. Marks are allocated for method in this school.'

I shot a glance at Nicole, to see how she felt about the new class brain-box. But she had her head studiously down, checking her answers.

As for me – finally, I'd got my pencil sharpened properly. The show was about to hit the road! Laboriously, I wrote the number '1' in the margin, the full stop neatly next to it.

'Right, everyone, pens down,' rapped out McCracken. 'Let's see how you've all done. Hands up for the answer to number one.'

And so the day went on. Weevil's hand, with its smooth, clipped nails, was always first in the air with an answer . . . and the answer was always right. Not that I cared.

And now a visit to Matron. And I knew one thing for sure: whatever it was, it wouldn't be good.

Reluctantly, I knocked on the office door.

'Come in.'

Matron was at the desk, filling in some kind of a form. As usual, she totally ignored me. After a minute or two – still without looking up – she barked, 'Don't slouch. Stop fidgeting and take your hands out of your pockets.'

Eventually she looked up. You've never seen eyes like Matron's: flat and hard as flint, with about as much warmth. There were these sharp lines from her nose to her mouth, as if she was constantly smelling a bad smell. Often – especially in the winter – there'd be this little drip trembling on the very end of her nose. She wore bright red lipstick that came off on her teeth, like she was some kind of a vampire – that's what I used to think when I was little. She was skinny as a stick, with loose grey skin on her neck, like a lizard, and her breath smelt of drains, overlaid with onions.

'I have received a letter from Mr Quested in Winterton, inviting you for the holidays.'

I nearly fell over. My mouth dropped open so my jaw practically hit the floor. My heart did a triple somersault, and this mammoth grin pasted itself all over my face. 'Really?' I croaked.

Matron sniffed. 'Yes, *really*. It is hard to believe, but nonetheless, it is the case – although he has met you previously and should be fully aware of who – and what – he is taking on. And frankly, Adam, I would be glad to be rid of you for two weeks.'

Two whole weeks?

I couldn't believe it. 'You're going to *let me go*?'

Twelve years of history hovered like ghosts in the musty air between us. Not once in all those twelve years had she ever made a decision that might possibly make me happy. And now – this.

My first reaction – excitement, joy, amazement – was settling down to a more realistic one – disbelief, suspicion, distrust.

'Certainly, I am going to let you go. Why should I possibly want to keep you here when you have such an exciting opportunity, Adam?' She spat my name out like it was something rotten.

Silence. I waited – I didn't know what for, but I knew there'd be more.

Matron looked down again, flipped over her form, and uncapped her pen. I shifted and shuffled my feet, wondering whether I should go.

I'd reached the door when the single word came after me, like an icy dart. '*Unless* . . .'

I turned back, my heart settling in my stomach as if it were made of lead.

'Unless you behave in such a manner that you oblige me to cancel this privilege. I am a reasonable woman, Adam: a charitable, generous woman, as well you know. Naturally, I have your best interests at heart.

'There are three weeks until the beginning of the holidays. Three weeks in which you will prove to me that you are worthy of this invitation, and can be relied upon to be a credit to myself and to Highgate while you are away.

'I am giving you a chance. Not one, not two, but three chances. We shall see whether, for the remainder of term, you are able to stay out of trouble. If you are, well and good. You go to Quested Court. Slip up once, or even twice, and still you go. But slip up three times . . . and you stay right here.' She smiled. 'Do you understand?'

I stared at her, trying to see a glimmer of what was going on behind those cold eyes. Did she really want to get shot of me for two weeks? Was she trying to use the visit as a lever to guarantee my good behaviour? Or was she playing some elaborate game of cat and mouse that she knew she'd win?

I nodded dumbly, looking as hangdog as possible. Because I figured that was *exactly* what she was doing. She'd done it before – nothing was ever simple with Matron; she got her kicks in subtle ways. But this time, she'd been too clever. I had a trump card up my sleeve. The new, freshly minted, newly invented, totally reformed Adam Equinox: an Adam so unlikely, so impossible, there was no way she could possibly guess he even existed. The Adam who was learning to turn away from trouble every single time. *I knew I could do it.* Looking as miserable and surly as possible, I shuffled out of the door . . . but the minute it closed behind me, I raised one fist in a triumphant gesture of victory: *YES!*

At the door of the rec room Weevil was watching me, his eyes sharp and inquisitive.

MY GLADIATOR PROJECT

I pushed past him into the rec room. Mondays and Wednesdays were my allocated days for the computer – I was only allowed to use it for half an hour, and only for homework. My meeting with Matron had eaten a big chunk out of my computer time, so I'd need to be extra quick to make up.

Although weekdays between three and four were officially supervised playtime, my computer time was from three to three thirty. For anyone else, it would have been the worst possible time – right after school, with no time to relax in between. Also, it meant you had to rush straight back, no dawdling, and even then you'd always lose a couple of minutes – all reasons I'd been given that particular slot, of course.

But it suited me perfectly. I got peace, privacy and a precious chance to do my own thing with no one peering over my shoulder.

I slid onto the grey plastic chair, whipped the sheet off the computer onto the floor and switched it on. Hang on a sec, though – I hastily grabbed the sheet back, folded it up as tidily as I could, and put it on the

22

table as if it were made of glass. Grinning inwardly, I gave myself a mental pat on the back. Matron wasn't going to catch me out, not with the tiniest thing – not when so much depended on it.

With a quick glance over my shoulder to check no one had snuck up behind me, I tapped in my private, super-secret password – the one Q had helped me set up before I left Quested Court. I hadn't told him much about Highgate, but he was one of those people who didn't need to be told things to understand them. In his usual mild, absent-minded way he'd suggested that with other people using the computer, privacy might be an issue. He'd told me to choose a password I'd be sure to remember, and keep it completely secret, even from him.

I'd thought long and hard about what to choose. It had to be something really cast-iron; something super-cool and special to me. It had to be something no one would ever guess – not in a zillion years.

There it was on screen: ★★★★★★★★★★★.

Wicked!

Quickly, I checked my mailbox. Maybe there'd be something from Q.

There was!

hello adam hope all is ok have written to mrs whatnot asking you here for holidays hope it wont cause any problems wed love to have you especially h who is getting chubbier and cheekier by the day she has something to show you but i will say no more must dash q

It was the way Q always wrote – the way his mind

worked, I guess. I tapped out a reply, quick as a flash – my typing had come on a blue streak over the past few weeks.

Thancks a zilyon Q and gess wot I CAN CUM!!!!!!!!!!! C U soon!!!!!!!!!!! Adam

Zapped it off.

Checked the clock. Yeah – I just about had time, if I was real quick. I tapped in the first two letters of Richard's name, and the computer filled in the rest.

Hey ther Ritch, I typed hastily. *Hows it gowing? Gess wot – Im gowing to sta with Q and hanna 4 the hollidays!!!!!!!!!! Iyll miss yoo guys thow – just imajin if we got 2 go 2 karazan agen! Not mutsh chans of that thow! Sumtims I cant beleev it rearly happnd can yoo. Rite soon from Adam E.*

Blat! Away it went. Darn – only five minutes left!

Quickly, I hopped off the Internet – fully paid courtesy of Q, access restricted to me and protected by my password, all unknown to Matron – and called up my gladiator project.

For a long moment I sat back and gazed at the title page with this goofy little smile. I scrolled carefully down, looking for where I'd left off last time. Scrolled down page . . . after page . . . after page. I couldn't believe how long it was! Looking at that project, you'd never in a zillion years have guessed it had been done by Adam Equinox, class blockhead.

We'd been given the assignment at the beginning of term. We had the whole term to work on it, the McCracken told us, and she expected a top job. 'At *least* five pages – and preferably legible, and bearing *some* relation to the topic, Adam Equinox.'

Well, was she in for a shock!

Before, I'd have shoved the worksheet right to the back of my desk and forgotten all about it – until Nicole or someone 'happened to mention' how many hundred pages they'd done, on the day it was due.

But this time I got stuck in straight away. I made up my mind to do a little bit each time I used the computer. Right at the beginning I typed in ROMAN GLADIATORS and hopped on the Internet to see what I could find – and after a couple of false starts it was like an open sesame to a whole new world. I got so hooked into the whole thing I even cruised by the school library to see what books I could find, so I could carry on with it at weekends. The librarian had acted kind of startled, looking at me as if I was an alien from another planet. Which in that library, I guess I was.

By now, weeks down the track, it was a total masterpiece. It had special headings, and it was illustrated with pictures from the graphics library Q had installed. I'd even numbered the pages with Roman numerals – that idea had breezed into my head one night when I couldn't get to sleep.

Every session before I quit I ran it through Q's special Spell Checker and Grammar Fixer, to make double sure there were no mistakes. It worried me how many it seemed to find, and I sometimes wondered if there was a fault in the programme. I couldn't wait to see the McCracken's face when she saw it, and read my name on the front page.

Today, I was doing a section called *The Venatio*, about a special kind of combat to do with hunting and killing exotic wild animals. I'd just started typing – pecking away with two fingers, but way faster than when I'd started – when someone spoke behind me, so close his breath tickled the back of my neck.

'You can do more exciting stuff than that wiff computers if you know how.' I practically jumped through the ceiling. I knew who it was without turning round – I'd know that voice anywhere, with its distinctive little lisp. Weevil.

I scowled at him. 'Shove off. I'm busy.'

He ignored me. 'A *lot* more.' He craned his neck to see what was on the screen. I shifted so my body was shielding it.

'I mean it. Leave me alone.'

But he pulled up another chair and sat down with his arms across the back, resting his chin on them. 'I know all about you,' he said cosily. 'How you won that competition, and went to Quested Court and everyfing. I entered too – nicked an entry form from a girl in my class. Computers – they're my fing. I could have learned heaps on that course. But *I* didn't get picked: *you* did. What a waste – you're as thick as peanut butter. Tell you what, though: it's not what you know, it's who you know that counts. You know the right people – people like Quentin Quested. That's why I want to be your friend. How about it? Want to be mates, you an' me?'

'No thanks,' I said abruptly. 'I've got all the friends I need.'

I might as well have saved my breath. He carried on as if he hadn't heard. 'Bet you're wondering how I got my nickname. Know what a weevil is?'

Impatiently, I shook my head. Over his shoulder I could see that the minute hand of the clock was creeping closer to the six.

'It's a bug – an insect that burrows into stuff that's stored away. Weevils can get inside lots of places. Private places. Anywhere – anywhere at all. I could show you fings about computers you've never even dreamed about. Know what a hacker is? Bet you don't. Look it up in the dictionary – if you know how.'

'Weevil,' I said wearily, 'go away.'

The minute hand had reached the six. I turned my back on him, pressed Control S to save, and quit. I gave a long, luxurious, phoney stretch, like a guy without a care in the world. When I turned round, he was gone.

THE PRINCIPAL'S AWARD

For the next week, I concentrated on staying out of trouble. I felt like a tightrope walker . . . and every step I took, I watched my back.

I made myself stop and think before I did things. Before I said things; before I practically even *thought* things. As much as I could, I stayed out of everyone's way – except for Cameron. Having a goody-goody for a friend was a bit like having a magical talisman: Cam had a natural talent for keeping away from trouble, and as long as I hung out with him, it seemed to rub off on me.

Then, on Sunday night, I was in the boys' bathroom cleaning my teeth when suddenly another reflection appeared next to mine in the mirror. I just about choked on the toothpaste. Scowled at him, bent, spat in the hand basin. Rinsed my mouth, then turned, ready to push past him and out of there.

But what he said next stopped me dead in my tracks. 'I know where you're going in the holidays. You're going to Quested Court. And I want to come wiff you. You'd be allowed to take a friend. Especially a friend who knows as much about computers as I do – a new boy wiff nowhere else to go. What do you say, Adam?'

'Where I'm going in the holidays is my business,' I growled. 'And if I was allowed to take a friend, you'd be the last person I'd choose. Now butt out and leave me alone!'

'Remember what I said about weevils? I know more than you fink.' He smirked. 'Like I said, weevils can get inside lots of places. Private places. Anywhere at all.'

'Oh, shut up!' I snarled. 'You've been sneaking through Matron's papers – and I hope she catches you!'

I shoved past and padded through to the dorm. Slid between the cold sheets and turned my back on the room, staring at the familiar pattern of flaking paint on the wall.

Weevil or no Weevil, Matron or no Matron, a whole week had gone by safely. There were only two weeks left till I'd escape to Quested Court – and a whole different life.

I tightrope-walked my way through Monday . . . Tuesday . . . Wednesday. On Wednesday after school, I ran all the way back to Highgate and shut myself in the rec room to finish my project. For once, I worked for the entire half hour without a single thing disturbing me. I even managed to do the index. Then, with five minutes to go, I clicked on the *Print* icon and watched page after perfect page scroll out from the printer.

I didn't have time to admire it – instead I snuck into the dorm and hid it under my mattress, where it wouldn't get crumpled. That night, when everyone else was asleep, I slipped it out and read it under the blankets in the dim glow of my pencil torch.

First thing on Friday morning, I handed it in. All XI pages: *Roman Gladiators*, by *ADAM EQUINOX*. The McCracken's eyebrows just about hit the ceiling. I'd slouched up real casual, of course, like it was nothing special; but then I watched her out of the corner of my eye. Once we were safely settled down doing silent reading I saw her flip through the pile and find it again, and leaf through it with this stunned, disbelieving look on her face.

Watch this space, McCracken, I told her in my mind. *There's more where that came from – you ain't seen nothing yet!*

The weekend dragged by. For the first time I was looking forward to school on Monday. I couldn't wait to get my project back. To hear what Miss McCracken would say about it, and read the comment she'd write at the end. Maybe she'd even read it out! And maybe, just maybe, there was the minutest chance – one in a squillion – that it might get a Principal's award.

Hardly any kids in my class had been given one, they were so rare. Cameron had, twice; Nicole had a truckload, of course. They were these big round shiny stickers that looked like they were made of real gold. They were stuck onto your work, and then it was displayed in the front office for everyone to see.

Your name was called out in assembly, and you had to go up and shake the Principal's hand. And your name got pride of place in the next school newsletter, on the front page.

Monday: nothing. Tuesday: not a word. But then, on Wednesday, Miss McCracken walked into the classroom first thing and said, 'I will be returning your projects this morning, children. But first: William Weaver and Adam Equinox, will you please come with me to the Principal's office.'

My heart did a quadruple somersault. I felt myself blush bright red as I followed her to the door, my heart hammering. I caught a quick glimpse of Cam's worried face; I gave him a reassuring grin and a wink. Little did he know!

We waited in silence outside the closed office door. The secretary was busy typing and ignored us, as usual. I was a regular customer – I was used to the tense, doctor's-waiting-room atmosphere. It was interesting to see that it didn't change, even when you were there for something good.

Eventually the intercom on the secretary's desk beeped, and a tinny voice said, 'I am free now. Send them in, please.'

In went Miss McCracken . . . then Weevil . . . then me.

There on Mrs Sharp's big, bare wooden desk were two projects, side by side. *Roman Gladiators, by ADAM EQUINOX*; *ROMAN GLADIATORS, by William Weaver*.

I wondered when she would put the stickers on.

31

'Please sit down, Miss McCracken, William,' goes Mrs Sharp, in a voice like silk. 'Adam Equinox: what is the meaning of this?'

I stared at her dumbly, not even beginning to understand. But slowly I was realising something was wrong . . . something was very, very wrong. I felt like someone falling from a high building, spinning over and over as I hurtled towards the ground.

Stared at her dumbly as her hands neatly, methodically, in perfect time, flipped over the pages of the projects, two by two. Eleven pages, complete with perfect spelling, full-colour clip-art and neatly centred roman numerals. Eleven pages . . . all completely identical.

ANYWHERE

There was a long, terrible silence. They were all looking at me, waiting for me to do something . . . say something.

'It . . . it's not how it looks,' I stammered at last. My voice sounded shaky and small.

'Oh, really, Adam? And how does it *look*?'

'It looks . . . you're both thinking . . .' Even as I said the words, I knew it was useless. 'You're thinking I copied Weevil – William, I mean. But I didn't. It was the other way round. He copied me.'

Miss McCracken and Mrs Sharp exchanged a glance. 'Oh, come now, Adam,' said Mrs Sharp, in the kind of voice you'd use to talk to a baby. 'Don't insult our intelligence. Here we have a superior piece of work, and a highly gifted straight-A student. On the other hand we have a boy who, frankly, has been nothing but trouble since he joined the school . . . a boy who can barely write his own name. Do you seriously expect us to believe for one moment this is *your* work – that *William* copied it from *you*? That is ridiculous. William: do you have anything to say?'

'Not really, Mrs Sharp,' said Weevil, sliding me a

sidelong, injured glance. 'Just that – well, Adam, I'm really disappointed. After I tried to be friends wiff you, and everyfing.'

'Miss McCracken?'

'Oh, Adam,' said Miss McCracken wearily. 'Do you know, sometimes I really do come close to giving up on you. And you know what discourages me most? You never even bother to try.'

Miss McCracken and Weevil left soon after – but not before a shiny gold Principal's award had been stuck onto the front of Weevil's project, and Mrs Sharp had torn mine in half and dropped it into the bin.

I had to stay on and listen while Mrs Sharp phoned Highgate and told Matron the whole story. While they discussed whether I should be suspended for the rest of the term, and agreed a more appropriate punishment would be a fail in history, and to have all my computer privileges suspended until further notice. Words like *sheer audacity* and *abuse of trust* flew through the air like arrows, but I was way past the stage where they could hurt me. I felt as numb as if I'd been turned to concrete.

After school, I dragged myself up the hill back to Highgate. Dumped my lunchbox on the tottering pile on the kitchen servery – and the whole lot came crashing down. Numbly, I bent and started picking them up. 'Let me take care of that, Adam,' said Cookie from the kitchen. She looked up from peeling potatoes, her face heavy with sympathy. 'You're to pop through and see *Her*, as soon as you get in. Right away, she said. Best hurry, dear, the state she's in.'

I knocked on Matron's office door, the wood sounding hollow under my knuckles.

Matron was at her desk. She'd had her hair done, I noticed automatically – it sat in tight grey rolls, like rows of steel tubing arranged on her head. Her eyes were like bullets. For a long moment, she said nothing.

Before, I would have shuffled my feet and dropped my eyes. But now I met her gaze levelly. I hadn't done anything wrong, and nothing Matron could do or say would change that.

'Well, Adam Equinox. It seems no matter how poor an opinion of you I have, you manage to surprise me by sinking even lower. This means the end of that computer for you. You cannot be trusted, therefore you will never touch it again.

'As far as your proposed plans for the holidays are concerned, I am sorely tempted to cancel it as punishment for your behaviour. But I am a woman of my word. I promised you three chances, and I need hardly tell you one is gone. With a boy like you, the others are certain to follow. However, I shall be obliged to notify Mr Quested of your actions. He should be aware of the kind of child he is inviting into his home.'

She paused, waiting for a reaction. I said nothing. What was the point?

'You disgust me. Get out of my sight.'

I felt myself flush, but still I didn't say a word. Just turned and walked out of there, down the passage, and out into the garden. Automatically, my feet took me towards the silence and solitude of my secret hide-out. It had been my bolt hole and refuge as far back as I could remember, a place that had saved my sanity more times than I could count: peaceful, private, and completely mine.

I headed for the shrubbery at the side of the house and double-checked no one was watching. I dropped to my knees and pushed my way into the flax bush guarding the entrance. The smooth leaves stroked my burning face like cool, comforting fingertips, and the familiar scent of damp earth rose up to greet me. As I burrowed deeper, my brain began grinding into gear. *What* Weevil had done – that was obvious enough. But *how*? How had he accessed my directory on the computer? How had he bypassed my secret pass-word? What was it he was always saying? *Weevils can get inside lots of places, Adam. Private places. Anywhere – anywhere at all*. It couldn't be true . . . could it?

I wriggled round the last bed of the tunnel, and the hidden cave of my hide-out opened out in front of me.

Right in the middle of the smooth earth floor, a word had been gouged in deep, jagged letters.

ANYWHERE

The magic bubble of my secret sanctuary shattered like glass. A pain sliced through me like a knife, so real that for a moment I thought it had actually happened – an invisible sphere had smashed, and one of the shards had lodged deep in my heart.

For an endless moment I knelt there, head bowed, paralysed. My eyes had squeezed themselves shut, but the crude letters burned in my mind like fire. It was wrecked – forever. Even if I scrubbed the letters out – even if Weevil never set foot there again – it would never be the same.

First Weevil had stolen my project. And now he had ruined the one place I'd thought was mine, and only mine. I had nothing left . . . or did I?

Instinctively my hand moved to my chest, and felt the ridged outline of my heavy metal ring under my shirt. Before Quested Court – before Karazan – I'd kept it in my bedside drawer, with my other special treasures. And that's where it would have been that night at Quested Court . . . if I hadn't taken it out to rub and hold, as I often did for comfort in bed at night, and fallen asleep with it in my hand.

Kneeling in the dirt, I thought back to that night for what seemed like the millionth time . . . and felt the back of my neck prickle and the hairs on my arms rise. For the millionth time I told myself I must have been dreaming, or at least half asleep – but I knew I hadn't been. The invisible presence I'd felt in the dark room . . . the drawer open just a crack, when I knew I'd left it shut . . . the stealthy click of the door snicking shut behind an intruder I couldn't see, but knew in my bones was there. Logic told me it must have been a dream . . . but instinct told me something different. And following my instinct, I'd kept the ring round my neck on an old bootlace from that day on.

But my other treasures – would they be safe from

Weevil? I turned and crawled back through the tunnel for what I knew would be the last time.

I straightened up and brushed away the dirt and bits of dry leaf. I checked no one was around, then crept into the dorm. Slid open my bedside drawer . . . and felt a dizzying surge of relief. My shawl was there: the shawl I'd been wrapped in when I was found on the steps of Highgate nearly thirteen years ago. Creamy-soft and light as a cloud, still holding a trace of the spicy, powdery perfume of the hands that had wrapped a tiny baby and then deserted him . . . the perfume of the mother I had never known.

My torch was there . . . and my dog-eared old *Bible* in its usual place. There was an identical one for every child at Highgate, courtesy of the Board of Trustees – I doubted even Weevil would give mine a second glance. Still, just to be sure, I flipped it open and checked that the yellowed old newspaper cutting was safe. My eyes rested on it for a moment, catching on a word here and there, though I knew it all by heart – it was the only history I had.

. . . left on the steps of the home probably only hours after being born . . . calling him Adam Equinox . . . born on the day of the Equinox – 22nd September . . . dusky complexion, with dark hair and unexpectedly pale eyes . . . lamb's wool shawl . . . silver penny whistle and unusual ring . . .

The day of the Equinox. The day when night and day are equal, and the sun is in the sky for exactly twelve hours. My special day – less than a week away.

I pushed the thought away impatiently. There were no birthdays at Highgate. Most years, 22 September passed by without me even noticing it. Sure, when I was small I'd made a private ritual of my Naming Day, as I'd thought of it: reading the newspaper cutting over and over again . . . closing my eyes . . . reaching out with my thoughts . . . trying to pretend there was someone out there somewhere who thought of me still and remembered me with love. I didn't bother with that baby stuff any more. *Until further information comes to light, the baby remains in the care of the Highgate Children's Home.* That's how the cutting ended. Well, 'further information' never had come to light. So here I was, stuck with Matron and Geoffrey – and now Weevil – for keeps.

Closing the *Bible* with a sigh, I reached my fingers to the very back of the drawer, where my silver penny whistle always rolled. Double-checking, though I knew it would be there.

It wasn't.

My fingers scrabbled on the smooth, flat metal. My heart gave a sickening lurch. Frantically, my hand swept from one side of the empty drawer to the other. I grabbed the drawer and yanked it out with a clatter. Empty. Stupidly, I upended it over the threadbare blanket, in case by some miracle the penny whistle might drop out of nowhere. It didn't. I turned it right way round again and stood staring into it, my mind as cold and empty as the drawer. A word was sounding in that bleak, empty room, but it wasn't in my mind – it was sounding over and over again with every slow, painful beat of my heart: *Weevil. Weevil. Weevil.*

I found him in front of the computer.

'Weevil,' I said, my voice sounding flat and strange, 'I need to talk to you.' He looked up at me with an innocent little smile. I could feel anger swelling up inside me, but I struggled to hold it down. I couldn't afford to lose my cool – not now, with the holidays so close. 'You went into my hide-out.'

'*You went into my hide-out!*' Weevil mimicked in a squeaky, ridiculous voice. 'Is that all you've come to say?'

'No, it's not!' I could hear the anger in my voice, and Weevil looked uncertain, inching his chair away from me. But I didn't lose my temper. 'You know it's not. You looked in my drawer – the drawer of my bedside cabinet. You took something of mine. I want it back.'

His eyes widened innocently. 'Oh, really? What did I take? Why would I want anyfing of yours?'

I'd hardly expected him to admit it. I looked at him steadily. 'I don't know why you would. I don't know why you stole my project, either. What's more, I don't care. I've come to ask you to leave me alone.'

'This isn't about what you want. It's about what *I* want – and I want to go to Quested Court. You fink you're going on your own, but you're wrong. Either you take me wiff you, or . . .'

'Or what?' But I already knew the answer.

'Or you won't go. I'll make sure of that.'

40

'So that's it. You're trying to push me over the edge so I'll do something bad, and Matron will stop me going. Well, it won't work.'

'Won't it? Why don't you just take me wiff you? I don't want to be stuck here all holidays, any more than you do. Come on: last chance . . . what do you say?'

'I'm not taking you anywhere. I'd rather not go to Quested Court than go with you. I don't want you near any part of my life. And I've got news for you. You think you can manipulate me, but you're wrong. You can't. I'm not going to put a foot wrong between now and Friday, and nothing you can do will make me. In two days I'll be packing my bags.'

THE SECOND THING

I didn't even bother looking for my penny whistle. I knew who had it, and I knew there was no way I'd ever find it. Instead, I concentrated on being careful. Very careful.

It was easier than I'd expected. The afternoon dragged to an end, dinner came and went. Weevil said nothing, did nothing. I didn't trust him – not one bit – but by breakfast next morning, when he was still behaving as if I didn't exist, a tiny hope was beginning to surface in my mind.

All day at school, he didn't even look at me once.

At last the bell rang, and I hefted my bag and trudged up the hill to Highgate. Only one more day to go! And all it had taken was a little firmness . . .

The white gate creaked open under my hand, and I crunched my way up the gravel driveway towards the house. Matron's snazzy new car was parked outside the garage . . . she must be planning to get one of us to clean it. It was one of the few chores we all queued up for, even with Matron watching every second and growling at us to be careful not to scratch the paintwork. It was a job strictly reserved for big kids, but even so I'd never had a turn. Surprise, surprise.

I glanced up. There outside the front door stood Matron. For a second – just a second – my heart did a funny flip-flop, because that was where Matron always waited after school to choose her car cleaner. But then I saw the look on her face. My heart froze in mid flip, and flopped down through my guts with a sickening, sinking feeling. In all the years I'd known Matron, I'd never seen her look quite like that.

I stopped dead in my tracks. We stared at each other for what seemed like forever, Matron up on the veranda, me down on the driveway, my bag dangling in the dirt. Then Matron's eyes swivelled away from me, along the driveway, towards the garage. Not wanting to – dreading what I was going to see – my eyes followed hers to the shiny red car, as if it were a magnet.

There, spray-painted on the side of the car in huge bright yellow fluorescent letters, were two words:

MATRON SUKC2

The blood drained out of my face so suddenly the whole world swam. Even though I was standing in bright sunlight, I felt like I'd been turned to ice. When she spoke, Matron's voice sounded as if she was made of ice too.

'Empty your bag onto the driveway.'

'But . . .'

'*Now.*'

I unzipped my bag with clumsy fingers and turned it upside down. Out tumbled my lunchbox . . . my homework books . . . a couple of crumpled notices . . . an apple core . . . a broken pencil . . . a rumpled old sock. Matron stared grimly at it all. A saying I'd once heard floated into my mind: *Innocent until proven guilty*. But for Matron, it worked the other way round.

'Put it back and come with me.'

I picked my stuff up and put it back in the bag, piece by piece. At first my mind had been numb, reeling with shock – but now it was racing. *Weevil did this, and made it look like me*. Somehow, some time since yesterday, he'd snuck into the garage with a can of paint . . .

Anywhere.

I was dead meat. Dead if I tried to defend myself, dead if I didn't. I risked a glance up at Matron from under my hair. Took a shallow, careful breath.

'Mat–'

'Shut your mouth. Get up here.'

Unwillingly I climbed the steps, my bag bumping behind me until I stood in front of Matron. With part of my mind I realised I was taller than her . . . when had that happened?

She reached out and took hold of my ear with her thumb and index finger, digging the nails deep into the soft lobe, twisting and pulling. My eyes watered, and my neck bent itself into an agonising angle. Matron half led, half dragged me into the house, down the long passage towards the boys' dorm. Every doorway was jam-packed with kids, utterly silent, their huge, horrified eyes following our progress through the house.

We stopped in front of my bed. It was neatly made, the threadbare blankets tucked into tight right angles in the corners, the lumpy grey pillow dead centre above the regulation turnover of sheet. Between the beds, squeezed in so tight it touched them, stood my bedside cabinet.

'Take out the drawer.'

Feeling the eyes of every kid at Highgate on my back, I shuffled slowly forward and reached out for the cold metal handle. Slowly I slid the drawer out. My few possessions lay there forlornly for everyone to see: my torch. My *Bible*. My special shawl, rolled up neatly. Nothing else. I set the drawer carefully down on top of the cabinet.

'Now strip the bed. All of it. Every stitch.'

One by one I pulled the two blankets back, shook them out, folded them, and piled them on the bed next door. Picked up the pillow, stripped off the pillowcase, shook it out, folded it. Gave the pillow a shake, and laid it on top. Peeled off the top sheet . . . the bottom sheet. The moth-eaten under-blanket. There was the mattress, patched and darned. I glanced at Matron. For the first time, I thought I could see the tiniest hint of uncertainty in her eyes. 'Now the mattress.'

I took hold of the edge of the mattress, lifted it, and turned it on its side. It was thin, and light as a feather. There was a metal lattice of springs underneath, bare and rusty. Slowly, I replaced the mattress.

Matron stared down at it, thinking. I didn't dare

45

move a muscle. Then suddenly, she stepped forward to the drawer. Reached out for my shawl with a hand like a claw, grabbed hold of one corner, and gave a sharp yank upwards.

A metal canister with a yellow fluorescent lid flew from its soft folds and landed on the floor with a hollow thunk, like the falling blade of an executioner's axe.

IN THE DEAD OF THE NIGHT

'There will be no third chance.'

'But you promised! You said I'd have three chances, and only two are gone!'

'Don't you dare throw my words back at me, Adam Equinox. You have had all the chances you are going to get. *You will not go to Quested Court.* You will not go anywhere. You will stay here with the other children who have no one to take them in, and I personally will do everything in my power to make these the worst two weeks of your life.

'And if you're thinking of sneaking off like you did last holidays, think again. You won't be going to school tomorrow, for a start. You are going to be so closely supervised you won't be able to take a breath without my hearing it.

'And now I shall take great pleasure in calling Mr Quested, and telling him . . .' for a moment, she hesitated. 'Telling him . . . you have had a better offer. That you have chosen to go to . . . let me see now . . . your new friend Cameron for the holidays. You may listen while I make the call.'

'*No!* Please – please, believe me just this once!'

Even as I heard myself beg, hating myself for doing it, I knew it was useless. 'I didn't do it! Truly, it wasn't me! Why would I? I've been trying so hard . . .'

Matron walked over to the bookcase and lifted down her cane. The words dried in my mouth. I felt the skin on my bum crawl and flinch in on itself, and cold sweat pop out on the back of my neck. Quickly, I looked away, down at the ground. I saw Matron's feet walk themselves over to her desk. I heard the rattle of the receiver being lifted from its cradle, and the bips as she dialled the number.

I listened as Matron explained to Q that I wouldn't be coming to Quested Court after all. That while it was rude of me to let him down at this late stage, the policy at Highgate was to allow children to make their own decisions. I listened to her apologise on my behalf, and say she hoped this wouldn't mean the invitation would never be repeated, though of course that would be quite understandable in the circumstances.

Then, just as she was about to ring off, I heard something unexpected: silence. Warily, I risked a quick glance at Matron's face. She was listening to Q, tight-lipped. 'You . . . you want to talk to Adam?' she blustered. 'I – I'm not sure that's possible. He may be out . . . some of the children went down to the . . . the shopping mall for an ice cream – as an end-of-term treat. You – you *insist*? Well, really, Mr Quested . . . *If you don't talk to him personally, you're coming to get him anyway?* I – I – hold the line, please.'

My heart was hammering with wild hope. Q wasn't

going to let Matron get away with it! I was saved! I felt my face split into a grin of delighted disbelief . . . and then I saw the look in Matron's eyes. She put the receiver down on the desk, and picked up the cane. Flexing it between her hands, without taking her eyes off me, she said silkily, 'Adam, dear . . . why, here you are. Would you please be kind enough to speak to Mr Quested for a moment, and explain the change in your holiday plans?'

I picked up the receiver, my hand clammy with sweat. 'Q?' I croaked.

'Adam? Is that you?' I could hear the smile in his voice.

'Uh . . .' I glanced up at Matron through my fringe. She was watching me the way a cat watches a mouse, tapping the cane lightly on the edge of the desk. *Tap* . . . *tap* . . . *tap* . . . 'Yeah. It's me.'

'Adam, my boy – I'm concerned about this. Not about the change in plan, if it's really what you want. But I felt I should talk to you myself, to confirm that it *is* your decision, and that everything is . . . all right. That you're well . . . and happy.'

I felt the sting of tears in my eyes and blinked them furiously away, turning my back on Matron. I would not cry – *would not* give her that satisfaction, on top of everything else! 'Everything's fine,' I lied miserably. 'I want to go to Cameron's for the holidays. His dad invited me.' My voice sounded weird, like robot, or a tape recording with a flat battery.

A sigh gusted down the line. 'Well, we'll miss you. I won't try to change your mind – I'm sure a boy your age does have better things to do than be stuck at the back of beyond with an old man and a little girl. Though Hannah will be disappointed . . . ah, well. Enjoy yourself, my boy. Maybe next holidays, eh?'

'OK. Bye.'

I stood there for an endless moment with the receiver clamped to my ear, the words I longed to shout out burning in my chest. *'No! It's all a lie! Come and get me! Take me away from here – please!'* The silence drew out like a rubber band . . . I drew a deep, shuddering breath, but I could feel Matron's eyes boring into my back like a drill.

'Q –'

'Yes, my boy?' His voice had never been gentler.

'I –' My courage deserted me. 'Tell Hannah . . . I'm sorry.' I put the receiver down in its cradle as gently as if it was made of glass, cutting off contact with Q and Quested Court with a tiny *click* of finality.

Without another glance at Matron and her cane, I turned and walked out of there.

The idea came to me in the dead of the night. It was so simple, so obvious, I couldn't believe I hadn't thought of it before.

The computer.

I lay for what must have been over an hour, staring at the dark ceiling . . . but it wasn't what I was seeing. I was seeing myself doing it . . . imagining every step, every possible thing that might go wrong. I'd have to be absolutely certain everyone was asleep. I'd need to be utterly silent. I'd have to do it all in the pitch dark.

50

How much noise does a computer make when you turn it on? I couldn't remember. I imagined myself sitting up, swinging my legs out of bed, padding in my bare feet over the cold floor. The passage had a wooden floor that creaked. Would Matron hear me? And if she did . . . Did I dare risk it?

I thought of the next two weeks, at Highgate with Matron. I thought of Weevil's face, with its smug, satisfied smile. Of Hannah.

I sat up. Looked over to the left, down the long line of beds. Weevil was a shapeless lump under the blankets, motionless. I couldn't see whether he was facing towards me or away . . . whether he was awake or asleep. But the night had that deep, velvety stillness that meant it was late – really late. He *must* be asleep.

I could pretend I was going to the toilet. But once I passed the toilet door . . . then there'd be no going back.

I slid out of bed and crept to the door. There was just enough moonlight to see my way. I reached out and took hold of the doorknob . . . squeezed my eyes shut and turned it, millimetre by millimetre. There was the tiniest metallic click, loud as a gunshot in the sleeping room. I froze. Someone mumbled something and turned over with a creak of bedsprings. Then silence.

One last check behind me, and I slipped through the door like a shadow. Tiptoed down the passage, keeping close to the wall where the boards were firmer. To the toilet door . . . past it. Down the dark passageway to the rec room door. Matron's bedroom was the next one down, at the end of the passage. The crack under her door was dark. *Good*.

Hardly daring to breathe, I eased open the door and slipped inside. The dusty old curtains were drawn, and it was pitch dark. I shuffled cautiously across the room towards the computer table, feeling my way forward step by step. The computer, shrouded in its sheet, looked like a ghost in the darkness. At last I reached it, slid the sheet off, felt for the on switch. This was it – the moment of truth. I pressed the switch. Obediently, the computer hummed to life, buzzing and chattering. I watched the door, my heart hammering. Nothing.

The computer screen gave the room an eerie blue glow. If anyone woke up and came into the passage, they'd notice it for sure. Taking a deep breath, I slid onto the computer chair and tapped in my password, every keystroke loud enough to wake the dead: ★★★★★★★★★★★

I logged into my e-mail. The connection hummed and buzzed. It had only been two days since I'd last been on the computer, though it felt like a lifetime; but there were five messages, all from Q, each more urgent-sounding than the last. I didn't have time to read them all; couldn't risk it. I clicked on the last one.

adam please confirm all is well are you getting my e-mails is this all open and above board h. says youd never cancel and were worried sorry to harp just wanted you to confirm one last time but don't feel bad youve got your own life to live and youre only young once but please do respond to this even if its just one word to say youre ok love q

Love, Q.

It was the only time in my life anyone had ever used that word to me. Even though I knew it was just a polite way of ending a letter, my heart swelled. Q never said anything unless he meant it. Staring at my screen, I imagined him in front of his own computer . . . he could easily still be awake, working on the next instalment of his Karazan computer game series. The connection between the two computers hummed. I glanced down at my keyboard, memories flooding back. There were the keys: *Alt. Control. Q.* The magic formula Q had developed on the same computer mine was linked to now . . . the keystroke combination with the power to transport you into another world. *Karazan*. It wouldn't work on this computer, of course – only on a computer like Q's, with a VRE Interface. I knew that. But still, if only . . . If only there was a keyboard command that would whisk me out of Highgate and into the library at Quested Court, in front of the fire . . .

Was I crazy? I had no time for dreaming now!

I checked the door. Clicked on New Mail. Typed in: *PLEEZ CUM AND GET ME!* I didn't dare write more. For Q, that would be enough.

I clicked on Send. The computer made a ghastly GLUNK! – its warning when you did something wrong. The sudden jolt of noise sent a spurt of adrenaline through me like an electric shock. I checked the

53

door: nothing. Then the screen: *The message could not be sent. You must specify a recipient for the message.* I clicked on To, and typed: *Q*. Send.

Checked the door.

A dark figure was standing in the doorway, watching me.

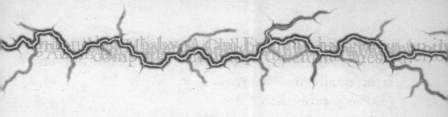

WAITING

We stared at each other in silence. All I could see was a dark silhouette in long winter pyjamas, but I could imagine the look on his face as clearly as if it was broad daylight. The smile . . . the shine of triumph in his eyes.

All the anger I'd been fighting surged up inside me in a giant wave. 'Get away from me!' I hissed. 'Leave me alone! I hate you!'

The figure took a step backwards. 'S-s-sorry . . .'

I blinked. The wave of rage gurgled away like bath water disappearing down the plug hole. I gaped at him with my mouth open. It wasn't Weevil – it was Frankie, a little kid with a stammer, his bunny clenched under one arm. 'Frankie?' I was out of the chair now, padding towards him in the cold light of the computer. He backed away from me, his eyes wide and frightened in his thin face.

'I th-th-th-thought I heard a b-b-b-b-b—'

'Shhhh. There's no burglar – only me. I didn't mean to yell. I thought you were . . . someone else. Frankie – no one must know I was here. Don't tell, OK?' He shook his head wordlessly. I put my hand on his shoulder. He was shivering. 'Back to bed now. Quiet as a mouse, huh? And remember – not one word to anyone. Promise?'

'P-p-p-promise.'

He turned and stole away down the passage like a little ghost. I turned the computer off, covered it carefully with its sheet, closed the rec room door, tiptoed back to bed . . . and lay there in a cold sweat of relief, my heart hammering hard enough to wake the whole of Highgate.

I knew Q would come. Probably just after three o'clock, when I'd normally be getting back from school. Or during afternoon tea . . . or maybe just before dinner. One thing I knew for sure: he'd come.

I spent the morning locked in the bathrooms on my hands and knees, cleaning the shower stalls and toilets. I thought of the other kids at school: the end-of-term lip-synch concert . . . the staff-versus-kids softball match . . . the sausage sizzle. Most of all, I thought of Q roaring along the highway in the big green four-by-four, his bodyguard Shaw at the wheel, every second bringing them closer to Highgate.

Matron and Cook had pies for lunch, from the corner bakery. I sat by myself at the far end of the dining room, making my slice of bread and jam last as long as possible, breathing in the smell of rich gravy and flaky golden pastry. Matron didn't take her eyes off me once.

After lunch, though I knew it was way too early, I found myself starting to listen for the sound of the car. I was spring-cleaning the kitchen under Cook's supervision, and it was hard to hear anything above the sound of my scrubbing brush, with my head stuck in the back of cupboard after cupboard. But at last I heard the slam of the front door, and the excited chatter of voices. Who wouldn't be excited, getting away from Highgate for two weeks?

Any minute now . . . any minute now, they'll come.

That whole afternoon my senses were on super-alert, my ears pricked for the sound of a car engine, or a door slamming. And there were plenty of those, as first one kid, then another was picked up by guardians or foster-families for the holidays. But when the doorbell rang, it was never for me.

By dinner time my heart felt like a lead weight in my chest. My fingers were wrinkled up like old prunes, my eyes were red-rimmed and stinging, and my skin had a tinny, chemical smell of bleach and detergent that no amount of soap could wash away. Breathing in the fumes all day had given me a headache and left a strange, metallic taste in my mouth that made dinner – liver, onions and cabbage – taste even worse than usual. I pushed it around my plate, trying not to look at Weevil sitting opposite, chewing tidily, his face smooth with satisfaction. For once, I didn't finish my grey, greasy plateful. When at last dinner was over and I left the table to do the washing up, the hollow feeling under my ribs had nothing to do with hunger.

He isn't coming . . .

Chores finally over, I mooched into the rec room

and over to my favourite chair. The stuffing was coming out here and there, and it had a funny, mouldy smell, but it was comfortable enough as long as you avoided the springs. I flopped down with my back to the room, opened my library book, and stared at the first page, sick with disappointment. The words blurred and swam and disappeared. My mind drifted . . . over the high wire fence of Highgate . . . over the roofs and twinkling lights of Redcliff . . . over the dark countryside, to Quested Court and beyond: far, far beyond, to a land where rivers sang and twin moons hung in a purple sky.

The doorbell rang.

Instantly, my book jerked into focus again. My ears mushroomed as huge as an elephant's . . . my heart stopped beating, and my breath caught in my throat. My head hummed with the echoing silence of the listening room. Everyone who was leaving for the holidays had already left . . . so who could this be?

Matron's footsteps marched down the passage to the front door: *clack clack clack clack*. The key turned in the heavy lock; the bolts drew back: one . . . two. The door creaked open.

The minutes dragged by. I imagined raised voices . . . shouting . . . Shaw bursting into the room with Sabre bounding and straining at his leash, teeth bared . . . an escort of uniformed policemen with a warrant for my instant release . . . the sound of a car drawing away, and Matron appearing in the doorway, cane at the ready. *Please – not that*.

But there was nothing – nothing except the murmur

of the television and the subdued, curious whispers of the other children.

Then, after what seemed a long, long time, the doorknob turned. The room froze, every eye on the door. It opened. A tall, dishevelled scarecrow in scuffed corduroys and a baggy green sweater stepped hesitantly into the room, searching it with eyes that were mild and interested behind smeary specs.

Q.

Behind him, a hulking giant of a man, shoulders so wide he turned automatically sideways as he entered the room, head ducking under the lintel of the door. Shaw, bald head gleaming under the electric light, face impassive as ever. Stopping just inside the doorway, arms folded, surveying the room through narrowed eyes.

Then I was standing, my book falling to the floor . . . crossing the room as if I was walking on clouds . . . arriving in the safe haven of Q's open arms with a feeling like coming home.

Ten minutes later we were coasting down the hill and through the centre of town, heading for the northern highway. I gazed out at the lights flashing by, hardly able to believe it was true. Here I was, cocooned in leather-scented luxury, music playing softly on the stereo, leaving it all behind . . .

Weevil, stunned, his face as blank as if he'd walked into a wall. Scuttling up to Q as we headed for the front door, reaching to tug at the frayed hem of his jumper – 'Excuse me, Mr Quested, sir, excuse me –'

while Q smiled down at me, shepherding me pro-
tectively to the car, not even noticing Weevil was
there.

The look on Weevil's face as we roared away down
the driveway, gravel spurting from the tyres.

Matron's closed door.

'*Matron!* She'll be so mad! She'll kill me when I get
back! What did you say to her? You didn't tell her,
did you? About the e-mail?'

Q's slow, peaceful smile. 'Relax, Adam. Don't worry
your head about her. I don't like what I sense about
that woman, to be honest, and I don't like the feel of
Highgate. I think you've had a tough time, one way
and another, you poor fellow. Places like Highgate
aren't run like that any more, or shouldn't be – this is
the twentieth century, after all.'

'The twenty-first century, ain't it, Q?'

'A minor detail, Shaw – but thank you all the
same. My point is, you can't run a children's home
like a prison. There are laws in place to prevent it.
I shudder to think what a competent investigation
of that place would turn up, starting with an audit
of the finances . . . tempting, isn't it, Shaw? I said as
much to your Matron . . . and I do believe she felt I
had a point. Seemed quite happy to allow you to come
with us, in fact. And now, my boy, sit back and relax.
The holidays are here – and Hannah and I are going
to make sure you enjoy every minute.'

HANNAH

It was as if a heavy weight was slowly lifting off me, growing lighter with every turn of the wheels. Most of that weight was Weevil. He was stuck back there at Highgate whether he liked it or not – there was nothing he could do about it now. I wouldn't see him, or even need to think about him, for two whole weeks.

I was in the middle of a detailed description of my gladiator project when a huge yawn just about cracked my jaw. Q smiled down at me. 'It's late, I know. So rather than drive all the way through to Quested Court tonight, I thought we'd stop off at a little country hotel a couple of kilometres further on. I've stayed there once or twice – the rooms are comfortable, and the food's not bad. We'll make an early start in the morning, and be back home in time for lunch.'

Home. It was a word I'd never have dreamed of using to describe Highgate, even though I'd lived there all my life. But somehow it fitted Quested Court perfectly – and it warmed me even more than the prospect of a cosy bed. But suddenly a thought came into my mind – an unwelcome thought I tried to push away before it took root and grew.

Quested Court: Q's home. A place where he and Hannah were safe and private, surrounded by the small group of people he trusted completely – almost like family, he'd told us once. A place where I'd felt safe.

But one of them had been in my room that night. Though I hadn't actually seen anyone, I knew it had been someone in Quested Court. But who? Not Q. Not Hannah. Not one of the other children, I was sure. That left the adults. Shaw: solid, reassuring, reliable, hands steady on the wheel as he guided the big car safely through the rushing darkness. Nanny, who loved Hannah like her own child, and who'd looked after Q himself when he was small. Withers, the accountant. I'd never met him, but I knew Q trusted him completely. Veronica Usherwood, Marketing Manager of Quest Enterprises. Brisk, businesslike, efficient; someone Hannah once told me *would like to be her mother* . . . but who neither Hannah nor her little cat Tiger Lily liked. Someone whose eyes I had noticed more than once resting on me with a cool watchfulness I didn't even begin to understand.

I ought to tell Q. But how could I – and what was there to tell? How did you tell your host that you believed someone in his home had . . . spied on you?

Now or never. I took a deep breath. 'Q –' I began hesitantly.

At that moment, the car slowed, and the indicator

flicked on. 'Ah – here we are,' said Q with satisfaction.

Perhaps that was the answer: you didn't tell him.

As Q had promised, we made an early start the next morning, fortified by a scrumptious breakfast of bacon, eggs and something I'd never had before called devilled kidneys. 'Food fit fer a king,' Shaw declared with his mouth full – and he was right. Several cups of steaming coffee and frothy hot chocolate later, we were off.

Early morning mist lay in thin veils across the road; the long grass sparkled with dew, and everywhere birds wheeled and spun in the clear air. As before, Shaw drove, leaving Q and me to relax in the back, dreaming, gazing out of the window, and occasionally talking about whatever came into our heads. Now, in the bright light of morning, the memory of that night at Quested Court dissolved like a forgotten dream.

Q was working flat out, he told me, often late into the night. The newest title in his award-winning Karazan Series was underway, and going well. 'Top secret still, of course, Adam,' he said, almost shyly. 'This will be the last one – the most powerful yet, and the best. The culmination of all my years of work . . . sad in a way, I suppose. But everything has to come to an end, and every end is a new beginning.' Something about his words sounded familiar . . . and unsettling.

'Yeah, I guess,' I mumbled. It was weird to think of Q writing another Karazan computer game. Sure, it was a world he'd invented, out of his imagination: a pretend world to thousands of kids all over the world. But not to me. Because it was a world I'd been to, whose air I'd breathed and whose food I'd eaten . . . a world with people in it as real as I was. But Q hadn't been there. Did that mean it was still a game to him?

And how did the computer-game fantasy tie in with the reality of Karazan? If Q invented something in his game – the game he was working on now – did that mean it would suddenly appear in Karazan, like magic? Could he influence things that happened there . . . or did his games operate in a different dimension from the real world Karazan had become – in a simple world of make-believe?

The thought of a new Karazan computer game gave me a strange feeling of unease . . . a queasy, uncomfortable feeling under my ribs . . . a kind of superstitious dread. I knew I'd struggle to explain the feeling to anyone, even Q. I didn't even begin to understand it myself. For a second I thought of asking what the new game was called . . . but 'top secret', Q had said, and I didn't want to pry, so I pushed thoughts of Karazan out of my mind, and went back to watching the world go by.

The last time – the only other time – I'd made this journey, I'd been fast asleep, a stowaway in the back of a horsebox. Now, I drank in every detail of the scenery as it scrolled smoothly past the window. It wasn't often I had the chance to get out of the city, and I was determined to make the most of every moment.

We stopped in Cranmer for a break, another cup

of coffee for the grown-ups, and a cold drink and an iced bun for me – crammed with raisins, with thick white icing on top that cracked into slabs when I bit into it.

And then it was only an hour and a half to Winterton. The big car gobbled up the kilometres to Quested Court as effortlessly as I'd gobbled up my bun. I smiled to myself when I remembered my endless walk along this same road – wet, bedraggled, and very unsure of my welcome.

Today couldn't have been more different. The sun was shining, the huge gates stood open, and Quentin Quested himself was beside me, as impatient as I was to arrive. The car slowed and turned into the driveway. I'd pictured Hannah waiting by the gate, swinging on it, maybe . . . the same gate I'd had to climb over in the pouring rain two months before.

I could tell Shaw was half expecting her to come darting out from the woodland that lined the drive – he slowed down to a crawl once we were through the gate, and in the rear-view mirror I could see his watchful bodyguard's eyes scanning the trees, alert for any movement.

Beside me, Q was leaning forward in his seat, eyes glowing with anticipation behind his cloudy specs. 'You won't believe how she's grown, Adam,' he was telling me for the zillionth time. 'Taller, stronger every day – a sturdy, healthy little girl with rosy cheeks – *rosy* – the first time I've ever understood the true wonder of the word. And her hair, wait till you see her hair – fluffy and golden, like duckling down. You won't recognise her! And we never get a moment's peace, of course. She was full of mischief even before, when she was so ill . . . well, you know that as well as anyone. But now she's . . . *bubbling* with nonsense, overflowing with the joy of life. And we have you to thank for it. And surprises! She's such a one for *surprises* – just you wait! She's been living for this visit ever since you left – she talks about you every single day. You – and the other four. My little Chatterbot . . . what you did for her can never be repaid, Adam. Never.'

Finally Shaw drew up outside the huge old house and we all piled out, stretching the stiffness of the long drive out of our arms and legs. Sabre, Shaw's fearsome-looking Rottweiler guard dog, waggled over to say hello. I patted his heavy shoulder and pulled his ear; he looked up at me, forehead crinkled in a worried frown, and gave a funny little whine.

Q bounded up the steps to the heavy wooden door. 'Hannah! Hannah!' he called. 'Chatterbot, look who's here! We're home!'

He flung the door open.

An elderly, dry-looking man like a kindly vulture stood framed in the doorway, his smile of welcome fading into an expression of dawning bewilderment.

'Withers!' cried Q. 'Come and say hello to Adam! Hannah! Where's that little monkey hiding? *Hannah!* Has she been making your lives a misery while we've been away? I was sure she'd be up at the gate . . .' Like a wind-up toy running down, Q's voice trailed off and stopped. He stared into Withers' face for what seemed a very long time. 'Where is she?' he breathed.

Withers cleared his throat: a soft, apologetic sound like rustling paper. 'But Q,' he said, 'Hannah – she went with you to fetch Adam, yesterday afternoon.'

SURPRISES

Q's face turned grey. 'No,' he whispered. 'She didn't come with us.'

The trim figure of Ms Usherwood appeared in the doorway beside Withers. 'Hello, Adam,' she said briefly. 'Now, Q, what's all this about Hannah?'

'She . . . I . . .' Deep lines were etched on Q's face. He'd aged twenty years in the last few seconds – he looked like an old, old man.

'Seems Withers thought she'd come with us ter fetch Adam,' growled Shaw, 'but she didn't. Last we saw of 'er was when we was leavin' yesterday afternoon.'

'She'll be hiding away somewhere to give us a fright, the little madam,' Usherwood said crisply. 'For goodness' sake, Q, sit down before you fall down.'

'The 'ole night? Not bloomin' likely, Usherwood. Kid's been missin' close on twenty-four hours. I reckon we search the house and the grounds, then call the cops. This set up says one thing ter me, and that's . . . *kidnap*. Sorry, Q, but that's my fix on it. Think about it: you an' me both away, gate wide open . . . might as well put out the welcome mat an' start countin' the ransom.'

68

Withers wrung his hands. 'If we'd known she was still on the property, we would have kept the usual security measures in place . . . but from what she said I was convinced you'd taken her with you, and that's what I told the others. How will I ever forgive myself?'

'Wot she said?' barked Shaw. 'An' wot was that?'

'She came into my office shortly before you left – about three o'clock or so. I was busy with the tax return at the time, or I would have questioned her more closely. She said . . . let me see . . . "I'm going to fetch someone I haven't seen for a long, long time." Adam, obviously. Then she prattled on, as she does – about a surprise, and a secret; I shouldn't tell anybody . . . I'm afraid I simply assumed you'd agreed to take her with you after all, Q – or that she was planning to stow away in the back seat. This is all my fault.'

Q shook his head. 'Don't blame yourself, Withers,' he said dully. 'Anyone would have thought the same. How could you possibly have known that for once I was determined to leave her behind? I was afraid there might be unpleasantness when we collected Adam, and I didn't want her exposed to anything upsetting. And she seemed surprisingly happy to stay. But now . . .'

'Well, there's nothin' to be gained by beatin' yourselves up about it,' growled Shaw. 'Wee 'annah's always full o' nonsense . . . it'd be a full-time job to make 'ead or tail of 'alf she comes out with. Wot we need ter do now is get movin' – search for an hour. And if we 'aven't found 'er by then, call the cops.'

'I agree,' said Ms Usherwood. 'Let's not waste any

69

more time. You and the groundsmen search outside. Withers and I will gather the house staff and allocate search areas indoors. Go on to the library, Adam – you know the way. We'll join you directly.'

I walked up the wide stone steps into the echoing hallway, my feet like lead. Hannah kidnapped? It's the kind of thing you read about in newspapers, not something that happens to people you know, in real life. Yet how many other strange – no, impossible – things had happened since I'd first come to Quested Court? Q was one of the richest men in the world, according to Cameron – though that was easy to forget. But surely it was more likely that she'd gone up to one of the disused rooms on the upper floors – an attic, maybe – and somehow locked herself in by mistake . . . or fallen and hurt her leg – even knocked herself out, somewhere in the huge grounds . . .

I opened the library door and stepped inside. The heavy velvet drapes were closed, the room dark and deserted. I groped for the light switch beside the door and flicked it on. The crystal chandelier hanging from the ceiling blazed into brilliant life – and in the same instant, the room exploded into a hubbub of shouts and laughter, of stamping, dancing feet, waving arms and crazy yells. 'Surprise! *Surprise!*'

It couldn't be . . . *it was*! Richard, popping up from behind Q's leather armchair like a jack-in-the-box, his blond hair tousled and his face one massive grin . . . Kenta peeking from behind a curtain, her dark eyes sparkling . . . Jamie trundling out from behind the suit of armour, his chubby face flushed and beaming with excitement.

And another girl – a stranger – straightening up from her hiding place under Q's computer desk and walking towards me, hands held out.

I gaped at them all . . . goggled at her. Questions jostled with the beginnings of answers in my numb brain. Hannah's surprises – this must be one of them! The whole thing of Hannah missing – was it part of it too? A trick – a carefully planned, not-very-funny joke? But then – where *was* Hannah? And the stranger – who was she? And why was she behaving like she knew me? I took her hands reluctantly in mine, feeling like a colossal fool. Behind her, Richard was grinning fit to bust, an expression on his face as if he was waiting for something. I stared at the girl. Hair a tangle of tawny gold . . . huge eyes as blue as cornflowers . . . a delicate, oval face . . . a smile that took my breath away. I gawked at her like an idiot, battling to make sense of it all. Her smile reminded me of someone . . . but who?

'Well – *are* you surprised?' she was demanding, in a voice that sounded weirdly familiar. 'Aren't you pleased to see us? You don't *look* pleased!'

'He doesn't recognise you, like I said!' hooted Rich.

'Oh, shut up, Richard – don't be ridiculous!' The blue eyes flashed, and at the same time a blush spread over her lovely face . . . a faint pink tide that started at the end of her nose and worked its way outward, till even the tips of her perfect ears were glowing like traffic lights.

My mouth fell open. '*Gen?*'

'I don't see what all the fuss is about, you guys,' Jamie said staunchly, waddling up to me and holding out a slightly sticky hand for me to shake. 'You ought to stop teasing Gen. It hasn't got anything to do with being bitten by the Serpent of Beauty. I think she looks just the same as she always did – she's always been real pr–' And he blushed bright pink too.

Seeing them all again . . . the unexpectedness of it, on top of the thing with Hannah . . . even though I was smiling, I could feel tears in my eyes. 'It's great to see you all,' I mumbled. 'It's the coolest surprise ever. But Hannah . . . is she . . .'

I guess part of me still hoped she might pop up out of her hiding place and skip over to give me a hug. But I knew, with cold certainty like a knife in my heart, that however many surprises had been planned, Hannah's disappearance wasn't one of them.

Just then Q appeared in the doorway, Usherwood and Shaw grim-faced behind him. He was holding a piece of paper, but his hand was trembling so much I was sure he would drop it. Gently, I reached out and took his arm. 'What is it, Q? Is it . . . a ransom note?'

He shook his head helplessly. 'This is all too much,' he croaked. 'I don't even begin to understand.' The paper fluttered to the ground.

Out of the corner of my eye I saw a little silvery-grey shape scamper through the door and across the carpet. A kitten. I felt a stab of sadness – it must be Hannah's, one of the surprises she was planning for me. And now . . .

I bent and picked up the paper. It was small and square, pale pink, with purple writing. It didn't look like a ransom note. Hesitantly, I read it out, my voice sounding very loud in the silent room.

> *Dear Bluebell,*
> *I love you very mutch, but I miss Tiger Lily two.*
> *When you meet her, you will umberstand egzactly*
> *how speshal she is.*
> *Be good wile I am gone.*
> *Love from*
> *Hannah*
> *XXXXX*

My mind was racing. What had Hannah told Withers? *I'm going to fetch someone I haven't seen for a long, long time.* Withers thought she meant me, but she didn't. She meant Tiger Lily.

Looking round at the others' blank faces, I couldn't believe they didn't understand at once. Hannah had this planned all along: the biggest surprise of all in what I knew would have been a long list of surprises.

'Hannah's gone to Karazan,' I heard myself saying. 'On her own. And if she's gone without the micro-computer . . .'

We knew what we would find in the computer room, and we were right. All the computers dark and lifeless . . . except one. Mine: turned on, the cursor blinking patiently on an empty screen. And half under the table, face down on the carpet, Hannah's teddy.

We watched Q walk slowly to his desk at the front of the room. He slid open a drawer, took something out, and stood staring down at it as if he'd been turned to stone. We all knew what it was. We would have recognised it anywhere. It was the microcomputer we had taken with us into Karazan: a prototype, the only one of its kind. On its tiny keyboard, on keys the size of grains of rice, I'd input the command that catapulted us back from Karazan: *Alt Control Q*. It was a lifeline, a passport back to our own dimension . . . and it was here, in Q's hand, in the computer room at Quested Court.

Hannah was alone in Karazan, with no way of getting back again.

'My clothes – have you still got them?'

At the sound of my voice, a tiny smile appeared on Q's face, but his eyes were far, far away. 'I beg your pardon, dear boy?'

'My gear – the stuff I wore to Karazan,' I repeated impatiently. 'Have you still got it, or did you chuck it all out?'

'I – of course we still have it. But . . .'

'Where is it?' I looked up at the clock on the computer room wall. 'I reckon it'll take me maybe . . . five minutes to put it all on. In six minutes – five and a half if I'm quick – I'll be there.'

Q was still staring at me as blankly as if I was speaking a foreign language. I didn't have time to waste. She'd been gone nearly twenty-four hours . . . time enough for anything to have happened. I turned and ran out of the computer room . . . along the passage . . . up the stairs, two at a time.

'Hey – Adam! Adam – wait up!' Without slowing down, I glanced over my shoulder. Richard was half-way up the stairs, arms pumping, face a scowl of determination. Behind him puffed Jamie, already puce in the face. Hot on his heels, Kenta . . . and Gen bringing up the rear. Something in their faces made me slow and stop. I stood there on the landing, arms folded, looking down at them. They stopped too, staring up at me . . . and on every face, the exact same look.

I opened my mouth to say: 'What is it?' To say: 'Forget it.' To say: 'One person will attract less attention than five – especially three with pink skin and blond hair. Especially one who looks like Gen.' But there wasn't time to argue. What's more, there wasn't any point.

So instead, I found myself grinning back down at my four friends like a prize idiot. 'OK then – have it your way! But quick – we have to hurry!'

Nanny was struggling with the buckle of Richard's broad leather belt. 'Well, I declare, you *have* grown,' she was muttering. 'I might just need to put another hole in this . . .'

'Yes, grown fatter,' teased Gen, rapidly braiding her hair into a tawny rope in front of the mirror.

'This isn't fat, it's muscle,' Richard retorted. 'And you should stop preening. Typical girl – any mention of going anywhere, and it's "Ooh, my hair!" and

"What shall I wear?", whether it's a desperate rescue mission or a trip to the mall . . .'

The door opened and Q stood there, looking at us. The dazed look was gone. His blue eyes were bright and piercing behind his specs – fresh smears made me wonder whether he'd tried to clean them on the way up the stairs.

'I'm not going to argue with you,' he said quietly. 'As you know, I'm not a practical man. I was annoyed with myself last time for not thinking of your pale skins, and how they'd stand out in Karazan.' For a second, he looked almost embarrassed. 'I thought – too late, of course – that I should have provided something to darken you up . . . make you look less conspicuous. But I looked into it, and came up with this.' He walked over to the top drawer of the dresser, opened it, and produced a small bottle, holding it up for us to see. 'Tyrotemp, used by theatrical companies, I believe. Based on the natural skin-darkening enzyme tyrosinase . . . guaranteed to last a week, then fade completely. I –'

But Jamie was reaching out an eager pink hand. 'Awesome, Q! I've always wanted a tan! Bags I first go!'

Ten minutes later we were ready to go. At Nanny's insistence we'd each wolfed down a steak pie – 'I've never let a child head off on an adventure on an empty stomach yet, and I'm not about to start now!' – in fact Rich and Jamie had gobbled down two, in record time. The weight of my backpack felt familiar and reassuring.

It had given me a weird feeling of excitement to see it again . . . I bent my head to sniff it, and sure enough, there was the faint, indescribable fragrance that was Karazan. I checked quickly through the contents: compass, sleeping bag, compact aluminium cooking pot, lighter . . . and there, in the front pocket, a replacement for the pocketknife I'd given Kai. Rich was holding up an identical one, a grin of delight on his broad brown face. *Brown face* . . . I stared round at the others. Gen's pale prettiness had darkened to a golden glow – with her mane of sandy hair, she looked as wild and beautiful as a young lioness. Kenta, naturally darker-skinned like me, was the same as ever; Rich looked like a real beach bum, his teeth startlingly white in his beaming bronzed face.

As for Jamie . . . he was peering anxiously into the mirror with his back to us. 'Well, come on, Jamie,' goes Rich, 'let's have a look at the new, improved James Fitzpatrick!'

Slowly, reluctantly, Jamie turned round. His hair was its usual neatly combed blond pudding-bowl . . . and beneath it shone a woebegone moon-face, bright orange as the setting sun. Richard gave a splutter of laughter, which he quickly turned into a cough when he saw the tears in Jamie's eyes. Kenta was at his side in an instant. 'Jamie – what happened? However did you do that? What went wrong?'

'I – I just . . . like I said, I've never had a tan before. I always burn, then peel,' said Jamie miserably. 'So I thought I'd put on a double dose – just to be sure it'd take, you know . . . seeing I have such a fair skin.

A *delicate* skin, my mum always says,' he added, a touch defensively. He rubbed uselessly at his face with orange fingers. 'But now . . .'

'Now you look like a carrot,' said Rich cheerfully. 'A walking, talking carrot – or an orange turnip, more like. Still, never mind, Jamie – what did Q say? *Guaranteed to last a week, then fade completely*. Let's hope he's right! And meanwhile, we can use you as a torch if our batteries run out . . .'

'Oh, give it a break, Richard,' said Gen crossly. 'He doesn't look too bad . . . and if he keeps his cloak on and the hood pulled forward, no one will even notice. Now, has everyone got everything?'

'Perhaps you should each take a good book . . .'

'Groundsheets, water bottles, dehydrated food – and plenty of it – sunscreen, insect repellent, polypropylene underwear, something for runny tummies . . .' recited Nanny, ticking things off on a list.

'Oh, come on, come on – can't we just *go*?' begged Gen, in an agony of impatience.

'I'm sure there's something I've forgotten – something really, really obvious, that I'll remember the moment you leave. Oh dear, whatever can it be . . .' lamented Q. 'I wish I were more practical!'

I pulled out my shawl from my school bag and stuffed it down deep into my backpack, along with my *Bible*. No one was going to sneak a look inside *that* while I was away. Rich watched me, grinning, but didn't say anything. I looked at him levelly, daring him to comment, running through my personal checklist in my mind. *Shawl*, Bible, *ring* – yes, there it was, cold and comforting under the rough fabric of my shirt – *penny whistle* . . . I felt a pang of loss. Who knows when, if ever, I'd see it again . . . A mental image of Weevil flashed into my mind, but I pushed it roughly away.

And finally we were back downstairs, each in front of our computer, screens on and ready to go. I tried to tune out Q's anxious voice: 'Do be careful. I shouldn't be letting you go, I know I shouldn't. I'd go myself, but I still haven't managed to modify the programme to allow adults to make the transition . . . to tell the truth, I haven't even been trying, what with *Power* . . . what with working on my new game. Now whatever you do, never forget things aren't always as they seem . . . and remember spontaneous evolution, children – things change, and the changes are not always for the good . . .'

'Ready?' I asked. Four heads nodded; four faces, in varying shades of tan, stared intently at their screens.

'OK then –'

'Wait!' yelped Q. Our hands froze above the keyboards. 'I've remembered! Don't go yet! I won't be a moment –'

He turned and sprinted, with surprising speed, out through the door. 'Quick – let's go before he gets back, or he'll never let us leave,' grumbled Rich.

'I think we should wait,' quavered Jamie. 'Maybe it's something really important. Or perhaps he's thought of somewhere else Hannah might be. Maybe we won't have to go to Karazan after all!'

Richard snorted. 'Maybe orange turnips can fly,'

he retorted. 'Anyhow, no one's *making* you go.'

'I know,' said Jamie with dignity. 'But a man's got to do what a man's got to do. That's what my dad always says . . .'

At that moment Q burst back into the room, something glinting in his hand. 'Here they are!' he panted. 'Thank goodness I remembered! There's only a little bit left of the healing one, but even that . . . you never know . . .'

Solemnly, he held out the crystal phials. One glimmered with a strange, milky-blue fluorescence: the last remnants of the magic healing potion that had saved Hannah's life. More useful than Nanny's medicine by a long shot, I thought grimly. The other, still full, was blacker than ink: the Potion of Power. Wrapped in my shawl, they were the only two to have survived the transition back from Karazan to our world. I dug for my shawl again and tucked the phials snugly into its soft folds, then packed it safely away.

'And now –' said Rich.

'Yes, now I suppose you really had better be off,' said Q reluctantly.

Rich looked over at me, fingers poised. I gave him a grin. Across the room Jamie was staring at his computer screen, eyes bulging like an exotic goldfish. Gen's face was tense and focused, Kenta's self-contained and still. 'Ready? One . . . two . . . three!'

Five sets of fingers came down on five sets of keys . . . and the computer room at Quested Court vanished in less than an instant, as if it had never existed.

AN OPEN DOOR

'Any one of you could pass through from our world to Karazan as easily as walking through an open door,' Q had once said. It was true. Making the transition from our world to Karazan was even more effortless than that, for me at least. Like blinking: eyes open – our world; blink and open them again – Karazan.

My eyes blinked open on a crisp autumn morning. The red-gold Karazan sun shone down from the pale bowl of sky without any real warmth. Above me, the endless cliff reared up as far as I could see – in a few hours the rock I was sitting on would be in deep shade, and bitterly cold. Snow lay in crystal patches at its foot, and in a deeper drift on the western side of the standing stone a few paces away, protected from the morning sun by the stone itself, and the afternoon sun by the looming cliff.

The air had a frosty bite, making my cheeks sting and my eyes water. Eagerly, I drank in its wintry freshness, my eyes searching for the far glint of the sea and the distant walls of Arakesh above the gold and copper carpet of forest stretching away below me.

81

I strode over to the tall stone and laid my forehead against its cold, unyielding surface. Closed my eyes, and breathed in the strange, familiar scents of Karazan. It was good to be back.

'Adam! Adam – I bumped my head on the way through!'

'Don't be stupid, Jamie – what could you possibly have bumped it *on*?'

'Let me look. There *is* an odd-looking splodge on your forehead, though it's hard to tell for certain under the oran– hard to tell for certain. Does it hurt when I touch it?'

'I feel like my insides have been taken out with an ice-cream scoop and left behind at Quested Court!'

'My pants are all wet – I landed in a patch of snow. I don't suppose I could pop back quickly and ch–'

'*No!*' The chorus that met Jamie's tentative suggestion brought me suddenly back to earth – or at any rate, back to reality – with a grin. I straightened, stretching, and watched my four friends picking themselves up and dusting away the ice crystals that clung to the boys' breeches and the girls' ragged tunics.

Back to reality . . . *Hannah*.

Frowning, I scanned the russet tussock that covered the hillside. Richard followed my gaze. 'Yeah – let's not forget why we're here! What say we spread out like a proper search party,' he suggested cheerfully. 'Hunt for signs, like trackers: a button, or a footprint; a message written in the snow . . . maybe even an arrow showing which way she went!'

'Or she could have left a trail of breadcrumbs so she could find her way back, like in *Hansel and Gretel*!' said Gen eagerly.

So we spread out and searched . . . but we found nothing. Not the tiniest clue that anyone other than ourselves had ever set foot on the deserted hillside.

After half an hour or so, Jamie plumped down on the low, lichen-covered rock. 'What say we have some morning tea?' he said hopefully.

'We should carry on looking,' objected Richard. 'We're not on some kind of boy-scout camp, or a picnic.' Jamie turned a deeper shade of orange, and lumbered reluctantly to his feet.

'Do you think we should try calling?' Kenta suggested. 'If she is still within earshot . . . injured, or trapped somewhere . . .' So we cupped our hands round our mouths like loudspeakers and called, over and over, our voices thin and lost-sounding in the cold air: 'Hannah! Hannah! *Hannah!*'

There was no answer, not even an echo. But deep down I knew all along there wouldn't be. In my heart I knew that by now Hannah would be far away. She'd have stood where we were standing and would have looked out to the east, towards the sea. Like I had, she would have seen the distant walls of Arakesh. She knew that was where we'd last seen Tiger Lily, so that's where she would have headed. But there was just one other possibility. 'You don't suppose . . .' I said tentatively, 'You don't suppose she might have somehow stumbled across the cottage I told you about?'

Rich's eyes lit up. 'The one where those two weird old people lived – Thingy and Whatsit –'

'Argos and Ronel,' I said slowly, remembering. They'd helped me when I was in trouble, however reluctantly – on Argos's part, at least. If Hannah had cried out, like I did, for whatever reason . . .

'Good thinking, Adam. Let's head on down and ask them if they've seen her. She's probably sitting in front of their fire having a nice hot drink.'

We left the open hillside and headed down into the trees, instinctively clustering closer together in the chilly shadows. I led the way, listening for the sound of the stream that would lead me to the cottage. Jamie stumbled along after me, breathing down my neck, standing on my heels, tripping over roots, and managing to squelch through every puddle on the forest floor. Our progress was almost completely silent apart from his huffing and puffing and grouching – any sound our footfalls might have made was completely muffled by the springy layer of red, bronze and brown leaves that carpeted the ground.

'Do shut up, Jamie,' said Richard good-naturedly. 'The racket you're making, we wouldn't hear Hannah if she was behind the next tree yelling her head off!'

Yes, I thought. *And who knows what might hear you?* Because no matter how peaceful and safe the forest looked, I had an uncomfortable feeling of being watched – that if I spun round quickly enough . . . The growl of Argos's gruff voice sounded in my mind, as clear as if he was beside me: *You have been making enough noise to wake the dead . . . and let us hope you have not.* The quieter we were, the better. And the sooner we were out of the forest, the happier I'd be.

'*Ouch!*' yelped Jamie. 'No need to throw things at me, Richard!'

'I didn't!'

'Yes, you did! It hit me on the head! Look – even through my hood it's left a lump the size of an egg!'

'Shhhh!' I said in a low voice. 'The river's over on the right – can you hear it? This is the way I went with Argos – down this slope, I'm sure of it –' At that moment something cracked me on the head – a sharp rap that made me flinch and duck away. 'Yeowch! *Richard . . .*'

Rich held out his hands, a look of innocent bafflement on his face. One thing for sure, it hadn't been him. I looked up. Between the leaves, way up in the forest canopy, I could see them clearly – dense bunches almost like grapes, of something that . . .

'Ow!' yipped Gen.

. . . of something that was falling all around us like fat hailstones, landing without a sound on the cushioning leaves. I picked up the one that had hit me. It was a round, purplish-coloured nut, bigger than a chestnut and round as a marble – and as hard as a marble too, with a shiny, polished skin.

'Nuts! I wonder if you can eat them?' said Jamie.

'Nuts to you too – and next time, be sure of your facts before you go blaming me for everything bad that happens to you!'

Taking care to stay together, with our hoods over our heads for protection, we tramped on through the trees in the direction of the cottage – or at least, the direction I was sure the cottage had been. But no matter how many times I retraced my steps, or how many landmarks I thought I recognised, there was no sign of it anywhere. Sure, it had been tucked away . . . but I'd have bet I could find it again, no problem.

At last I slowed and stopped, frowning, listening for the ring of an axe on wood, sniffing for the scent of woodsmoke. Nothing.

'It's a big forest, Adam. And if it's so well hidden, I'm sure Hannah wouldn't have found it either,' said Kenta comfortingly.

Unless it wanted to be found . . .

Impatiently, I shook the thought away. 'It ought to be here . . .' I said, more to myself than the others.

'But it isn't,' finished Richard, practical as always. 'And neither is Hannah, as far as I can see. She may be only five, but she's sharp as a tack – she'd know her best shot at finding her cat would be to head downhill towards Arakesh. I vote that's what we do too – then we'll have plenty of time to scout around for clues before dark.'

'We *could* try calling again, I suppose . . .' said Gen doubtfully. But the others looked around uneasily at the listening forest, and didn't answer.

'I know!' said Jamie, sounding suddenly more cheerful. 'Let's go to Arakesh and find Kai, and ask him for advice. We wouldn't have got anywhere last time without his help. And who knows – he might even give us more of those bread rolls!'

Rich gave me a grin and a wink, and I felt my spirits

86

rise. Looking round at the others, I could tell they felt the same. It wasn't the thought of the rolls, but Kai himself – his cheery face, his perky cow's-lick, his permanent smile. His knowledge of Arakesh – its streets, its nooks and crannies . . . its secrets, and its dangers. If there was so much as a murmur of Hannah's whereabouts, Kai would have heard it. But more than that, Kai was a friend. *Friends forever . . .*

Yes, Kai would be as good a starting point for our search as any – probably better.

THE BREWER'S BUTT

'I f Hannah tried to get into Arakesh through this gate, she'd have been caught before she went two steps,' said Richard gloomily.

It was true. To a five-year-old, there would have been something reassuringly normal about the steady trickle of traffic entering the city – handcarts and wagons, work-stained farmers leading glonks with panniers of produce on their backs, their lop ears lolloping with every stride . . . even the occasional child. Hannah would have seen the guards at the gate, stopping and searching the wagons and questioning the owners. But would she have noticed the pikes leaning up against the wall, their razor-sharp blades glinting in the sun? Would she have seen how the children clung close to their mothers, burying their faces in their skirts as they drew near the gate? Most of all, would she have seen the grey shapes huddled like vultures beneath the city walls? I doubted it.

What Hannah would have seen was what I'd described to her: cute glonks, higgledy-piggledy houses, quaint cobbled streets, the magnificent Temple rearing up in the centre of the city like a gigantic pink wedding cake. When I'd told Hannah the story of our quest – a few days after our return, when she was well enough – I'd made Arakesh sound like a fairy-tale city, full of excitement and surprises. I'd made the Curators out to be like Q had originally intended: wise, caring and kind. One of them would have found Tiger Lily, I told Hannah, and they'd love and care for her as much as she would herself. The reality was very different – and now I wished I'd told Hannah the truth. Sure, it would have frightened her . . . but that fear would have protected her. Who knows, if she'd been scared enough, she might still be sound asleep in her own four-poster bed in Quested Court, instead of here in Karazan.

But we knew a safe way into Arakesh – a secret way. The way Kai had shown us. And we intended to use it.

The tunnel under the city wall was harder to find than we remembered. The bushes concealing it had grown into a dense mass of tangled vegetation, and the mouth of the tunnel – when we eventually found it – was almost completely hidden under a network of twigs, cobwebs and fallen leaves. 'Looks like Kai hasn't been here for a while,' muttered Rich.

'No – but neither has anyone else. And that has to be good news,' I said, with what I hoped was a reassuring grin. The last time we'd used the tunnel – when Kai had met us at the entrance with a bag of fragrant rolls – seemed very long ago.

From the mournful look on Jamie's face, I could tell

he was remembering it too. 'It's pretty cobwebby, isn't it?' he said.

'Never mind, I'll go first. I'm not scared of a spider or two. Rich, you take up the rear.'

I lay down on my stomach and wriggled into the narrow opening. It had a fusty, stale smell. The earth under my palms was dry and dusty, and I could feel cobwebs brushing against my face like ghostly fingers. It was pitch dark. The tunnel sloped steeply downwards, then levelled out and rose again. At this point the dry, earthy smell changed abruptly, and I coughed and felt myself gag. The stink of the glonks was worse than I remembered – and suddenly I was back in Highgate again, on hands and knees on the toilet floor, ammonia fumes burning my eyes and stinging my sinuses. One thing was for sure: I'd rather be *anywhere* than there – even in a glonk stable. Smiling, I crawled out of the mouth of the tunnel and squatted down behind the hay bales to wait for the others, my cloak over nose and mouth to try and mask the stench.

My eyes had adapted to the total darkness of the tunnel, and I could see clearly in the dusky gloom of the stable. One by one the others crawled out into the open, gasping and choking. In the stalls, I could hear the comforting farmyard sound of hooves moving on soft hay, and the occasional whickering snort and explosive fart. Cautiously, we stood up and dusted each other off, picking bits of straw out of our hair and trying to make ourselves look like solid citizens of Arakesh, instead of interlopers from another world.

'At least we look the part this time,' muttered Rich, with a sidelong grin at Jamie. 'Most of us, anyway!'

In theory Kai could be anywhere. It was late afternoon, and trentice – the Karazan version of school – would be out for the day. He could be roaming the streets, or off somewhere with his friends – a sudden memory of Hob's grinning face flashed into my mind. Or he could be helping his father in the inn . . . and from what he'd said about his dad, I was betting that's exactly where he'd be.

We crept to the big double door and peered cautiously out. The courtyard was deserted, its cobbled floor swept clean, the drinking trough full of fresh, clean water. Glancing to the left, I noticed steep wooden steps leading up the side of the barn. Hadn't Kai said . . .

'His room's up there, isn't it?' hissed Richard in my ear. 'Remember him laughing about being kept awake all night by the racket when the glonks got into his father's veggie patch and ate the beans? Should we go up and have a look? Who knows, maybe we'll get lucky and find him there, doing his homework.'

We snuck up the stairs and hesitated outside the heavy wooden door. I lifted my hand to knock – and suddenly a weird feeling of unease swept through me, making the back of my neck prickle. Instinctively, I glanced over my shoulder . . . but there was nothing to see except the tense, expectant faces of the others clustered behind me. 'Go on – hurry up!' whispered Gen.

As softly as I could, I knocked on the door, my

knuckles making barely any sound on the rough, pitted surface. 'If he is in there, he won't have heard you,' breathed Kenta. 'Can't we just . . .'

We could. The door was on the latch, and swung open with the faintest of creaks when I pushed it. I peered round, then slipped inside, beckoning the others to follow me. The room was deserted. If it had ever been Kai's bedroom, it wasn't now. Sacks of grain lined the far wall; glonk harnesses hung from the rafters. There was no sign of a bed – or of Kai – anywhere.

'Maybe the stink got too much for him, and they let him move into the inn,' said Jamie with feeling.

The inn. My spirits sank. Like it or not, that's where we were headed next. That's where Kai would be – serving ale to weary travellers, peeling vegetables for the evening meal, making up beds for guests . . . there'd be enough work to keep him busy till bedtime.

I looked across at Rich, and he pulled a face back. 'Do you think we can get away with it?' he whispered.

'What? Get away with what?' quavered Jamie anxiously.

'With going into the Busted Butt, or whatever it's called, and finding him,' Rich answered grimly. 'I'm betting that's where he is – and where he's going to stay until tomorrow morning. And we haven't got that kind of time to waste.'

Hearts hammering, trying desperately to look casual, we sauntered through the courtyard gateway and out into the street. For the time being at least, it was empty, rows of houses curving away on either side, their upper stories almost touching in places over the narrow lane. 'Look!' Jamie pointed to a wooden sign hanging from a rusty double chain, the words *The Brewer's Butt* in flaking red and gold paint. A sturdy wooden barrel stood beside the door, bound with hoops of rusty metal. 'A brewer's butt, I'll bet,' said Rich with a grin. 'One kind, anyhow. Let's hope we don't come across the other!'

'If we do, we must just pretend to be travellers,' Gen whispered as we hesitated in front of the door. 'Drama's one of my best subjects at school. I'm going to imagine I'm in a play – and after all, they must be used to all kinds of strangers arriving, being an inn.'

'Maybe Kai's on reception duty,' said Jamie, ever hopeful, 'and he'll be the first person we see when we walk in.' I tried to see through the windows on either side of the door, but the small, diamond-shaped panes of glass were thick and irregular, and hadn't been cleaned for a while. Another job for Kai, I reckoned.

'Come on – let's do it!' Rich squared his shoulders, pushed back his hood, and flung open the door. In his drab tunic and weatherworn boots, his face dark with Tyrotemp and scowling to conceal his nerves, he could easily have passed for a traveller from a distant city arriving for the night.

Just don't let's blow it, I thought, and followed him into the inn.

We were in a small, stone-flagged reception room. A desk opposite the door held a lantern, a small, dented gong, an inkwell with a feather sticking out of it and a thick, leather-bound book. Two barrels, smaller versions of the one outside, held what looked like rolled-up parchments, with some kind of notice tacked to the wall behind them.

Double doors led off to the right; I could hear the rattle of pots and pans and the sound of someone singing. A rich, meaty smell hung in the air, making my stomach growl and my thoughts turn to dinner time. There was a different, yeasty scent too – one I didn't recognise.

'The pub,' hissed Rich, with a nod at the half-open door opposite the kitchen. Beyond it I could hear voices, and sense the comforting warmth of a log fire.

The door banged open and a big man bustled out, sleeves pushed up over his forearms, drying his hands on his apron. One glance was all it took to tell that this was Kai's father. His good-natured face was a carbon copy of Kai's . . . except it had a defeated, jowly look that reminded me of a bloodhound. The eyes were Kai's, too – at least the set of them, but they looked weary, and the sparkle was missing. If there'd been any doubt left in my mind, his wiry grey hair stuck up in a cow's-lick that was an exact mirror image of Kai's.

'Well, young 'uns, and how may I be of service to you?' he asked, folding his arms and looking down at us enquiringly.

We shuffled our feet and exchanged uncomfortable glances. Then Rich spoke up, astounding us all. 'Good day to you, good innkeeper,' he said boldly, striking a swashbuckling attitude, his voice clear and strong. 'We were wondering . . .' he paused, quickly regrouping . . . 'we be travel-stained and hungry, and in search of a . . . a warm fire, and . . . a place to rest our weary feet.'

I blinked at him, impressed. I could tell he was pretty pleased with his own performance, too – he'd obviously taken Gen's acting comment to heart.

'You be young to be abroad alone,' grunted Kai's father. 'Too young to join the menfolk by the fire, any road. But food I can offer you – if you have the gelden to pay for it.'

It was obvious Rich hadn't been expecting to be asked for money, but he was on a roll, and tried gallantly to bluster his way through. Digging a hand into the pocket of his breeches, he fumbled for coins we all knew weren't there. 'By Zephyr!' he said in ringing tones. 'I believe I have –'

But the words died on his lips. The innkeeper's expression had changed in an instant from grudging welcome to horrified alarm, bordering on what looked almost like fear. 'Be you mad to speak thus – to use *that name* in this place?' he growled, glancing over his shoulder at the door standing ajar behind him. 'You will bring disaster on us all. I can give you no welcome here!'

Rich gawked at him, totally dumbfounded. Whatever had gone wrong? Here he'd come out with a real slice of vintage Karazan – one I could tell he'd felt real proud of, that we'd heard Kai and Hob use countless times – and if he'd said the worst swear word he knew, it couldn't have had a more dramatic effect. 'B-but . . .' he stammered.

'Nay – you have said enough! Be gone – and take your companions with you!'

Well, we had nothing to lose. Looking as harmless as I possibly could, I stepped hesitantly forward. 'Excuse me, sir,' I said apologetically, 'we . . . we were wondering whether we could maybe have a quick word with Kai . . . if he's not too busy, that is.'

I was looking up into his face as I spoke, and that's how I saw it: a flicker deep down in his eyes that had nothing to do with his next words. It was an expression I recognised instantly: sorrow, almost too deep to endure . . . and pain too great to bear. But then he spoke, and his words were harsh and grating, carrying clearly to every corner of the room and beyond.

'I do not know of whom you speak. I have no son. I have never had a son. I have never had a child, or children.

'Leave now, and never return!'

HOB

'Well, so much for that,' said Rich rather shakily. We were standing in the entrance of an alley a few streets away, and Richard's were the first words spoken since we left the inn. 'I'd have put money on him being Kai's father. I guess they must have sold the inn and moved away.'

'I'm not so sure,' said Jamie thoughtfully. 'It seems weird to me. Something about it just doesn't . . . feel right.'

'I agree,' said Gen. The whole thing has a . . . sort of sinister feeling. Nothing I can put my finger on . . .'

'Hang on a moment,' I said slowly, replaying the scene in my mind. 'What was it that guy said? *I have no son* . . .'

'Yeah, and he seemed pretty sure about it,' grumbled Rich, still smarting from the turn things had taken.

'*I have no son*,' I repeated. 'I didn't say I wanted to speak to his *son*; I said I wanted to speak to *Kai*. And he comes back with *I have no son* quick as a flash. He should have said, "Who's Kai?" or, "There be no one of that name here," or something.'

97

'You're right, Adam,' said Kenta. 'It's as if he *did* have a son, once, and it *was* Kai . . . but now something's happened . . .' her soft voice trailed off into unhappy silence.

'And the way he went all weird when I said that about Zephyr,' muttered Rich, rather sheepishly. 'I thought . . .'

'Of course you did,' said Gen. 'Anyone would. Don't beat yourself up about it, Rich. It wasn't your fault the wheels fell off.'

'So what do we do now?' asked Jamie glumly. 'We've got a missing cat, and a missing Hannah, and now Kai's disappeared and his dad's denying he ever existed . . . and . . . and I wish we'd never come!' His chin wobbled ominously.

'I'll tell you what we do now,' said Gen decisively. 'We pay our old friend Hob a visit. There's nothing strange or sinister about Hob. He's Kai's best friend: he'll know where he is.'

Finding Second Chances – Hob's father's junk shop – was easier said than done. We trudged around the streets for what seemed like hours, watching the light slowly fade, staying as much out of the way of other people as possible, and trying to ignore the cooking smells that wafted from every doorway we passed. It was getting steadily colder too – a hard, metallic chill that seemed to sink into the marrow of my bones.

Then suddenly, just when I thought we were totally lost, there it was: the familiar faded wooden sign above the door, and – to my huge relief – faint light still shining dimly through the thick panes of glass in the window. 'Working late,' said Rich with satisfaction. 'Looks like our luck's about to change!'

'Just so long as his dad doesn't answer the door and say *Who's Hob?*' muttered Jamie.

Hob's dad was there. Peering through the glass, ready to make a run for it if necessary, we could make him out all too clearly: a bald, bespectacled man who reminded me with a pang of Q, perched on a tall stool with his nose deep in a pile of parchments. There was no sign of Hob.

Richard said a very rude word.

'Here we go again,' said Gen with a certain amount of relish. 'My turn this time.'

'Hang on, Gen,' I said. Truth was, I wasn't keen to try out our acting talents again. It hadn't worked too well so far. 'There's a wooden door here in the wall. It might lead through to some kind of courtyard. What say we have a quick snoop around before we do anything rash? Who knows, maybe they live above the shop or something. Maybe Hob's round the back. It's worth a try.'

We edged the door open and slipped silently through. It felt good to be off the street, away from the hooded grey shadows I was beginning to imagine round every corner. Best of all, I was right. It was a courtyard – cobbled, with a rickety washing line at one end with a few drab garments hanging forlornly from it. 'Late to leave the washing out,' Gen murmured disapprovingly . . . and at that moment, right on cue, a door at the back of the building opened and out came Hob, a wicker basket dangling from his hand.

He looked taller than I remembered, but otherwise just the same – skinny and red-haired, with an up-turned nose and a jaunty air of self-confidence. Without so much as a glance at the doorway where we stood in a breathless huddle, he sauntered over to the washing line and started taking the clothes down, whistling between his teeth. We all exchanged a lightning glance of complete agreement.

'Pssssst! *Hob!*'

Hob squawked and dropped the basket, whipping round with a face suddenly whiter than the shirt he was holding. He saw us, and his eyes widened in disbelief. Grinning, I stepped forward, holding out a hand in greeting.

But to my horror Hob's mouth tightened and his eyes narrowed. Shaking his head slowly from side to side, he backed away towards the open door, both hands held out in front of him as if to ward away something evil.

Suddenly, he didn't look at all like the Hob we'd known. He looked way, way different. Adult . . . suspicious . . . and afraid.

'Hob?' quavered Gen uncertainly. 'It's us – Kai's friends. Don't you remember us?'

'Stay away from me! Haven't you done enough?'

Behind me, I heard Jamie give a stifled snuffle of dismay. And then suddenly I felt my confusion give way to anger. What was it with everyone? Why were

100

they all treating us like we had some kind of terrible disease? And what was with all the mystery?

I stepped forward, scowling. 'Hang on one minute, Hob,' I said, my voice low, but with an edge to it that stopped him in his tracks. 'Run away if you want. But first tell us where Kai is, and why his dad says he's never heard of him. What's going on – why is everyone being so weird?'

Hob hesitated, a look of uncertainty crossing his face. Then his expression hardened again. 'You ask that?' he spat. '*You?* When it be your fault? And now you come to the door like friends . . . when a true friend would stay away! Kai helped you – he trusted you! And now . . .' suddenly his face contorted, and he made a strangled hiccuping sound.

Kenta was at his side in an instant. 'Poor Hob,' she said softly, looking anxiously up into his face. 'We *are* your friends – we truly are. We don't know what's gone wrong – what's happened to change the way you feel – or what's happened to Kai. And if you don't tell us, we can't help.'

She was speaking over the anguished, wrenching sound of his sobs. And then we were all around him, Kenta with a comforting arm round his shoulders, Gen offering him the handkerchief Nanny had insisted on us bringing, Rich patting his arm awkwardly. Me standing there like a spare part, all hands and feet. But: 'Adam – *the gate!*' Hob's voice was low and urgent. Quickly I crossed the courtyard and closed it, first checking there was no one in the street.

Two minutes later we were all hunkered down

on the stone step outside the back door, and Hob was his old self again. 'First things first,' said Rich, taking charge. 'Where's Kai?'

Hob wiped his nose on his sleeve and sniffed, ignoring Gen's hanky. 'Kai . . .' he whispered, 'Kai . . . is gone forever. He was . . . taken, two sunsets after I gave you the parchment.'

'Taken where? Who by?' Gen's face was pale in the darkness.

'By the Followers – the Faceless.' Hob's voice was almost inaudible.

'Because . . . of us?'

Hob nodded. 'Aye. There be nothing their eyes do not see – if eyes they have – or their senses cannot seek out. I have been fortunate. Yet if they saw us now . . .'

A shiver ran down my spine. Finally I understood: by talking to Hob, we were putting him in deadly danger. The girls knew it too – they searched the courtyard with wide, frightened eyes, as if a grey shadow might materialise from the very walls. Jamie gave a muffled whimper. Rich scowled. 'OK then – tell us quick,' he demanded. 'Where is he? Where have they taken him? Will he still be . . .'

Alive. The word hung, unspoken, in the air.

'And why did his dad – his pa – say he'd never heard of him? I don't understand . . .' said Jamie plaintively.

'It is death to speak the names of those taken by the Faceless. It must be as if they have never lived at all. And does Kai live, you ask? There is no knowing.

Maybe it is better that he does not. There be worse fates than death – where he has gone, any road.'

'Where is that?' Kenta's question was the merest breath.

'Where all be taken who are of . . . *interest* . . . to King Karazeel. Beyond the shroud . . . to Shakesh.'

At his soft words a chill ran through me. Shakesh . . . where had I heard that name before? Suddenly it came to me: Kai's voice, grim and low: *It would be the axe and entrails on the walls of Shakesh, children or no. That – or worse.* Or worse . . .

'*All* are taken?' Gen was asking. 'You mean – anyone who does anything wrong?'

'Wrongdoers . . . strangers . . . those that speak forbidden names. Believers; the innocent. Any man or woman – aye, or child – who draws the Faceless to their trail. There be ways without number to fall under their shadow – and none I know of to emerge again.'

Hannah.

'We know of someone –' I said hesitantly – 'a young girl – a friend of ours. We believe she may have come here – dressed differently . . . pale-faced, like we . . .'

'Once were,' Hob finished, with the faintest glimmer of a smile. 'Aye – you be learning, any road. Your friend – she too will be gone. Taken north to Marshall . . . and beyond. Forget her. Do not speak her name again. She is lost forever.'

'Well, we're going to Shakesh to find them both,' Richard said angrily. 'We're going to prove you wrong, Hob. This *never speaking names* and *passing beyond the shroud* is rubbish. Who does this King Karazeel think he is? Where we come from, no one would dare carry on like that! We'd have him out on his backside in no time, king or no king! Haven't you people heard of dem– dem–'

'Democracy,' Jamie offered helpfully.

'And what's with this guy *Zephyr*?' Richard ranted on. 'Who is he, and why did Kai's dad look like he'd swallowed a fishbone when I said his name? I'm sure glad I don't live in Arakesh – it'd drive me bananas!'

'You spoke the name of Zephyr at the inn?' Hob stared at Rich in disbelief. Then he gave a snort of laughter. 'Rich, you are – were – a friend of Kai's, and of mine. Therefore, Friend, I say this to you: as you value your soul, do not breathe that name where any but the most trusted and true may hear it.'

'But – *why?* Who *is* he? Is he so bad . . .'

'Bad?' Hob's eyes shone in the darkness. '*Bad?* Nay . . . not bad. Zephyr –' he said the name with awe bordering almost on reverence, his voice so low I had to lean forward to catch his words, feeling his warm breath on my cheek, 'Zephyr is the Lost Prince – the Prince of the Wind. Legend has it such a one was born to the fair Queen Zaronel half a hundred spans ago. You speak of overthrowing King Karazeel.' His voice was grim. 'None can accomplish that – none save the Lost Prince. There be whispers of a prophecy: a prophecy held true by those that believe all goodness is not gone forever. A prophecy that foretells, after two score spans and ten, Prince Zephyr will return again to claim his throne. On the day the warrior prince returns from exile, riding tall and proud upon a winged horse – on that day, the crown of Karazan will return to its rightful head.

'And now, my friend, do you see why none dare breathe the name of Zephyr where it may be over-heard?'

The sound of a door banging somewhere inside the building made us all jump. Hob clambered to his feet. 'I wish you good fortune, my friends – but above all, I wish you common sense and caution,' he whispered. 'The common sense to forget those that are lost, lest you join them – and the caution to keep your mouths shut, or at the very least your voices low. Now, I bid you farewell. And I beg you, do not seek me out again.'

'But Hob – we don't even know the way to Shakesh. I don't suppose you happen to have a map or something . . .' Gen said hopefully.

One look at Hob's face, and I knew we'd had all we were getting. And who could blame him?

I held out my hand. 'Hob – thank you. You have helped us more than we had any right to expect.' For a long moment our eyes locked in a smile. Then he clasped my wrist briefly, turned, and let him-self quietly into the house, the door clicking shut behind him.

The courtyard seemed suddenly very empty. Then Jamie's voice spoke up out of the gloom, trembling slightly: 'We aren't really going to go to Shakesh, are we?'

'You betcha,' said Rich.

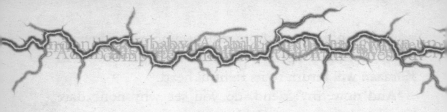

A DISHONEST MISTAKE

'This Five Grain Pan Bread looks more like instant brick mix to me,' Rich said dubiously, poking at the contents of the saucepan. 'Are you sure we've done it right?'

We'd decided to set up camp in the woods to the north of Arakesh, have a slap-up rehydrated meal and a good night's sleep, and set out for Shakesh at first light.

'I'd feel a lot better about tomorrow if we at least knew the way,' Gen frowned, stirring the pot of MeenXtreem Souper Minestrone that was bubbling over the fire. 'What was it Hob told us? *North to Marshall . . . and beyond.* Not an awful lot of help.'

'I don't know.' I took the spoon from her and had a taste. 'I doubt there's more than one north road, and once it gets light it should be easy to find.'

'I still wish we had a map,' she said wistfully.

Jamie was rummaging in his rucksack. He turned to face the fire again, his hands behind his back, with a funny, secretive look on his face.

'Hey, guys,' he said, 'I'm not keen on going to Shakesh, but one thing's for sure: if we're going anywhere, I'd rather we knew the way. Like Gen says.' He gave her a shy, sidelong look. 'Remember what Q once told us about keeping our eyes open for things we might find useful? Well, looks like I'm the only one who listened! You wish we had a map, Gen? And now . . . ta-da!' He brought his hand round with a flourish. We goggled at him. He was holding up a scroll – a rolled parchment, neatly tied with a leather thong.

'Where did you get *that*?' croaked Rich.

'From The Brewer's Butt,' smirked Jamie, bursting with pride. 'While you guys were nattering away to Kai's father, I had a look around. And it's just as well I did. There were two little barrels on the reception desk – not that any of you noticed. But I did. *Maps*, it said – so I took one. And guess what else? It's not just a normal map. Feel!' He held the scroll out to me. Automatically, I took it . . . and felt a faint tingle, almost as if the scroll was humming to itself under its breath. *Magic*.

'Yeah – it's a magic map,' crowed Jamie. 'A magic map, courtesy of Jamie Fitzpatrick, the only one to keep his eyes open and his wits about him!'

Rich was grinning from ear to ear. Gen was beaming at Jamie, impressed. But Kenta's face was very serious, and her eyes grave. 'Jamie,' she said gently, 'those maps weren't free. You were supposed to pay for them.'

Jamie's mouth dropped open and he gawked at her. 'But – it didn't – there wasn't . . .'

'There was,' she said. 'Underneath the big sign was

a smaller one and it said, *New: 5 gelden. Used: 10 gelden.*'

Jamie's face had flushed a rosy apricot. 'It can't have said that,' he muttered. 'You must have read it wrong, Kenta. Why would a new map be cheaper than a used one? That's dumb! And anyway, even if it did . . .'

'Even if it did, it isn't Jamie's fault,' I interrupted. 'We all know Jamie'd never steal anything on purpose. OK, he took a map without paying for it – but it was an honest mistake.'

'A dishonest one, more like,' grinned Rich. 'But remember what Kai once told us – about patterns, and things happening for a purpose? Maybe Jamie was *meant* not to see the price on the maps. Maybe he was *meant* to take one. Anyhow, it's done now. Let's have a look at it!'

Jamie untied the thong with careful fingers, and unrolled the scroll. Kenta and Gen huddled beside him as Rich and I peered over his shoulder. The five of us stared down at the map in total silence.

'Well, Jamie,' said Rich, 'you might have saved yourself the trouble of pinching it, for all the use it's going to be.'

I didn't say anything. I felt sick with disappointment. Some of the map was how I'd expected it to be – old-fashioned, hand-drawn in black ink on buff-coloured parchment. Sea, rivers, towns . . . a normal map. But the part of the map we needed – the part north of Arakesh, where Kai had said Marshall and Shakesh lay – was completely covered by a solid black splodge. The stain started about where we were now, just north of the city, and extended up to the very top of the map, and westwards to the entry point to Karazan and beyond.

Cautiously, I looked at Jamie. His lips were pressed tight together, and I could tell he was struggling not to cry. I knew just how he felt. Gen put one arm round him and gave him a hug. 'Cheer up, Jamie – it's not your fault it's a dud.'

Jamie blushed scarlet. Then Richard started to laugh. 'You have to admit it's got its funny side,' he chortled. 'Typical Jamie. Tries to be a hero . . . steals a map without meaning to . . . and chooses the only one with ink spilled all over the important bit! We might as well chuck it away – it's no use to us, and precious little use to anyone else. But at least we're no worse off than we were before. Here, Jamie – shove it back in your bag and perk up. We can always use it as toilet paper if we run out! And now, who's for some Five Grain Gobstopper and a bowl of hot soup?'

RUSTLES IN THE DARK

In spite of Richard's attempt to put a brave face on things, the disappointment of the map changed the mood around the campfire. It was almost as if some of the darkness from the map had found its way into the forest surrounding our little campsite. The flickering flames that had seemed so comforting before now seemed to make the shadows deeper and more threatening. Without noticing, we'd all drawn closer to the fire. 'I only want a little, please,' said Kenta when the soup was ready. 'I'm not very hungry.'

'All the more for me – us, I mean,' said Richard cheerfully.

Spicy steam tickled my nose, and I eagerly spooned up my first mouthful of soup. Silence fell as we ate – at least, as close as the rustling forest would ever get to silence. Kenta pushed her plate away almost untouched. 'Do you suppose . . .' she said hesitantly, 'do you suppose there are . . . *things* living in these woods?'

'Course there are,' said Rich with his mouth full of bread. 'Lots of different little animals, like at home. Think of all the stuff you find in forests. Owls, and bats, and rats and mice and ferrets and here in Karazan there'd be sn . . .' – he gave Gen a quick glance – 'things like that. Nothing to worry about.'

But that wasn't what Kenta meant, and we all knew it.

'Why did you ask?' Jamie quavered.

'Oh,' said Kenta, trying to sound casual, 'it's just . . . I keep hearing funny little rustles, as if . . . something's trying to creep closer, without being seen.' She gave a forced laugh. 'Silly – it's my imagination, I know. I'm just not used to camping out at night.'

'That's right – it *is* silly,' said Rich staunchly. 'Pass your plate. I hate to see good food wasted.'

I didn't say anything but I'd heard it too. Just beyond the ring of firelight – a stealthy brushing sound rather than an actual rustle: the sort of sound something would make pushing slowly and secretly through the undergrowth. Not a little thing like a mouse or a ferret or a sn . . . but a bigger thing. About the size of a human . . . or something that had once been human.

I could see the girls were dreading the moment when we'd have to let the fire die down, unroll our sleeping bags and try to sleep. But the food was finished, the clearing up was done, the talk had gradually wound down . . . and all too soon Richard gave a big, phoney stretch and said, 'Well, guys – I guess we'd better hit the sack. Big day tomorrow, and all that.'

'I'll take first watch,' I offered quickly. The way I figured, if there was something out there, it would

111

make its move sooner rather than later. I reckoned attack was the best form of defence . . . and I had a plan.

'Rich,' I said casually, 'let's scout around for a bit more wood before we settle down. We don't want people wandering off alone in the middle of the night looking for firewood.'

Together we moved out of the circle of light into the surrounding darkness, searching for fallen branches and dry sticks. We were on the opposite side of the clearing from where I'd heard the rustling. Through the tree trunks we could see the little campsite as clearly as if it was spotlit on a stage. The fire glowed warm and red; beside it were the logs we'd perched on to have our meal. Our backpacks were dark lumps on the fringes of the firelight, and beside them we could make out the shapes of Jamie, Gen and Kenta huddled as close as they dared to the fire.

I touched Richard's arm. 'Rich . . .' He turned to me at once. 'Kenta was right. There *is* something out there, just beyond the campsite. On the other side of the fire from where we are now. I heard it – and I think I caught a glimpse of it. Something pale and . . . greyish, about the size of a person, hunched over.'

'I know.' Richard's face was grim. 'I didn't want to scare the girls . . . and I didn't want *it* – the thing – to know I'd seen it. I planned to stay awake, then come and talk to you when the others were asleep.'

I swallowed, hoping my voice would sound as calm and steady as Richard's. 'We need to make the first move,' I whispered. 'Take it by surprise . . . whatever it is. That way, at least . . .'

'At least we stand a chance. Good thinking. What do you reckon?' Richard's eyes gleamed. 'A pincer move, maybe? You on one side, me on the other? Then . . . *whammo*!'

'Yeah,' I echoed, trying my best to mirror the enthusiasm in his voice: 'whammo.'

I picked my way cautiously through the undergrowth. In daylight the forest had been easy to walk through – we'd automatically registered obstacles and navigated our way round them without a second thought. But at night it was different – way different. Even once my eyes had adjusted to the darkness, I could hardly see a thing. More than once I bashed my head on a low branch, or almost tripped over a protruding root. But because the campsite we'd chosen was so sheltered, the ground underfoot was soft, damp and springy with decomposing leaves, and my footfalls made no sound.

I crept through the darkness, keeping our campsite the same distance away from me, circling it warily. My eyes burned from staring blindly into the darkness; my ears strained for the faintest rustle and my heart thumped in my throat. Sweat popped out on my forehead, freezing cold in the icy air; my breath plumed out in front of me, pale smoke in the blackness. I crept on.

Now I was halfway round. I imagined Richard picking his way through the trees opposite, sneaking closer to our quarry. I tried not to think what it might be . . .

or what would happen if we captured it. I wished I had my pocketknife and a length of strong rope. I stumbled and almost fell, lurching forward onto my hands and knees, grazing my knuckles on the branch I'd tripped over. My hand closed instinctively round it. *About the size of a baseball bat, solid and heavy . . .* I straightened and stole soundlessly on, my makeshift weapon at the ready.

And then all hell broke loose in the silent forest. Ahead of me, I heard a sudden rustle and the hiss of indrawn breath. At the same time, beside the campfire, Gen's voice, small and frightened: 'Adam . . . Richard? Where –'

In the same moment from ahead of me in the darkness came an animal roar. *Rich.* Something huge and heavy crashed through the undergrowth; wood splintered, and the night was torn apart by a single, terrified cry.

AN UNINVITED GUEST

'*Adam! Where are you?*' – one of the girls, shrill with panic.

'Gaaaaargh!'

'Sssssssssss . . .'

Desperately I lunged through the trees towards the sounds of the struggle, terror for Richard washing through my brain in a icy tide. '*Richard! Hold on! I'm coming! I'm here!*' My lungs were raw; adrenaline burned like acid in my blood. I smashed through the bushes, branches tearing at me, twigs whipping my face, my clothes ripping. At last they were in front of me, shapeless in the dark – a writhing, twisting, struggling shape convulsing on the ground. I skirted the dark mass with my weapon raised, waiting for a clear strike.

Then one of the shapes reared up over the other, straddling it, its face – dimly lit by the distant fire – a mask of blood. 'Stop struggling, or I'll throttle you within an inch of your life! *I mean it!*' The face was unrecognisable, but the voice – harsh and gasping, savage with pain and triumph – was Richard's.

The dark shape on the ground lay still, face down in

115

the dirt. I advanced on them warily, stick raised. 'And I'll smash your head in for good measure,' I growled, hoping I sounded as fierce as Richard. Slowly, stiffly, he clambered to his feet, wiping a hand across his mouth and staring down at the dark blood.

'Rich – are you –'

'It's by dose,' he said briefly. 'I'b fide.'

He aimed a none-too-gentle kick at the figure on the ground. 'On your feet, whatever you are – one false move, and you're mincemeat. Come into the light where we can get a look at you.'

I followed the two silhouettes into the circle of firelight. The other three were clutching each other on the far side of the fire, eyes wide. I stepped up beside Richard, my weapon at the ready. And then every nerve in my body went numb, and the stick fell from my hand. As if from very far away I heard Richard's voice, anger edging into disbelief: 'Who are *you*?'

I didn't need to ask. I already knew.

It was Weevil.

Muddy, bloody and shivering, standing there in the firelight in his striped pyjamas.

'Who *are* you?' Richard repeated.

'Yeah – and how did you get here? Because you're from –' Jamie hesitated.

Our world.

Weevil smiled. 'Adam knows who I am,' he said. 'I live at Highgate wiff him. I'm his friend.'

'Well, come closer to the fire then,' said Kenta with her shy smile. 'You must be freezing. And look at your slippers – they're in tatters. Here –' she dug in

116

her backpack – 'you can use my spare top if you . . .'

'Hang on one second, Kenta.' Richard was scowling. 'This guy says he's Adam's friend . . . but Adam doesn't seem very pleased to see him. And how did he get here in the first place? Not with his *friend* Adam, that's for sure. And what was he doing sneaking around our campsite, punching me on the nose when I . . .'

'When you tackled me,' finished Weevil. 'In the dark, when I was all alone.'

'Adam?' said Rich. 'Is this guy – what's your name?'

'Weevil.'

'*Weevil?* What kind of a name is that?'

'My name. Don't you know what a weevil is? It's a fing . . .'

Suddenly, numb shock gave way to fury. 'Don't listen to him!' I yelled. 'He's not my friend! He's snuck in here somehow – he said he could get in anywhere, and he was right! He wanted to come to Quested Court, but I wouldn't let him! He – he steals everything! My penny whistle – my project – my hideout – and now this!' My words were harsh and jagged, and tears burned my cheeks. Everyone would see them – Weevil would see them – but I didn't care.

'I know you're surprised to see me, Adam. But you're forgetting your manners. Won't you introduce me to your friends?'

'*No!* Get away from us! Go back where you came from! You've stolen everything else – you're not stealing them too!'

The others looked helplessly from Weevil to me

117

and back again. 'I can't get back,' said Weevil. 'I don't know how.' His voice trembled slightly, as if it was on the edge of tears. 'I'm cold – and hungry.'

'Oh, for goodness' sake!' said Gen impatiently. 'What do we do now? As if things weren't bad enough! Adam – can you put your differences aside while we get to the bottom of this? And you – whatever you call yourself – I suppose you'd better come closer to the fire before you get hypothermia or something. I think you owe us all an explanation – especially Adam.'

'He can give the explanation where he is,' I growled. I could feel the new Adam sloughing away like a dry snakeskin. The old one was right there underneath – bitter, angry, unforgiving. 'If he comes near this fire, I'm going. I'll set up camp on my own. I won't be with him – *I won't!* I won't let him burrow his way in – you don't know him! You don't know what he's like!'

'Adam.' Kenta's voice was very gentle. 'I can't believe . . . this isn't like you. Surely he can't be so bad? It's frightening enough for us, being here in the dark. And we have each other. Imagine . . .'

'The problem is, it's dangerous,' said Richard slowly. 'Whether we like it or not, he's here. And this . . . this is Karazan. There might be things out there, in the forest . . . Adam, we have to offer him the protection of our fire, at least. If we don't, something might happen to him – and it would be our fault. But I don't understand how he's here at all. Did you go to Quested Court and convince Q to let you follow us?'

'If you'll let me sit by the campfire, I'll tell you. Adam already knows part of it, don't you, Adam? It's all to do wiff computers. You can burrow inside and find out all sorts of fings, if you know how. That's what I did. Not at Quested Court – at Highgate . . . on Adam's computer.'

I gaped at him. 'I don't believe you,' I said flatly. 'There isn't a VRE Interface on that computer. There isn't even a single computer game – Matron sold them all. There's no way you could get to Karazan from there.'

'Fink about it, Adam. Not about what there *isn't*, but what there *is*. Quentin Quested's e-mail address – a hotline to his personal computer system at Quested Court. Did you ever find out what a hacker was? I said I could get in anywhere, Adam – and it's true.'

'But . . . my secret password . . .'

Weevil snickered. 'Password? I found that out in less than five minutes. You silly fing. Trying so hard to make it secret – and then giving away two secrets in one! It gave me access to Quentin Quested's computer – *and* it told me the key combination to bring me here to Karazan.' He smirked round at us all. 'Saved me a lot of trouble, that did. Fanks, Adam. *Alt Control Q.* Clever password – I don't fink.'

I still didn't believe it could be true. 'But . . . how did you even *know*?'

Weevil smirked at me. 'It started off wiff me just wanting to come to Quested Court and meet Quentin Quested. But then I read your e-mail to Richard . . .'

'You *what*?' growled Rich.

'. . . and it made me fink. *Imagine if we got to go to Karazan again*, you wrote. Was it just an imaginary game, or could it have something to do wiff Quentin Quested's "top-secret breakfrough in computer-game technology"? And now,' he finished with a smug smirk, 'I know.'

I didn't know whether to be angrier with Weevil or myself. How could I have been so dumb? But then, how could I ever have guessed what he would do? Suddenly I felt exhausted, as if my body and my brain had turned to putty. The day had gone on forever – all I wanted now was for it to end. Kenta stepped forward, as if she'd read my mind. 'Well, it was very wrong of you,' she told Weevil severely. 'Like reading someone's private diary, only worse. No one invited you here, and you shouldn't have come. You deserve to be left out in the cold. But right now, we all need to sleep.' She passed him her sleeping bag. 'You can use this – but you can take it over to the other side of the fire, on your own. I'll share with you, Gen – there's plenty of room for two, and it will be warmer that way. Perhaps things will look better in the morning.'

Jamie looked over at me and pulled a sympathetic face. 'Yeah – and in the morning, when it's light, we'll have a *private meeting*,' he said importantly. 'Just the five of us – to decide what to do. But now, I'm sleepy – and I vote we don't let this *Weevil* have a turn on watch. Not till we're sure he can be trusted. And that –' he said with a meaningful glare at Weevil – 'just might be *never*!'

But the only thing that looked better in the morning was Jamie's orange face, which had faded overnight to

120

a more natural-looking tan. Apart from that, things looked just the same – to me, anyhow. Weevil's presence cast a shadow over the whole forest – the whole of Karazan. A shadow even the rising sun and the dawn chorus of birds could do nothing to lighten.

The freeze-dried scrambled eggs we made tasted slimy and bland and reminded me of Highgate. My eyelids felt as if they were made of sandpaper, and my head ached from lack of sleep.

The five of us squatted together round the fire, nibbling at our eggs and sipping our mugs of cocoa, having Jamie's secret meeting. Weevil sat a few metres away in Kenta's sleeping bag, his back to a tree, watching and doing his best to listen.

'Whatever we do, we can't win,' muttered Richard. 'There's no two ways about it: Weevil – what a dumb name! – was wrong to come. But he's here now – and the only way for him to get back would be to use –' he lowered his voice to a whisper so low we could barely hear the words – 'the microcomputer.'

'But *we* need that,' hissed Jamie in alarm. 'What if he nicked it? Then we'd be sunk! I vote we don't even tell him about it.'

'He probably already knows,' I said bleakly. 'He seems to know everything else. And anyhow, he doesn't *want* to go back – he wants to be here, with us. And if he doesn't want to go, he won't.'

'So what do we do?' asked Gen. 'Ignore him, and hope he goes away? Pretend to be friends, but keep an eye on him?'

'I hate excluding people,' Jamie muttered, not

meeting my eye. 'It's happened to me often enough, and I know how it feels. It's a kind of bullying, my mum says. Sometimes people really do just want to be friends – but they haven't had any practice at it, so they don't know how.'

I snorted, but said nothing. Jamie blushed.

'What about food? And water? We can't just leave him to drink from streams and things – it might not be safe. It seems unkind, having our breakfast while he sits there with nothing. I feel really uncomfortable about it. I'm not hungry – can't I give him . . .'

'For heaven's sake, Kenta – you'd give him the shoes off your feet if you had the chance,' said Gen. 'Adam – you're very quiet. What do you think we should do?'

I sighed. 'I don't know,' I said dully. 'I really don't. What I'd like to do is go back to Quested Court, dump him off, and start all over again. But every minute we waste is a minute more for Kai in Shakesh – and for Hannah.'

'Do we have to make a decision now?' asked Richard slowly. 'Can't we get moving – find the north road, at least? What he does is his problem. He can tag along or not – his choice. If you feel bad about him being hungry, Kenta, you can give him the left-over bread – that'll make him wish he hadn't come, if nothing else. We're talking in circles. We might as well do that at the same time as we walk – but we can do the walking in a straight line, at least.'

★

Richard's straight line was surprisingly easy to find.

The north road turned out to be a broad, well-worn track, winding over a rickety bridge and away into the forest. We headed back into the shade of the trees with heavy hearts, sorry to leave the blue sky and sunlight behind. 'It's a shame about that map,' Kenta murmured. 'I wish we knew exactly where we were going . . . or at least how far it is. Will we be walking for a day? Two days? For all we know, this forest could go on forever.'

'It probably does,' grumbled Jamie. 'And my feet are hurting already.'

None of us said so, but I knew we were all thinking of Weevil. He was trailing behind us like a shadow, Kenta's sleeping bag wrapped round his shoulders to keep out the cold, shuffling along in his tattered slippers. We'd all seen Kenta drop back and slip the last of the pot bread into his hand, and knowing her, giving him a kind word along with it. So at least he wouldn't starve – though it would serve him right if he did, I thought bitterly.

Anger and resentment mingled uncomfortably with the scrambled egg, making me feel sick, ashamed and miserable. My pack a lead weight on my back, my heart a lead weight in my chest, I trudged dismally on.

THE RIVER RAVVEN

The forest didn't go on forever. Before lunch time the trees began to thin, soon giving way to rough grassland. Apart from the rutted track stretching ahead of us there was no sign of life – just birds wheeling in the pale sky, and the sigh of the wind in the grass.

To our left loomed a jagged mountain range, the topmost peaks lost in a bar of white cloud. The stone cliffs behind the entry point to Karazan must be part of them, I realised; they stretched behind us to the south and ahead to the north, dissolving into the grey haze of the distant horizon.

'Hey – good place for a picnic!' chirped Jamie hopefully.

'It's way too soon to stop,' objected Richard. 'Think how long the afternoon would be – and then ages till dinner time!'

'Rich's right,' I agreed reluctantly. So we heaved our packs onto our aching backs and put one weary foot in front of the next until at last the sun was directly overhead.

'Now this *is* a good place for a picnic,' grinned

Rich – and he was right. We'd reached the banks of a river – wide, silent and slow-flowing. 'I'd be able to swim this, I reckon,' said Rich, surveying it with his hands on his hips. 'Doesn't look like there's much of a current – and I'm freestyle champ at school.'

'It's just as well you won't have to,' said Gen quietly. 'I don't like the look of that water. It's so dark it's almost black. That must mean it's deep – and who knows what might be under there . . .'

Gen was right: we wouldn't have to swim. A little way downstream from where we stood, a wooden raft was pulled up well out of reach of the water, partly hidden by the trailing branches of what looked like a willow tree. A thick rope stretched across the river near the raft's mooring place, from one bank to the other.

'Great!' said Richard with satisfaction. 'A shady picnic spot, a place to refill our water bottles – and built-in transport to the other side! Now this is what I call a *civilised* adventure!'

He pulled his flask out of his backpack, and strode cheerfully to the water's edge. 'Richard – don't!' There was an edge of panic in Kenta's words that stopped Rich dead in his tracks.

'What?'

'I remember this place from *Quest of the Dark Citadel*,' said Kenta. 'It seems so weird to be here – like being in a dream. I spent a lot of time here when I was trying to find the citadel – I'd convinced myself it was on the other side of this river, and kept trying to cross. But I only managed it way to the east, where it joins the sea.'

'Huh?' Richard looked confused. 'But . . .'

'It's called the River Ravven.' Kenta said the words with a quiet solemnity that made me realise at once there was some kind of significance in what she was saying – to her, if not to the rest of us. Looking at their blank faces, I could see they were just as puzzled as I was about what she was getting at. Like Rich, I thought it looked simple enough – hop on the raft, pull ourselves across, and away we go.

Then Jamie piped up. 'You don't say *ravven* to rhyme with *cavern*, Kenta,' he corrected her. 'You say it with a long a – raven. It's a kind of bird, a bit like a magpie. There's no such word as *ravven*.'

'Oh yes there is.' Weevil had fallen so far behind us on the long morning's walk I'd almost managed to convince myself we'd lost him. No such luck. 'A raven *is* a bird – a black-plumed, hoarse-voiced bird of evil omen that feeds on flesh. But if you pronounce the same word the way she did, then it means something different. It means to prowl for prey, to eat voraciously, or have a ravenous appetite.'

We gawked at him, mouths open. Even Jamie looked impressed. 'What does vor– vor– vor–' began Richard.

I interrupted him, scowling at Weevil. 'What's up with you – swallowed a dictionary? And who asked your opinion?'

Weevil shrugged, his eyes on the ground. 'I can't help it if I remember things I've read,' he muttered.

'It's called a *photographic memory*,' Jamie told us, with more than a hint of envy. 'I've sort of got one. I –'

'Hang on a sec, Jamie,' Gen broke in. 'We can hear all about your sort-of-photographic-memory round the campfire tonight. Right now, I want to hear what Kenta has to say. About this Ravven-raven River, and what happens when you try to cross it.'

Kenta had been listening quietly, nibbling on an apple. Now she took a final bite, chewed, and swallowed. The rest of us watched her impatiently. When she spoke it was directly to Gen, with a strange note of hopelessness I didn't begin to understand. 'I'll show you.' She pulled back her arm and threw the apple – less than half eaten – away across the water. It wasn't a bad throw, for a girl. The apple flew in a lazy arc about ten metres over the water, and landed on the black, greasy-looking surface with a *plop*.

In that instant the water erupted into life, bubbling and churning with what must have been thousands of tiny, scrabbling shapes, the sunlight flashing off them like a mosaic of diamonds. In less time than it takes to snap your fingers – less time than it took for the apple to sink below the surface of the water – it was gone as if it had never existed.

'Point taken,' said Richard grimly. 'Looks like the ferry's there for a reason. What are they, Kenta?'

'Piranhas, I'll bet,' said Jamie with gloomy relish.

'No, not piranhas. They're a kind of carnivorous water spider. But they eat . . . well . . . anything. Fruit, like you just saw. Leaves. Nets, if you try to catch them in one. Even wood.'

Even wood . . . 'So the boat . . .' I murmured.

'So the boat gets you part of the way across,' Kenta whispered; 'and then . . .'

There was an uncomfortable silence. Then Rich spoke up, his voice unnaturally hearty. 'OK, so the river's full of these vor-whatsit spiders. But people *do* cross it. And they use this raft – they must, or why is it here? So the question is . . .'

'The question is how.' Gen's face had an intense, distracted look I remembered from before. Though the face had changed, the look hadn't. It meant she was thinking – hard. 'How about we have a hunt around the riverbank. See whether we can find anything – any clue; any hint; any other way over. Because Rich is right. The one thing we do know is: there must be a way.'

We finished our lunch and then picked our way along the riverbank, keeping well away from the edge. In places it was sandy and smooth, almost like a beach. In other places trees grew down to the river's edge, damp drifts of autumn leaves trapped between their gnarled roots. Thick undergrowth grew down the bank here and there – undergrowth none of us seemed very keen to shove our way through.

I headed off to the left, in the direction of the raft. I wanted to have a closer look. First, I examined the rope. It was thick – as thick as my forearm – and in good condition. It was tied with an impressive knot round the trunk of a tall tree a fair way up the riverbank, giving it enough height and tension to stretch the entire way across the river without touching the water. Just as well, I thought grimly. The raft itself was a simple platform of rough planks laid across circular poles, held in place with rusty but solid-looking nails.

I straightened up and stared out across the water. It gave no hint as to the swarming life – or death – lurking below the surface. Here, the bank was bare and stony, sloping gently down to the water's edge; I could see drag marks in the pebbled beach where the last people to cross had heaved the raft up out of harm's way. The pebbles were all sizes, all colours – a salt-and-pepper mix of brown and grey and bone-white . . . *bone-white?* Abruptly, I stooped and picked up one of the white pebbles. It wasn't a pebble at all. It was a knuckle-shaped bone, bleached by the sun and worn smooth by wind and water. I picked up another . . . and another. Slowly I turned so my back was to the river, my eyes raking the banks on either side of me. Everywhere there were bones. Not just small bones like the ones on the riverbank – bones of all shapes and sizes, half hidden by the reeds and rushes, grass and undergrowth. A cold hand tightened round my heart. I could feel the hair at the back of my neck prickle as I picked my way cautiously among them, half recognising a leg bone here, a shoulder blade there. It was a graveyard . . . a graveyard around the raft's landing place. *Why?*

When at last I stumbled on the answer, it brought me quite literally to my knees . . . and face to face with a human skeleton, gleaming dull ivory in the dappled shade of the willow tree, a frayed and partly rotted rope still knotted loosely round what was left of its neck.

But it wasn't the grinning skull that made me cry out – a strangled cry of revulsion and denial that brought the others running to join me and stare down at what I had found.

It was the signpost. Half hidden in the undergrowth, cracked and rotted and covered in mildew and growths of tiny brown toadstools . . . but still legible. Just.

Live Bait Ford.

Richard's face was pale and set, and his eyes were narrowed angrily as he stared out over the oily-looking water. 'Now we know how they cross – *King Karazeel*'s men.' He spat the name out. 'They give the spiders something more . . . interesting . . . than wood to chew on.'

'Richard – don't.' Gen's eyes were huge in her white face.

'We know how they do it . . . but it won't help us. And yet we *have* to get across.'

'Now I understand what Q meant about evolution,' whispered Jamie. 'He'd never have put a solution like this in a game for kids.'

There was a pause. 'Let's see what we've got in our backpacks,' I said slowly. 'OK, I don't for a second believe that dangling a tin of condensed milk over the side of the raft would have the same effect as . . . the same effect, but there might be something else that could be useful.'

The girls bent down and started unpacking the bags, glad to have something to do to take their minds off my discovery. 'Baked beans . . . instant pancake mix . . . strawberry honey cereal . . . mountain chilli . . .'

'Don't, Gen – it's ages till dinner – and we may never have any at this rate!' groaned Jamie.

'Matches . . . string . . . sunscreen . . . can opener . . . insect repellent . . . long-burning fire-lighting fluid . . . dishcloths . . .'

'Hang on a sec, Gen.' The ghost of an idea was hovering on the fringes of my mind. Holding it there, scared to look at it too closely in case it evaporated, I stepped forward. Crouched down, and rummaged through the pile of stuff. Came up with two things, one in each hand. Gave the blank faces above me what I hoped was an encouraging grin.

'This is going to sound crazy,' I said hesitantly, 'but listen for a second, and tell me what you think . . .'

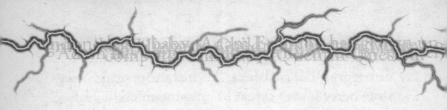

THE CROSSING

Half an hour later the raft was loaded, our packs piled in the centre, and we were ready to go. The girls hovered nervously near the water's edge, watching the launching with wide, frightened eyes. Weevil stood with them, huddled in Kenta's sleeping bag, looking sorry for himself.

Rich and I grabbed one corner of the raft each, and heaved. It weighed a ton. Gradually we tugged it down the gentle, stony slope towards the water. Jamie was capering about, getting in the way and giving advice: 'Look out for that big rock, guys! Oops, it isn't a rock, it's a . . . never mind. Careful, Adam – you don't want to get your feet wet! Watch that overhanging branch, Rich! Ouch – bet that hurt! Nearly there!' And at last: 'There we go! *We've done it!*' – to an ironic glance between Rich and me.

But we didn't have time to worry about Jamie – or anything else. 'Quick, girls – hop on! Right into the middle – and *hurry*!' Weevil and Kenta didn't need telling twice. Already, the places where the wooden base of the raft met the water were churning with ravenous, scrabbling life. But Gen stood frozen on the beach, hands up to her face, eyes huge. 'Adam – I don't know if I –'

Unceremoniously, I picked her up and dumped her in the middle of the raft. With our combined weight, it pitched alarmingly, dousing my foot in an icy wave of river water. Almost instantly, a pain like a bee sting shot through my ankle. 'Shoot,' I muttered under my breath.

'You OK?' Richard was balanced at the far end of the raft, both hands on the rope, ready for action.

'Yeah,' I grunted, ignoring the biting pain lancing through my foot. 'Let's go!'

With the girls and Weevil huddled silently in the centre with the gear, we set off across the smooth water, Rich at the front, me at the rear.

The current was stronger than it looked – way stronger. I'd estimated it'd take ten minutes or so to pull ourselves across – no more. More than estimated it – gambled on it. But as we approached the centre of the river, the raft started pulling to the right, in the direction of the slow flow of current. The rope curved outwards like a giant bowstring, creaking from the strain. If we'd stood upright, the raft would have swept out from under us and away downriver, leaving us dangling from the rope like clothes pegs on a line. But as the pull of the current increased we'd both automatically turned upriver to face the distant mountains, bracing our feet on the crossbars of the raft and leaning back against the river's pull. By the time we were halfway, my shoulders were on fire and my hands raw from the constant rubbing of the rough rope. The raft crept on at a snail's pace. Beside me, Richard heaved and panted and swore softly under his breath.

But the slow pace was the least of our problems. Almost as soon as the raft was waterborne it had started: a grating vibration that hummed through the wooden raft as though its bottom was being gently rubbed with coarse sandpaper . . . or as if a million – ten million – tiny mouths were gnawing away under the water.

Now Jamie spoke up, his voice trembling. 'Adam – it's happening . . .'

I shot a glance over my shoulder. He was crouched as close to the centre of the raft as he could get, his back to Weevil and the girls. He was holding a stick with a checked dishcloth bunched and tied tightly at one end, brandishing it in both hands like a weapon. His eyes were fixed on the edge of the raft.

They had come, just as we'd known they would. But nothing could have prepared me for the sight of them. A heaving, convulsing mass of spiders, each the size of a tiny grape, fat and transparent and bulbous like globs of phlegm with scrabbling legs, clawing their way up over the edge of the raft towards the cowering huddle in its centre.

'Toughen up, Jamie. You know what to do. Watch and wait – and do it if you have to!'

I turned back to the river. Was it my imagination, or was the raft starting to settle deeper into the water? Did the sandpapery, rasping noise seem louder – closer?

I shook the useless thoughts out of my head, gritted my teeth, ignored the searing pain in my ankle and the throbbing of my foot, and heaved at the rope. Hand . . . over hand . . . over hand . . .

'Adam! It's stopped them! Look!'

The entire perimeter of the raft was thick with spiders now – a bizarre edging of live lacework wider than my hand. But Jamie was right – it had stopped them. Like an invisible barrier, the thick line of insect repellent we'd sprayed was holding them at bay – for the time being at least. 'Good one, Jamie!' I grunted. 'Way to go!'

At last, it seemed the far bank was closer, and the pull of the current was letting up. So why did the raft seem so much heavier? Shooting a look across at Richard, I could see the muscles in his arms bunching and straining with effort; his face was bright red and covered in sweat, his dirty blond hair plastered to his forehead in dark strands. For a second, our eyes met. 'The raft,' he panted. 'It's settling . . . deeper into the water. As they eat . . . the wood off the bottom!'

At that moment, there was a shriek from one of the girls, and a warbling cry of horror from Jamie. Desperately, my flayed hands rasping over the rope, I looked down – and saw the spiders were crawling over one another, dragging their bloated little bodies over a layer of their wiggling, squirming companions to form a living carpet over the no-man's-land of insect repellent. They'd breached the first of our defences. Time was running out. 'Jamie . . .' I gasped.

'*I'm doing it!*' Out of the corner of my eye I saw that

he was: almost invisible, the fragile, flickering flame of the match in Jamie's wavering hand was licking at the tip of firelighter-soaked dishcloth. Then Kenta's slim brown hand was over his, steadying it, and the makeshift torch flared brightly into life. Legs straddled for balance, eyes round with horror, Jamie started brushing at the advancing tide of spiders in wide, awkward sweeps. There was a hissing, popping noise. I caught a glimpse of Gen cringing away, her face hidden in her hands. I turned my back and pulled with all my might.

But the raft was slowing. Sluggish, reluctant, it inched its way through the water. Behind me, Jamie huffed and puffed and whimpered; I could feel the platform tipping and swaying as he turned from one side to the other. Time crawled. A tide of panic was struggling its way up from somewhere deep inside. There was no going back now. The raft was settling deeper into the water. At first, the platform had been an easy hand's-span above the surface; now, little, greasy waves lapped over the edges, each one rimmed with a frothy edging of spiders, like the foam on the ripples at the seashore.

Suddenly, Gen screamed – a high-pitched shriek that turned my blood to ice. 'Jamie – there's one crawling on me! Quick! Help me!'

Jamie was losing the battle. As fast as he could swipe at the spiders, more came on. For a second, I hesitated; gauged the distance we still had left to the shore. Not far now – not far. Jamie's torch was burning low, starting to gutter . . . our options were running out. Rich and I exchanged a glance of grim agreement. 'Jamie – *now!*'

With a faint whimper, Jamie pushed the smouldering remains of the dishcloth down onto the deck of the raft, rubbing and turning it, searching for the second invisible line . . . Could the spiders have crossed it already? Had it soaked into the wood? Was the torch still burning?

The riverbank was a stone's throw away now. I closed my eyes and heaved . . . and all around me I felt rather than heard a running whoosh of flame as our last defence flared into life.

Together, Richard and I heaved the raft closer to the bank, our breath coming in agonised sobs, our eyes stinging with sweat. The raft with its paper-thin platform, its cargo of ravenous spiders, their scrabbling growing to a sizzling frenzy, and its last defence: a brave rectangle of flickering flame between us and the spiders, where we'd poured a thin barrier of fire-lighter what seemed like a century ago.

And suddenly we were there. The trees that had been tiny and far away were close enough to touch; I could see individual twigs and leaves and smell the rich, damp scent of earth. Then I felt ground under us – not the rough, harsh grating of wood on sand, but a squashy, squishing resistance. 'Quick – *jump!*' The raft bucked and jerked; I lost my balance totally and would have toppled headfirst into the water if I hadn't still been hanging onto the rope like a lifeline. Then Rich was leaping for shore like a champion long-jumper, and I was after him with an armful of bags, landing face-first in the powdery sand of the river-bank . . . rolling over and over . . . pushing myself up on my elbow to look out onto the river at the burning remains of the raft.

I couldn't believe we'd made it. There seemed impossibly little of it left, turning in a slow-motion circle like some kind of floating funeral pyre, a thin line of flame still stubbornly flickering, a wisp of blackish smoke swirling up towards the blue sky. The others were sprawled on the sand beside me: Weevil, Kenta, Rich, Gen . . . Jamie. From somewhere I summoned a wink and a grin. 'Good job, Jamie.' Jamie blushed an odd pinkish-green, then turned away and started to retch.

I pulled off my boot and my soaking sock and picked the spider off my ankle, fat and ruddy with my blood. A chunk of flesh the size of a pinhead came away in its pincers. I dropped it on the beach where it lay like a stranded whale, immobilised from gorging, its legs stiff and useless on either side of its grossly swollen belly.

Out of the water, the remains of the raft seemed to sigh softly as they tilted and sank forever beneath the sullen surface of the River Ravven.

'Lucky we won't be needing to come back this way, huh?' said Rich with an attempt at a grin. I thought of the microcomputer safely stashed in my backpack . . . thought of the long way we'd come, and the unknown distance still to travel.

I picked up my boot and brought it down on the

stranded spider with a satisfying *splat*. Then I heaved myself to my feet and held out a hand to Kenta.

'Come on, guys. Don't know about you, but I've had enough of this river to last me a lifetime.'

CHATTERING WOOD

On the other side of the river the ground rose steadily, then levelled out into a rolling plain that seemed to stretch on forever. The breeze rippled the blue-green grass, making the ground billow like the swells on the sea. At first the low autumn sun shone directly in our eyes; then gradually, as the long afternoon wore on, it sank to our left and disappeared behind the mountains. The moment it vanished, the temperature dropped like a stone. And so did our spirits.

'Is that what I think it is – that dark splodge up ahead?' groaned Jamie. I lifted my head and looked in the direction he was pointing. Sure enough, a dark shadow of trees spilled over the horizon.

'Let's stop here in the open for the night,' said Jamie when we reached the outskirts of the wood in the fading light of dusk. 'It's dark in there, and it smells damp. I'm sick of sleeping in forests, worrying about what's behind every tree and lurking under every bush.'

'I don't know, Jamie,' said Gen thoughtfully. 'I agree in a way – but we've been lucky so far. We've seen no one. Who's to say it'll stay that way? What if we're fast asleep by the side of the track and a whole gang of King Karazeel's heavies comes thundering past? I think we should play it safe: head on into the forest, light a fire, and take advantage of the shelter of the trees. Feel that wind – and what if it rains?'

She was right – the wind was freezing. The light breeze that had cooled our faces on the long walk had changed direction and sharpened into an icy blast, whipping over the plain behind us, freezing the backs of our necks and turning our hands to ice. It would be far more sheltered among the trees.

'Look at the track, though,' objected Richard. 'It forks – see? The main track carries on straight into the forest, but there's a branch going off to the left. Which is the right way, do you think?'

It was impossible to tell. I'd have given anything for a helpful signpost saying 'Shakesh – 5 kilometres', but there was nothing – no arrow or marker of any sort – to show which way we should take. 'The left-hand fork skirts round the forest, towards the mountains,' murmured Gen. 'Almost as if it was avoiding it for some reason. An alternative route, maybe – ending up in the same place?'

'But why would anyone want to go the long way round?' asked Rich. 'Far as I'm concerned, there's only one right way, and that's the most direct one.'

'We head into the forest then, I guess,' I said reluctantly. There was something about it I didn't like. It seemed odd to have one path going through it, and another going round. If it had been up to me, I'd have willingly walked twice the distance to avoid entering the shadows of those trees.

'Are we stopping here for the night?' Weevil limped up, dragging Kenta's sleeping bag in the dirt behind him. His slippers must have fallen to pieces somewhere along the way; his feet were bare, dirty, and obviously so sore he could hardly hobble.

'What do you mean, *we*?' I said gruffly. '*We're* going into the forest to set up camp. *You* can do what you like.' Kenta gave me a look that made me feel a bit uncomfortable, but I pretended not to notice.

We tramped on down the main track in silence, the dark walls of the trees closing in on all sides. The leaves above us whispered and sighed. A far-off chittering buzz ebbed and swelled through the trees. 'Almost like the sound a computer makes,' Kenta murmured. 'Bees, maybe, or a flock of birds settling down for the night.' As the darkness gathered, the sound dwindled and died. It was almost too dark to see . . . but at least the wind had finally dropped.

'What do you reckon? This as good a place as any?' We didn't even bother to answer Richard; just followed him twenty metres or so off the track and flopped down gratefully on the damp, mossy bank of a shallow stream. 'What if Weevil can't find us, tucked away here?' asked Kenta worriedly.

'No such luck,' I growled. 'Here he comes.' His pale shape was winding its way through the trees towards us.

'I wonder if we should move further from the stream,' said Kenta. 'I'm sure I remember it being a talking one. *Who drinks of me shall be a . . .* what was it now . . .'

Richard ambled over to the stream and bent down, his ear close to the water. 'Well, if it is talking, it's whispering. I can't hear a thing.'

'We're safe enough if we don't drink any water. I'm not moving anywhere,' groaned Jamie. 'Not ever again. My legs are one big ache, and I've got blisters. I'm going to sit right here till I die of old age.'

'Well, I'm not.' Gen heaved herself to her feet. 'I'm going to look for wood. No wood – no fire – no Kung Fu Oriental Noodles, Jamie. And no warmth or light, either. Up you get!'

Grumbling, Jamie struggled up and joined the rest of us in the hunt for dry wood. It wasn't easy to find. A dank chill was rising from the forest floor, and lacy grey lichen grew on many of the fallen branches, which were heavy and crumbling with damp. When at last we had a fire built and set a flame to it, the wood smoked sullenly and refused to light.

We squatted round the little tepee of sticks in gloomy silence, willing the flame to catch and wishing we'd saved a drop of the fire-lighting fluid. Weevil sat under a nearby tree, picking sulkily at his blisters. 'He hasn't even fetched a single twig,' whispered Jamie loudly, 'but I bet he'll be first in line for the noodles. I reckon you're right about him, Adam . . .'

'There won't be any noodles for anyone unless we can get this fire lit,' Gen pointed out.

'I know!' said Richard suddenly. 'How about we tear a couple of strips off the edge of the map? Just to get it going. The paper's real old and dry as a bone – it'll burn like blazes!'

'Are you crazy, Rich?' I couldn't believe what I was hearing.

'Adam's right,' said Jamie reluctantly. 'You shouldn't burn magic maps, even ones covered in splodge.' He gazed at the noodle packet longingly. 'Although . . . maybe just a teensy strip, off the black part. It's getting so dark – and I'm starving!'

It was dark – almost too dark to see the black stain and the lines on the map when Jamie opened it out. Almost . . . but not quite. 'Hang on a sec,' said Gen suddenly, just as Rich was about to make the first careful tear. 'Look at the dark bit – the black patch. Kenta, pass your torch.'

She shone the torch on the map, and we all saw what she had seen. The edge of the black area had moved. Before, it had begun just above Arakesh. Now, we could clearly see where the woods to the north of the city ended . . . the River Ravven and the ford . . . the fork in the track on the edge of this forest . . . even its name: Chattering Wood. But north of the forest's outskirts the map was the same as it had ever been: black and featureless.

'There you go!' said Jamie triumphantly. 'The stain's shrinking! Soon it'll all be gone and the map'll be as good as new!'

'Hmmm,' murmured Kenta. '*As good as new . . .* why does that worry me?'

'OK, OK, we know it's *not* new,' said Jamie defensively. 'We've been through all that before. I must have taken it from the *Used* barrel. But you shouldn't –'

'The new maps were cheaper than the used ones.' Kenta was thinking aloud, her eyes dark and intense with concentration. 'That isn't logical. Why should they be?'

'Maybe someone switched the signs round,' suggested Richard, 'as a joke – or to try and get a new map cheap.'

'No.' There was an undercurrent of excitement in Kenta's voice. 'The used maps were ten gelden, and the new ones only five. Why would a used thing be worth more than a new one? It doesn't make sense. Unless . . .'

We all watched her, waiting. But she shook her head, frustrated.

'Unless it somehow gained value by being used,' said Gen slowly.

'That's dumb. How could it?' scowled Richard.

'I've got it!' Jamie's eyes shone in the torchlight. 'Think where we are, guys!' He grinned round at our blank faces. 'In Karazan, right? And what *is* Karazan?'

'I dunno – a country? A world?' hazarded Rich.

'Yeah – but what else?'

'It's a computer game . . .' I said slowly, remembering. Remembering selecting 'New Game' on the PC that long-ago afternoon at Cameron's house, and my let-down feeling when the opening screen had been black, empty and featureless. Remembering Cam explaining it to me: *It moves when you move . . . the map reveals itself as you travel through it. It's called . . . shroud.*

'That's why used maps cost more!' Jamie was babbling excitedly. 'Because part of the map's been revealed already, by whoever's travelled there! I bet the new maps were just plain black! And the black stuff retreats as whoever's bought it . . .'

'. . . or nicked it!'

'. . . travels along! So wherever we go, the black stuff will disappear from that part of the map – and eventually, the map will be perfect!' he finished triumphantly.

'And that makes sense of something else too,' said Kenta slowly. 'Do you remember what Hob said . . . about shroud? *Beyond the shroud . . .*'

'Yeah!' Jamie jumped up. 'Right, Kenta – that's what the black stuff's called in computer games! I was scared to even think what Hob meant before! It sounded real creepy, cos shrouds are like . . . well, to do with dead people. They're those long white gowns you wrap dead bodies in, like ghosts wear. They –'

'OK, Jamie, we get the point,' said Gen impatiently. 'It's not *that* kind of shroud Hob meant. He meant we had to travel past the existing limits of our map – *beyond the shroud* – to get to Shakesh.'

'It's a pretty back-to-front way for a map to work if you ask me – but I don't suppose anyone's keen to burn it now, just the same,' said Rich. 'So I guess we'd better start hunting for dry kindling.'

I joined the others on the search, listening to their excited chatter as they wound through the dark tree trunks in the gathering gloom. I searched, and said nothing. There was something the others had forgotten . . .

None of us had known Jamie had taken a map . . . not until later that night, by the campfire. If we hadn't known, neither had Hob. And even if he had, he couldn't possibly have known what part of the map was still covered by the shroud.

And if he hadn't known, then what *had* he meant by *beyond the shroud*?

'WHO DRINKS OF ME . . .'

'*A*dam! Adam – help! Quick!*'

Richard's yell hit me in the face like a bucket of ice water. I jerked bolt upright, my heart twisting in a sickening somersault. 'Huh? What –'

'*Hurry!* Before it's too late!'

The campsite – the whole forest – was alive with sound: a chittering, jabbering din that made me clamp my hands over my ears. I struggled to my feet, stumbling over my sleeping bag, floppy and stupid with sleep, and stared wildly around. Rich was dancing around the clearing, a stick in his hand, shaking his fist at the trees above us. 'Bring it *back*, you little suckers! That's our stuff!'

'What – who –'

'I was on watch,' Rich growled, then looked sheepish. 'But I must have dozed off for a second. Next thing I knew, they were all around me!' He pointed up into the trees. It was still almost dark – that translucent, misty greyness just before dawn. Wide awake now, I focused on the canopy above us. The branches were rocking and swinging with movement, raucous with jibbering, chattering calls. 'Monkeys?' I croaked.

'Not monkeys – chatterbots.' Kenta spoke quietly beside me. 'I remember now. That was what the talking stream said: *Who drinks of me shall be a chatterbot.* In the game, they were cute little furry things – if you caught one, it could give you a wish.'

I thought of Q's special nickname for Hannah: Chatterbot. Had he called Hannah after the chatterbots, or the chatterbots after her? Whichever way round it was, gentle, bumbling Q would never have invented monkeys like these. Their voices were harsh and strident, their razor-sharp teeth bared aggressively, and their eyes glowed like red-hot coals.

'Like Q said, it looks like these ones have done a bit of evolving – downhill. I wouldn't call these guys cuddly or cute,' said Richard grimly; 'never mind the fact that they've ransacked our backpacks and made off with all our food!'

The five of us sat in a dismal huddle and watched the chatterbots swing through the trees, capering and chattering and flashing their bright blue bums at us as they ripped open our packets of dehydrated food, sweets, chocolate and dried fruit and guzzled the contents. They must have launched their raid on our campsite in absolute silence, with the planned precision of a military operation, and then burst into a triumphant clamour once it was finally done.

Nothing was left.

They stuffed handfuls of food into their gaping mouths, chittering delightedly to each other, grinning so widely the food fell out in a hail to land on the forest floor. They flung handfuls of rice at each other . . . they sprinkled dried noodles on one another's heads like confetti. They shoved raisins into each other's ears and up their own noses. Two adolescent chatterbots chased each other, teeth bared, the front one swinging by his tail from branch to branch, a jumbo pink marshmallow in each wrinkled fist.

At last, despite ourselves, we started to grin at their antics, then to laugh. 'Look at that one! He's pulled empty soup packets onto his feet, like boots!'

'There's a baby, look – smaller than my hand! Hanging onto the fur on his mum's stomach –'

'That one's twisted a toffee into the ruff round his face! Serves him right!'

Gen was suddenly serious again. 'They're really mean – look. The big one just snapped at that poor little one. I've been watching – they all keep turning on him and chasing him away. He's got something, I think – something shiny, and the mean one wants it. Look – he's chasing him again. Oh – he dropped it! Wait – I'll get it!' She darted into the undergrowth, flapping her hands at the chatterbots: 'Shoo! Shove off! Haven't you got enough, you greedy things?'

'Careful, Gen – they're vicious – look at those teeth!'

The chatterbot that had been doing the chasing swung by one hand from the branch above Gen, jibbering angrily. The other one – the one that had dropped the shiny thing – skulked a safe distance away, baring his teeth in a cringing grin of submission.

Beside me, Jamie sighed sadly as a gentle shower of

chocolate peanuts pattered to the ground around us.

Gen emerged from the bushes, holding something up triumphantly. 'Got it! It's not ours, but isn't it cool? Some kind of a flute – silver, with a pattern on the side . . .'

Far above us, high in the forest canopy, the outcast chatterbot stared down at us with brown button eyes . . . and stretched his monkey mouth into a smile that looked almost human.

It was as if, in that instant, the forest fell utterly silent.

I looked round at the others. They were staring up at the chatterbot with eyes like saucers. It was Kenta who whispered the words that were in all our minds: '*Where's Weevil?*'

'It can't be . . . can it?' asked Richard in a low voice.

I gulped. Gen gazed around wildly, as if hoping Weevil might leap out from behind a tree yelling '*Surprise!*' Kenta fixed me with a sorrowful look. 'Oh, Adam,' she said, 'how *could* you?'

'Me? What did *I* do? *I* didn't make him drink it!'

'Adam's right: we all knew not to drink the water, Kenta,' said Jamie righteously.

'Yes, Jamie – but Weevil wasn't here. He arrived afterwards, remember – when we'd already started looking for wood. He didn't know. And now . . .' Gen's words trailed away into silence.

As if one of them had given an invisible signal, the chatterbots were swinging away through the trees, their jabbering cries fading to the distant chatter we'd heard the evening before, and then to nothing.

But not all the chatterbots. Up in the forest canopy one remained, hunched forlornly on his branch, peering down at us through the leaves.

Kenta gave me a last, reproachful look. Then she turned her back on us all and picked her way through the undergrowth to Weevil's tree. 'Weevil,' she called, holding out her hand. 'Is that you? Come here – come down. We won't hurt you.'

'Be careful – he might bite,' cautioned Jamie.

Kenta ignored him. Slowly, branch by branch, Weevil clambered his way down. Watching him, my heart like a stone in my chest, I wondered how everything could possibly have gone so wrong. Was what Kenta had said true? Was this new disaster with Weevil my fault? Could I – should I – have done something differently? Sure, Weevil had been wrong. But did that make me right?

Jamie's cheery voice broke into my thoughts. 'Hey, guys – there is something left, after all! In the inside pocket of my pack – chewing gum, two whole packets! What's more, I've had an idea.' He lowered his voice to a loud whisper. 'The Healing Potion! Do you think it might work on Weevil? Should we try a drop and see?'

'I dunno, Jamie,' said Rich dubiously. 'I think it's for making sick people better – and he looks like a healthy chatterbot to me. Nah – we'd be wasting it. There's nothing wrong with him other than . . . well, other than the obvious. And I don't think there's much we can do about that.'

'Maybe it wears off after a while. Or maybe he'll change back once we get back to our world. But meanwhile, he looks happy enough. I wonder if, inside his head, he thinks like a chatterbot, or like he used to when he was a person?'

I wondered too – but there was no way of telling. What was going on behind that monkey face was anybody's guess. But my fault or not, as far as I was concerned he was still Weevil – I wasn't about to start liking him better just because his bum had turned blue and he'd sprouted a tail.

I walked quietly up to Gen and held out my hand. 'Gen – that penny whistle. Weevil . . . took it, back at Highgate. It's mine.'

'*Yours?*' Gen looked at me in astonishment. 'But . . . it's beautiful! Where . . .' Something in my face must have stopped her. She gave me a long, searching glance, then shook her head. 'Sometimes I feel we don't really know you at all, Adam,' she said softly, and pressed the penny whistle into my hand.

It fitted there just as it had always done – as if it belonged.

We packed up camp and pressed on through the forest with grumbling stomachs, Weevil loping along beside us. 'At least we don't have to waste time having breakfast,' Jamie puffed, toiling along beside me. I gave him a sidelong grin, and thought but didn't say, *or lunch . . . or dinner.*

And it was about lunch time when we finally

emerged from the trees and sank down thankfully for a rest and a drink of water. It was a grey day, fat-bellied clouds threatening rain. Ahead of us, the track wound upwards into low hills, then disappeared into the mist. 'I was worried this might happen,' Richard told me under his breath. 'Let's hope these aren't the foothills of the main range – it's hard to tell what direction we're going in, now the sun's disappeared. If we have to climb those mountains . . .'

'If we have to, we will.' I sounded a lot more confident than I felt. 'Let's get moving again. We should try to be on the other side by nightfall – it'll be freezing at the top, and the weather looks grim.'

The path climbed steadily. I led the way, Jamie puffing and panting behind me, the girls trudging along after him and Richard taking up the rear. Weevil bounded beside us, sometimes scampering on ahead and looking back to chitter at us, sometimes falling behind, never completely out of sight.

Soon we were completely enveloped in cloud – swirling mist that made it impossible to see where the path was headed, or how much further it was to the summit. Every now and then the track would level out, or dip down slightly; then it would round a bend and climb again. It grew colder. The mist gave way to light rain, the occasional snowflake swirling in the eddying gusts of wind.

Then suddenly I stopped. 'Look,' I said softly to Jamie. 'Over there on the left.'

'Houses!' Jamie's button nose was all I could see of his face, deep in the shelter of his hood. 'That means fire, maybe even a bed for the night. And *food* . . .'

'Hang on a minute. Let's not rush into anything we might regret.'

The others had come up alongside us now. We stood in a damp huddle, staring longingly at the squat shapes of the cottages, smoke smudging up from stone chimneys.

'It looks like a friendly little place to me,' said Jamie hopefully.

'If only we knew how much further we had to go . . .' I said.

'If only we knew how much daylight is left,' said Gen.

'If only we knew what the weather's going to do,' said Rich.

'*If* is one of the smallest words in the English language,' said Kenta quietly; 'and also the biggest.'

'Do you think this could be Marshall?' asked Rich after a pause.

'I guess it could. But we have to go to Marshall *and beyond*, so even if it is, we still have a way to go. Jamie – the map.'

'Look!' Gen pointed. 'The black stuff – the shroud – it's moved again! We're here – and here's the village. Drakendale.'

'Drakendale . . .' said Kenta thoughtfully. 'Where have I heard that name before?'

'On *Quest of the Dark Citadel*, I'll bet.' Rich gave her a grin. 'We all know you're the world expert, Kenta! But what interests me isn't Drakendale – it's Draken

Pass. I don't know much about maps and geography and stuff, but isn't –'

'Yeah! A pass is normally the uppermost point of a route – we learned about it in Young Explorers' Club at school! And if it *is* –'

'Then the track should start heading down pretty soon,' finished Rich. 'So what do we do?'

There was a short silence. 'I say we head on,' I said reluctantly. 'There's no telling who lives here. And even if they're friendly, it'll be more time wasted. Anything could be happening to Hannah and Kai. Every second could make a difference.'

Between life and death . . . or worse. I didn't say it, but looking round at the cold, pale faces of the others, I realised I didn't have to.

Without another word, we turned away from the cottages and headed on into the swirling whiteness. On, and down.

As if confirming we'd made the right choice, the weather began to clear. The mist shredded into ragged strands, revealing distant glimpses of blue-green hillside, yawning canyons and towering, rocky crags.

Down we slithered, loose stones skittering away under our boots. Then, without warning, the last of the mist lifted like a veil and a valley opened up below us, washed in the pale gold light of evening.

In the valley was a town.

And beyond the town was the weirdest thing I'd ever seen.

THE EDGE OF THE SHROUD

We stared down into the valley in silence, trying to make sense of what we were seeing.

The village was way smaller than Arakesh. It had the ramshackle look of a frontier town, like in an old Western movie. There was no wall, and the buildings seemed to be made of wood. There were a number of what looked like corrals, some with animals, some empty. On the main street I could make out a kind of hitching post, with a dozen or so horses – at least I assumed that's what they were – tethered to it. Tiny people scampered about like ants, scurrying in and out of buildings and fussing around a straggle of wagons and carts parked up at the far end of the street. Every now and again I caught the flash of watery sunlight reflecting off polished metal. *King Karazeel's soldiers.* Instinctively, my eyes searched for the hunched figures of the Faceless, a chill crawling spider-like down the back of my neck . . . but if they were there, they were invisible.

On the outskirts of the town were scattered several clusters of low buildings surrounded by tidy post-and-rail fences. *Farms*. In some of the paddocks animals grazed peacefully. Other fields were planted with crops. Over on our left I could see the main mountain range curving away to the west, its peaks lost in cloud.

A typical country scene, reassuringly – deceptively – familiar. It was what lay beyond the town of Marshall that chilled my blood.

'Just as well we got down off the mountain before that hit us,' muttered Rich. 'Talk about a storm . . .'

'I don't think it *is* clouds.' There was a tremble in Jamie's voice. 'I think . . . I think it's the edge of the world.'

It began a couple of hundred yards beyond the northern limits of Marshall, and stretched away on both sides as far as we could see. Rich was right – it looked like a bar of pitch-black cloud, dense and impenetrable. It lay over the land like a vast, billowing eiderdown, reaching far higher than the tallest tree or building ever could . . . but from our perch on the side of the mountain we were looking down on it, and could see that it extended unbroken as far as the distant horizon.

'I live up in the hills overlooking the city,' said Kenta quietly. 'Sometimes there's fog, and we're up above it. Do you think . . .'

'It reminds me of flying over cloud in an aeroplane,' said Gen, 'only no cloud in the world – in any world – was ever as black as that.'

But I knew what it was. I could hear Hob's voice as clearly as if he was standing beside me: *Beyond the shroud . . . to Shakesh*. 'It isn't a storm, or the edge of the world. It isn't cloud or smog.' I hadn't realised I was speaking my thoughts aloud till I turned to the others and saw they were all staring at me, eyes wide. 'It's shroud. Real shroud. Not a black stain on a map. Real blackness. We're going to have to go through it to get to Shakesh. We don't have a choice.'

'Well, let's hope it'll retreat ahead of us, like in the game,' said Richard. 'If it does – no problem, huh?'

But if it doesn't . . .

'Yeah,' I said grimly. 'Let's hope so.'

Our perch on the mountainside was the perfect vantage point, but being able to see also meant being able to be seen. There wasn't much shelter at this height – only a few low, grey-green thorn bushes clinging stubbornly to the sparse soil. Lower down, though, the slippery scree slope gave way to groves of gangly trees and denser pockets of scrub. We could make out glimpses of the track zigzagging its way through them, eventually joining up with the main street of Marshall.

We followed the track down to where the vegetation was thicker, and then branched off cross-country till we were almost directly above the town, well hidden by a tangle of prickly shrubs.

With sighs of relief, we shrugged off our backpacks and flopped down onto the ground. 'What wouldn't I give for a ham sandwich, with lots of mustard!' said Jamie mournfully.

'An apple for me – a bright red one, crisp and juicy – and a big chunk of cheese!'

'Don't, Rich,' groaned Gen. 'I'd settle for a crust of stale bread . . . but if I could choose anything, it would have to be chocolate. Milk chocolate, crammed full of hazelnuts.'

Jamie dug in his bag, producing a small, rectangular package. 'Chewing gum, anyone?'

Weevil had settled down on his skinny haunches on a flat stone in the sun, and was watching us with bright button eyes. 'He's listening to every word we're saying, aren't you, Weevil?' asked Kenta. Weevil chittered back at her. She tilted her head to one side, smiling at him. 'I wish we could understand you! What would you choose? You're trying to tell us, aren't you? Let's guess what it would be . . .'

'A banana – or maybe a crunchy beetle, huh, Blue-bum?' Kenta glared at me.

'Hey, guys – look! Something's going on down there. Come check this out!' Richard was lying on the ground, half hidden by a thorn bush. An undercurrent of excitement in his voice made me wriggle in beside him, my heart thumping.

The ground fell away steeply, giving a perfect, unobstructed view of Marshall, clear as a photograph, framed by prickly branches. Rich was right – something was happening. Whatever preparations had been underway before were complete. A caravan of laden carts straggled slowly away from us down the street, each drawn by a brace of harnessed . . . horses? Oxen? Glonks – or those funny llama-type things we'd seen before, in Arakesh? From this distance, it didn't look like any of them – but it was hard to be sure. Whatever

160

they were, they moved with a strange, swaying gait. I rubbed my eyes and squinted down, straining to see every detail. Were they tied together – or chained in some way? And each one seemed to have something dangling in front of it, almost like a long nosebag . . .

'Wish I had a pair of binoculars,' whispered Rich.

At the head of the column was what looked like a leader of some sort – a single animal with a rider. Behind it, the line of vehicles trundled slowly forward, some driven by figures that looked like soldiers, some led, some lurching forward in response to the cracking of whips that echoed into the foothills like gunshots. Behind the wagons, a rearguard of tall figures with pikes and gleaming helmets marched in tight formation. 'Headed for Shakesh, I'll bet,' breathed Rich.

Breathlessly, we watched the caravan approach the edge of the shroud. I stared, unblinking, my eyes watering, willing a magical tunnel of light to open up in front of the leader. The entry point to the shroud was marked by standing stones, half a dozen or so on each side like sentinels flanking the track. Five metres . . . two metres . . . one . . . and then the animal and its rider disappeared into the blackness. Close on its heels followed the next, and then the next . . . until the entire column had been swallowed by the shroud as completely as if it had never existed, leaving Marshall as empty and deserted as a ghost town.

I was turning away when I saw movement out of the corner of my eye. My heart flip-flopped; my skin was instantly slick with cold sweat. The standing stones were moving, drifting, floating away into the shadows of the buildings like ghosts.

They weren't markers at all. They were the Faceless, guarding the entrance to the shroud.

Cautiously, under cover of the deepening dusk, we scrambled down to level ground, staying well away from the outskirts of the town. It had seemed unthreatening before, but now it crawled with menace, filling us all with sickening dread. There was no way we dared take the same route as Karazeel's men. We'd just have to find our own way through. 'Maybe it's not as bad as it looks from above,' Rich said cheerfully. 'If they can do it, so can we.' But I could see the worry in his eyes.

With every wary step the shroud loomed closer, taller than a skyscraper, blacker than the blackest night. It seemed to lean over us as we approached, threatening and claustrophobic. Soon – too soon – we reached it, and stood in silence, face to face with the black wall. Far over to our right the buildings of Marshall crouched in the dusk like animals waiting to pounce.

Tentatively, Richard reached out one hand, palm outwards. For a moment his hand was resting flat against the solid wall of shroud; then, with an effort of will I could almost see, he thrust his hand elbow-deep into the darkness. It was as if his forearm had been amputated. Behind me, someone gave the tiniest whimper.

There was a gleam in Richard's eyes I was starting

to recognise. 'I'm going in, to see what it's like.'

'Richard – no!' Gen's eyes were huge and scared.

'I'll come with you, Rich. I agree – we have to know.' I rummaged in my backpack and found my torch. Dug in my pack again, and pulled out a coil of nylon rope. 'Jamie.' I handed it to him, twisting one end in a tight double loop round my hand. 'Whatever you do, *don't let go*. Rich –' I held out my other hand, fingers spread. Rich gripped it with his warm paw, our fingers tightly intertwined, solid as a rock. Our eyes locked. Together, we stepped forward into the shroud.

SHAKEŞH

It was worse than I'd imagined. Much worse. The shroud wasn't like normal darkness: it had a cloying weight that caught in my throat like steam, but cold as ice. It pushed in on my eyeballs with the suffocating pressure of a black pillow, making me want to kick and struggle free. I felt trapped – couldn't breathe. Taking a breath of shroud would be like taking a lungful of water – it would swamp me in darkness.

A sick wave of panic surged through me – and then Richard's hand tightened on mine. His voice came faintly out of the blackness beside me, muffled, but cheerful as ever. 'Pretty murky, huh? Can you hear something?' I could – the faintest undulating rise and fall of sound, the sort of white noise air conditioning makes, or waves breaking on a beach very far away.

I fumbled for the switch and clicked on the torch. Off; on again. But there was nothing – not the faintest glimmer of light, even when I held it right up to my face. It was impossible to believe the others were only a couple of paces away. I couldn't hear them at all; they could have been on another planet.

'So.' Richard's voice was grim. 'We're going to have to go in blind. Follow our noses, and hope we don't go in circles and get hopelessly lost.'

He was right: there was no other way. Or was there? I wished I could have got a closer look at the strange procession that had headed so purposefully into the darkness.

'Had enough?' I nodded, then remembered there was no way Rich could see me.

'Yeah,' I croaked. 'More than.' I could taste the shroud in my mouth, thick as treacle, tinny and metallic as blood.

There was a sharp tug on the rope. If it hadn't been for the double loop, it would have jerked loose for sure. Jamie, getting impatient – or worried. Then the rope went totally slack, and my heart stopped. What was he playing at? But then the pressure was there again, steady and strong, pulling me backwards out of the shroud like a fish on a line. I grinned, dizzy with relief. Good old Jamie! I was more than ready to breathe fresh air again.

We turned and took the few shuffling steps back to where the others were waiting for us. In moments the shroud gave way to the greyness of dusk . . . and with a numbing surge of terror I saw what had been reeling us in.

Not Jamie.

A hooded figure lurched out of the gloom, its cloak flapping like broken wings as it clutched for me. My mind took a split-second snapshot of the motion-less bodies of the others on the ground, faces white as death, dark shapes hunched over them like vultures at the kill. I gasped out one strangled cry of warning – too late.

The rope jerked and I stumbled helplessly forward into the suffocating embrace of the Faceless. The empty cowl of the hood bore down on me; a gust of fetid breath and the stench of carrion engulfed me. Something soft and smothering clamped over my face . . . and I was falling into a darkness deeper than the darkness of the shroud.

Awareness floated towards the surface of my mind, then drifted down again, rocking gently like a coin sinking into a deep pond. With the rocking came a hollow, pea-green queasiness that was part memory, part dread. I lay still, breathing shallowly, my heart thudding like a hammer in my chest. Where was I? Where were the others? And where were . . . *they*?

I opened my eyelids a chink. Utter blackness. My ears strained for a sound, but it was as if I'd gone deaf – they had a weird, tightly packed feeling as if they were stuffed with cotton wool, and I could taste shroud on my tongue.

I was sprawled half on my front, half on my side, with one arm bent painfully under me. Warily, I shifted my weight . . . felt metal grate on metal, and a sharp edge of cold steel dig into my wrist. Rough, splintery wood was bumping under my cheek with a familiar, regular vibration. I was moving. Being driven, in a cart, or a wagon . . . travelling through the shroud. *Towards Shakesh*. The Faceless were gone.

166

I could feel it – knew it as surely as if it was broad daylight. The weight of another body was pressed against my back. It felt loose, floppy, boneless – either unconscious, or asleep. *Let it be one of the others – please. Let them be OK.*

Something brushed my face – the faintest breath. I breathed it in. *Peppermint chewing gum.* My hand groped over rough wood; felt the softness of wool, and the smooth warmth of skin. I felt my chains shift and clank; then slender fingers tightened on mine, and the peppermint breath gusted out again in a soft sigh. I lay holding Kenta's hand, waiting.

Gradually the feel of the darkness began to change. The metallic stink of the shroud gave way to a heavier, dank reek. The vibrations changed from the jarring trundle of wheels over hard ground to a soggier, squishing resistance, as if we were travelling through sticky mud.

The dead weight lying against my back stiffened and shifted. Wriggled and squirmed, chains dragging. Suddenly it gave a convulsive heave, and a bullet-hard head smacked me on the nose, making my eyes water. Rich had woken up.

I closed my eyes against the darkness, shifted away from Rich's bony elbow, and waited. There was nothing else I could do – for the moment at least.

I opened my eyes to the faintest grey beginning of light. Kenta's face was pale as a ghost beside me; twisting my head, I could see other dark shapes huddled above me and at my feet. Up ahead, the broad back of a driver was silhouetted against the lifting darkness.

With every second it was lighter. Now I could see Kenta's brave attempt at a smile and the tear-tracks on her cheeks; the path winding away into blackness behind us; a vast, broken expanse of water stretching away like puddles of ink on either side, smudged with paler patches of reed.

Then the last remnants of shroud were behind us. It was early morning, just before dawn. The sky boiled with clouds, red-rimmed and shot with purple and gold. Ahead it was blotted out by the brooding silhouette of a massive, blunt-topped mountain, rearing out of the surrounding swamp.

And on its summit crouched Shakesh – not the bustling city I'd imagined, but a grim fortress surrounded by black walls, as dark and menacing as a giant tarantula about to spring.

A chill shadow fell over my face, and the rumbling vibration of the wheels changed to the jarring rattle of iron rims on rough stone. We lurched to a stop with a final bone-rattling bump. Armoured figures loomed over us. Rough hands grabbed me by the scruff of the neck and threw me to the ground. Fingers twisted cruelly into my hair, almost tearing it out by the roots. My head was turned one way and then the other and the packing that had been rammed in my ears was ripped out.

I couldn't understand it – a blindfold would have made sense, but why block our ears? What could there have been to overhear? But I was glad to be able to hear again – the grate of hooves on stone; the clank of chains; the snarling orders of the guards. And a strange whoofling sound . . .

Sprawled on the cobblestones, I stared at the creatures drawing the cart. They were the size of small horses, with antennae like snails, telescoping in and out . . . long trunks snuffling and questing . . . and pleated folds of skin instead of eyes . . . *So this is how they find their way through the shroud.*

A boot connected with my ribs. I struggled to my feet, rusty iron manacles weighing down my arms and dragging at my legs. Rich was flung out of the cart beside me onto hands and knees, glaring daggers at the guard; then Kenta. Jamie scrambled awkwardly down, red-eyed and trying hard not to cry. Gen came last, head held high and eyes blazing, yanking her arm away from the guard's hand with a furious toss of her head. There was no sign of Weevil.

We were in a gloomy, cobbled courtyard. A heavy chill hung in the air, more than just the cold of early morning. Rough stone walls reared skywards, streaked with dark patches of greasy slime. The deep shadow of the corners was stippled with creeping black mildew, edged with early morning frost.

A rattling rumble made me lumber awkwardly around. A massive portcullis was grinding its slow way down. I stared wildly around the claustrophobic space. Every instinct screamed at me to run – but there was nowhere to run to. With a final protesting squeal the portcullis thudded to rest . . . and a door, deeply recessed in the wall of the curved tower behind us, slowly opened. We wheeled round to face it.

The doorway was almost blocked by a huge figure cloaked in black. For a long moment he stood staring down at us, eyes in deep shadow. At last he spoke.

'This is Shakesh, Seat of His Eternal Excellency High King Karazeel of Karazan.' The words were cold and hard as steel. 'Look your last on the light of day. *Take them below!*'

Two guards emerged from the dark doorway. Jamie was shoved roughly in the back, stumbling forward into the shadows. Kenta and Gen were seized and thrown after him, stumbling over their heavy iron shackles.

'Hey – you don't have to –' Rich stepped forward with fists clenched, scowling furiously. The chief guard raised one gauntleted hand and smashed it across Rich's face in a brutal backhander that echoed across the courtyard with a sickening *thunk*. Richard dropped to the ground like a stone, the livid, mottled imprint of the steel glove on his cheek.

One of the guards hefted Richard's limp body in a fireman's lift and disappeared through the doorway. I shuffled after him onto a small, dark landing . . . then down a corkscrewing stairway lit by burning brands set deep into the walls. The steps were crumbling and slippery with damp, narrowing on the inside to a hand's-width. The heavy iron chain between my feet clanked along behind me, dragging at my feet and threatening to trip me and send me headlong down the steep stairwell. I groped my way down, concentrating on putting one foot in front of the next, trying not to think about what lay ahead.

After an eternity the stairway ended and we were shoved down a narrow stone corridor, through one clanking portcullis and then another, iron keys squealing in rusty locks. The passage opened into a wide rectangular chamber dimly lit by flickering torches. It stank of smoke and human waste, overlaying damp stone and the cold tang of fear. Moisture beaded the stone walls, trickling slowly downwards like tears.

We clanked to a halt, the rattle of our chains echoing into silence. Somewhere close by, something squealed and scrabbled away.

Along one long wall a rusty railing of iron bars stretched from the floor to the low stone ceiling, which pressed down on us . . . we were deep in the belly of the mountain. Beyond the bars, the narrow space was divided into smaller chambers – cells.

All of them were empty. If Hob was right – if Kai and Hannah had been brought here – they weren't here now. I closed my mind to what that must mean.

A key shrieked in a lock; a barred door creaked open. The guard carrying Richard's limp body shouldered his way in and dropped him on the floor, his head connecting with the stone with a crack that made me wince. The girls hurried after the guard, flinching away and keeping their faces down. Jamie sidled through the door and backed against the wall, his chin quivering. I stepped in after him. The door clanged shut; the key turned.

And suddenly the helpless despair weighing down

on me gave way to red rage, familiar, wild, and welcome as an old friend. Without thinking – hardly knowing I was doing it – I strode to the bars and gripped them in my fists, shaking with all my might. '*Let us out!*' I yelled. 'Who do you think you are? At least bring us some food and blankets! We'll freeze down here!' I hammered on the bars with my fists, and kicked at them with my feet till my toes were bruised and numb.

There was the last distant rattle of an iron grille falling, and the hollow echo of retreating footsteps, punctuated by an exchange of deep voices and a burst of harsh laughter. '*You've killed Richard!* And what about Blue-bum?' I was almost sobbing with helpless fury. 'He's out there somewhere, lost in the dark . . . and you don't even *care*! And the others – where are they? What have you done with them?' My voice rang out into the shadowy corners of the dungeon, the bleak walls bouncing my words back at me in a mocking echo.

And then my anger faltered and was gone as if it had never existed, leaving a hollow emptiness. It had all gone wrong – everything. Hot tears burned behind my eyes. I sank forward exhausted, hanging from the bars, feeling the cold fingers of the dungeon creep through my tattered clothes, through my skin, into the depths of my heart.

There was a long, long silence. Then a voice spoke behind me. 'Adam?'

I turned stiffly, not daring to believe what I'd heard. It was Richard, the marks of the gauntlet still raw on his cheek. 'Hey,' he croaked with a crooked grin, 'do you see what I see?'

Rich was pointing at my backpack, which was lying on top of a forlorn heap just inside the door, where the guards had dumped them. It twitched. Tipped. Rocked from side to side. Slowly, the flap of the bag lifted . . . and a pinky-brown monkey paw patted its way tentatively out. Followed by another . . . followed – very cautiously – by a single bright button eye.

Rich propped himself up on one elbow, his grin lighting up the gloom. 'Why not relax and enjoy the free accommodation, Adam?' he said huskily. 'After all, we're in Shakesh, where we wanted to be. We've got our sleeping bags, and plenty of chewing-gum . . . and now it looks like your old mate Blue-bum's hitched a ride in your backpack.

'What more could you want?'

THE PRINCESS

We slept huddled together for comfort like a litter of puppies, as far from the door as we could get, without stirring or dreaming: the sleep of utter exhaustion.

But tired as I was, when I woke it was as abruptly as if someone had turned on a light bulb in my brain. One moment I was in deep sleep, dark and silent as the still water at the bottom of a well; the next, my brain was racing, every sense alert.

Voices – there were voices in the dungeon.

I lay there without so much as twitching, listening.

'Be sure you understand the order of ceremony for the day.' I recognised the voice instantly: deep and harsh, with a ring of authority. The chief guard. 'First, the princess.' He gave the word a strange, almost sneering emphasis. 'A private audience – His Excellency is still amusing himself with her, or so it seems.'

'First, the princess,' repeated another, younger-sounding voice obediently.

'She is already in the first holding chamber. Remember: private audience, drapes drawn. Then . . .'

there was the sound of parchment shuffling . . . 'then we have these vermin – you will need to take them up to the second holding chamber.'

'Should I clean 'em up? They're awful stinky.'

'Orders are that His Excellency wishes to see them as they came in.'

'What will he do with 'em, do you think, Captain?'

'Who knows? The Faceless found them sniffing about at the edge of the shroud. His Excellency has no mercy on interlopers – especially now, as the time draws nigh.' He gave a cruel laugh. 'We will not be guarding these long, I'll warrant. Once they are done with, only the Mauler remains before mid-morning recess. Grilles closed, drapes open; Their Extreme Elegancies will wish to watch the display, but their safety is paramount. Be prepared to draw the drapes at a moment's notice should the spectacle become too overwhelming.'

'So: grilles closed, drapes open, but be ready to close 'em.' A new note crept into the business-like exchange. 'Captain . . . this Mauler. I've been up guardin' the slaves workin' on Arraz, and I ain't seen it yet. Is it really all they say?'

'All . . . and more. A killing machine. Teeth like sabres; talons of adamantine. Eyes of fire, and a body lithe and sleek as a spring . . . untameable, and ruthless in the pursuit of its prey. It is a savage beast spawned of your wildest nightmares; a legend sprung to life. Aye, the Mauler is a rare curiosity, a collector's piece . . . and at present, His Excellency's greatest diversion and indulgence.

'But remember, as your life depends upon it: *keep the guard-grilles closed*. And now, make haste!'

I opened one eye a slit. There was a heavy wooden table against the wall opposite our cell – a guard-station, I guessed. It held an untidy scatter of parchments, a couple of dirty-looking tankards and platters, and a jumble of rusty-looking chains. A smoky lantern hung from a bracket on the wall above the table, with a grimy slate next to it. Though it was hard to tell in the dim light, it seemed to be divided into boxes I guessed must refer to the cells . . . or to the long rack of heavy iron keys fastened to the wall beside it.

A burly figure heaved itself up from one of the rough wooden chairs and unhooked the key second from the left. Hefting a thick metal truncheon, he crossed the wide gap between the table and our cell in three long strides and ran the truncheon along the iron bars with a rattling clang that brought the others leaping to their feet, wide awake in an instant.

In seconds, the door was flung open and we were herded out and down the narrow corridor between the wall and the line of cells – this time, in the opposite direction to which we'd come. We skirted a heavy metal grille set into the floor with a sickening, putrid smell wafting up from it. I noticed a narrow stairway leading steeply downwards to our left, into deep shadow. Instinctively, I shrank away, shuddering at the thought of what desolate depths it must lead to. An echoing chant wound up from the depths – the same few words endlessly repeated, with the hollow desperation of a mind clinging desperately to its last shreds of sanity. We huddled closer and hurried on.

Through one portcullis and another, to a circular tower with a spiral stairway leading upwards. Waiting our turn to join the file clanking its slow, cumbersome way up the steps, Rich and I exchanged a glance. We didn't need words to know what the other was thinking. There was no way in the world we would ever escape from here. We'd be here for life, as long as it lasted . . . if it wasn't for the secret microcomputer, hidden in the depths of my backpack with Weevil curled on top of it, quiet as a mouse and hoping against hope not to be discovered.

We emerged from the top of the stairway into a curved passage. Our guard – a swarthy, bearded man in the black cloak which seemed to be the universal uniform of Shakesh – held one finger to his lips, indicating we should be silent . . . and then drew the edge of his hand across his neck to show what would happen if we weren't. Still in single file, we crept after him as quietly as our clanking chains would allow.

The wall to our right was unbroken, but studded wooden doors led off at regular intervals on the left. We followed the curve till only two doors remained. Our guard opened the first of these and pushed us roughly through, bolting the door behind him.

We were in a small antechamber, about four metres square. On the rear wall was the door we'd come through; the two adjoining walls were bare. The third wall wasn't stone, as the others were – it was a close-knit mesh of what looked like steel, intricately hinged and bolted . . . I guessed this was so that it could slide away to open the room to whatever lay beyond. On the far side of the grille was a heavy tapestry, drawn across like a curtain.

One thing was clear – for the time being at least, there was no opportunity to escape. Rich looked at me, raised one eyebrow, and shrugged. I shrugged back, and gave the others what I hoped was a cheerful grin. We were a pretty miserable-looking lot – pale with hunger and apprehension, faces smeared with dirt and dust from sleeping on the dungeon floor, clothes tattered and filthy.

I slid down so I was sitting with my back to the wall, a weirdly familiar feeling fluttering in my gut – and couldn't help a wry grin when I realised what it was. Here, in the holding chamber awaiting an audience with King Karazeel of Karazan – an audience I had a hunch could only end badly – I had the same feeling of sinking dread I'd had on my many visits to the Principal's office. For some crazy reason, the thought made me feel a whole lot more cheerful.

And then a man's voice spoke up on the other side of the grille, only slightly muffled by the heavy drapery, and every other thought was instantly banished from my mind.

'I ask again: *Who are you?*' The voice had a silken, almost hypnotic quality; a gentle, sinister insistence.

There was a pause; just the merest heartbeat. Then another voice – a gallant, staunch little voice that sounded as out of place in the bleak castle as a skylark's song. It was a voice that brought me leaping to my feet and over to the grille in a flash, mashing my face against the cold steel so as not to miss a single syllable, my heart thundering.

'I'm Hannah Quested.'

'Han-nah Ques-ted? A strange name for a little girl. Especially a little girl who told me only yesterday that she was . . . let me see now . . . *Princess Fenella Foo-Foo.* Yet today, you have a different tale.'

'I was Princess Fenella yesterday, and I'm Hannah today. People can be different things on different days. Depending.'

'Depending? Depending upon what?'

'Depending on how they feel.'

'So. Today you are Hannah Quested.'

There was a short pause while King Karazeel – as I knew it must be – digested this information.

Then, the merest whisper: 'I want my daddy.'

Quick as a striking snake – 'And who is your "daddy", sweetmeat?'

'*Don't call me sweetmeat!* And don't touch my hand! You feel all slimy!' I closed my eyes, beaming her a silent, desperate message: *No, Hannah – no! Hang in there – don't make him angry, whatever you do!*

But he was angry – I could hear it in the silkiness of his next words. 'Very well . . . Hannah Quested. Tell me where you come from.'

'I told you already. Quested Court!'

'Quested Court? A court is a king's residence. Who is this king? And you say your name is Hannah

179

Quested . . . daughter of the court . . . yet you deny you are a princess. You trifle with me, child.' I could sense his anger growing to a terrible, cold rage – but still he hid it from her. 'But come now. Let us be friends, hmmm? Perhaps if I know more, I can help you return to your . . . *daddy*. So tell me: where is Quested Court?'

'I told you – I don't know! It's at home. It's where I live with Q.'

There was a brief pause. 'Very well then. Tell me this: how did you journey to Arakesh? A little girl like you, all on your own?'

'I've already told you.'

'Tell me again.'

Hannah, with exaggerated patience: 'Through the computer!'

Richard and I exchanged a horrified glance. 'And what is a com-pew-ter, little one?'

Even on the other side of the thick drape, I could hear Hannah's sigh – a sigh that said clearer than words that she'd had enough. 'A computer is a *computer*, you silly billy! Don't you know *anything*?'

Instantly, the voice changed to a low hiss. 'You dare call me *silly*? Me, His Eternal Excellency High King Karazeel of Karazan, Ruler of the Realm of the Twin Moons, and Conqueror of the Lands Beyond the Distant Sun?'

There was a ghastly silence. We waited, hardly daring to breathe. Then Hannah's voice came again, very quietly, with a slight wobble. 'You sh-shouldn't yell at little girls.'

'We shall see, sweetmeat, what His Eternal Excellency High King Karazeel of Karazan should and should not do – *and who will tell him so.*'

As if at some invisible signal, the door behind us edged open and our guard reappeared. At the same moment, the heavy drape was drawn aside, revealing the throne room of King Karazeel, a fleeting glimpse of a small figure in an extremely dirty fairy costume being roughly bundled out of the huge double doors at the far end . . . and the king himself.

The throne room was horseshoe-shaped, with a raised dais at the open end. Holding chambers were ranged at intervals round the curved perimeter, each with a metal grille and a heavy drape that could be opened or closed as required. I took all this in at a glance . . . and then all my attention was fixed on King Karazeel.

I'd been expecting a throne. Instead there was a long settee on the dais, with a backrest at one end. On it lounged the king, flanked by four motionless guards in golden armour.

By now I was used to people wearing drab colours in Karazan – and staring at the king, I felt as dazzled as if I'd been watching an old movie in black and white and it had suddenly switched to brilliant Technicolor.

King Karazeel wore a loose shirt of golden silk, and breeches of silver cloth, with a wide scarlet sash – the colour of royalty, I remembered Kai saying – encircling his waist. From his shoulders fell a heavy cloak woven of every colour imaginable – an exotic, dazzling kaleidoscope of shifting colour that glimmered and shone in the bright sunlight beaming down onto him like a spotlight from a skylight far above. His hair was the deepest black, thick and luxuriant. He wore a crown – a design I had the weirdest feeling of having seen before: a heavy, interlocking circlet of gold and silver. Had it been on the box of *Quest for the Golden Goblet* – a kind of logo, perhaps?

But his face – I couldn't take my eyes from his face. It was harsh and utterly compelling: golden-skinned and strikingly handsome, with a thin, cruel mouth and a curved, hawk-like nose. On anyone else, the lines on his face would have been smile ones . . . but these were as different from Q's laugh lines as night from day. A voice spoke in my mind, with absolute certainty: *Those are lines drawn by pleasure in other people's pain.*

It was the face of a man in his prime . . . yet somehow it wasn't. There was something strangely ageless about King Karazeel, as if he was suspended in time. But most striking of all was the aura he gave off, so strongly my senses reeled from it: a stench of power, greed and corruption.

As I stared at him, at the same time fascinated and repelled, his pale, hooded eyes slowly swivelled towards us . . . and settled on me.

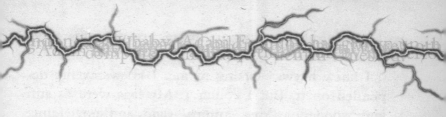

THE MAULER

It was as if no one else in the room existed. I stared into those pale, empty eyes and felt the world fall away under my feet.

Dimly, I realised the metal grille had been slid aside, and the others were being herded reluctantly towards the dais. Automatically I moved with them, my eyes still locked on Karazeel's. It was as if his eyes were made of cold, grey steel – magnets, drawing me forward.

We reached the raised edge of the platform, and stopped. Karazeel was no more than two strides away. I was dimly conscious of a strange, musky odour almost like incense, overlaying another smell – one I couldn't identify.

'*Kneel!*' It was the guard, his whisper loud in the silence. '*Kneel before the king!*'

There was a dull thump from beside me as Jamie thudded to his knees. I felt rather than saw the others follow his example. It was what we'd agreed – do as you're told. Buy time. Keep what options we still have open. Above all, don't make waves.

The order came again, more urgently this time. '*Kneel, imbecile!*'

I knew he was talking to me. I knew my life depended on it. But I couldn't. My legs were as stiff and wooden as tree stumps, rigid and unyielding. I could no more have bent them and knelt to King Karazeel than sprouted wings and flown up through the skylight.

'*Adam . . .*' Gen's desperate whisper.

Still, I stared into the eyes of the king. Then suddenly his lips curved into a smile, and he spoke. 'This boy . . . interests me. Let him stand if he will. Evor . . .' He held out one hand.

Our gaze broke. From behind Karazeel, a humpbacked, misshapen figure shuffled forward. I had a fleeting impression of a dark robe, purple as night and spangled with stars; sharp, calculating eyes glinting from a nest of long, matted hair; a twisted hand with nails curled like claws.

The hand reached out to a low, gilded table beside the king's seat. Ranged on the table was an array of phials . . . crystal phials that shone like diamonds in the shaft of sunlight. Shimmering phosphorescence . . . liquid ebony . . . crystal-clear transparency . . . distillation of emerald . . . and a dull mustard sludge, the colour of pus. The hand stroked over them, as if considering. The long nails made a faint rasping sound as they trailed delicately over the gleaming crystal, like the scritch-scritch-scratching of rats in a dungeon.

The hand settled on the sludge-brown potion, thick

184

as liquid mud. As the sorcerer touched it, a mottled shadow slithered into my memory, lifting its blunt head and tasting the air with its flickering tongue. *Inner Voices. The Potion of Insight.*

King Karazeel's heavily ringed hand reached hungrily for the phial, almost snatching it. He held it up to his nose and inhaled deeply, savouring its scent. Then abruptly he put the phial to his lips and upended it with a greedy, sucking sound. Instantly, his eyes rolled up in their sockets leaving only blank, bloodshot slits of white, a thin string of drool sliding from the corner of his slack mouth.

Alarm bells were jangling in my mind. Fragmented thoughts jostled with the growing panic on the edge of my consciousness . . . *This boy interests me . . . Evor . . . sorcerer . . . Inner Voices . . . Insight . . .*

Then I felt it. Sly and subtle, as if fingers made of jelly were probing my mind. Fondling, stroking, digging oh so gently into the deep reaches of my thoughts . . . deeper . . . and deeper. There was something comforting, soothing and luxurious about giving in to the soft searching. Pictures began to float to the surface of my mind, hazy and seductive as dreams, as if my memory was on slow rewind.

A distant view of a village from a mountainside . . . a stomach empty and hollow as a drum, and the minty taste of gum . . . searching, searching *. . . swirling mist . . . a burning raft . . .* searching, searching *. . . a small figure in striped pyjamas . . . a computer keyboard . . . a dog's hot breath on my face . . .* closer, closer *. . . the blue of Q's eyes, clear as the sky . . . a shabby brown book . . . a* *haunting tune, the melody clear and pure as raindrops, made by . . . made by . . .* yes? . . . yes?

A glint of silver hovered faint as a note of music on the edges of my mind, flickering and starting to take form . . .

. . . *the blue of Q's eyes* . . .

NO!

Denial rang through my head like a clash of cymbals, almost exploding my brain with its force. The trembling image shattered and was gone. Instinctively, in desperate reflex, I threw up a wall in my mind – a wall of stone, blank and featureless, stretching to the sky. All I saw was the wall. I stared at it, eyes squeezed shut, metallic echoes still ringing in my skull. I stared at my wall. It was solid, strong. My world was the wall.

Gradually, the echoes faded and died.

The groping fingers were gone. Warily, I opened my eyes. King Karazeel was lying back, head lolling. His pale eyes were half open, but vacant and empty.

The sorcerer hovered at his side, peering into the blank eyes. His bony fingers snapped once – twice. There was no response. He reached for the phial that shimmered with liquid mother-of-pearl, and held it gently, almost tenderly, to the king's slack lips.

I watched, sickened, remembering another time, in another world . . .

Karazeel sipped, coughed – then greedily sucked. At once colour flooded back into his face and his eyelids fluttered. His eyes opened, searching me out again with glittering intensity.

The hunchback fussed over him, straightening the crown, smoothing the rainbow cloak, dabbing at the pale lips with a silken cloth. The king murmured something to him. Evor hobbled forward with his awkward, lurching gait, and fixed me with eyes that burned dark as coal. He spoke in a hissing whisper that made the hairs on the back of my neck rise. 'King Karazeel bids me tell you there are more ways than one to unlock the secrets of the mind. Ways more painful for you . . . though not for him. But there is time enough . . . You will await his pleasure.'

At last Karazeel's gaze moved down to the others, huddled silently on the floor at my feet. His eyes rested on them one by one. His lips curved into a dismissive smile. 'Only the boy,' he said finally. 'He has a look about him . . . but now I am tired. Dispose of the rest.'

Evor gestured to the guard and murmured something to him – I caught the words 'boy . . . dungeons . . . others . . . *upon the eastern wall . . .*'

My heart froze.

The guard grasped the girls by their arms and hauled them roughly to their feet. Kenta's eyes were pools of terror in her ashen face. She'd heard what I had . . . maybe more. But Gen's eyes sparked blue fire. Her tawny hair was wild and tangled as a lion's mane, her teeth bared in a ferocious snarl. She fought the guard's grip on her arm, kicking and scratching like a wildcat . . . and then, unbelievably, she pulled free, leapt forward onto the dais, and spat full in the face of King Karazeel.

Instantly, the four soldiers were on her, her struggling figure surrounded in a second. Gen was helpless in their grip, a drawn sword at her neck, another at her heart. They turned to face the king, awaiting his order. Karazeel watched, face expressionless.

The moment stretched forever.

Then King Karazeel smiled . . . a smile that chilled my blood. 'Yes,' he murmured, as if to himself. 'How did I not notice her before? A little beauty – and the fiery spirit will be easily quelled. She will do very well as a handmaiden of the court, serving the king . . . and she will not spit so well, nor so far, when she lacks a tongue.'

Two of the soldiers dragged Gen away towards the huge doors at the far end of the throne room. 'Let me go!' she screamed. 'I want to stay with the others! I won't ever serve you! You're evil and hateful – I'd rather be dead!'

King Karazeel watched her go with cold, expressionless eyes. Then he inclined his head, and instantly the sorcerer was beside him, wiping Gen's spit off his face and bending to catch his next words. At a sign from Evor, pages sprang forward and drew back the heavy tapestries lining the far wall.

I gaped. Beyond the tapestries was a luxurious chamber, an extension of the throne room itself. It was thronged with ladies – twenty, thirty or more: a gallery of queens. My eyes were drawn from one face to the next, each more dazzlingly beautiful than the last. Some were dusky-skinned, some rose-petal fair . . . some had dark hair, loose and flowing, some hair like spun gold piled high on their heads . . . some had eyes as wide and dark as fawns', some eyes like angels, blue as heaven. Each wore a gown of a different colour – ruby red, bronze, rose, sapphire, silver, ivory – and a delicate crown of gold. They were like exotic birds of paradise, fluttering and preening and twittering among themselves as they cast sidelong smiles and sultry glances at the king.

'Remove the vermin!' Evor rasped. 'The king wishes to be entertained! Heralds: a fanfare for the entrance of the Mauler!'

The four of us were bundled hurriedly down the red carpet towards the door Gen had disappeared through. We stumbled along without protest, numb with the shock of being separated and dread of what lay ahead.

As we reached the doorway a bright chorus of trumpets rang out. Instinctively, I glanced back. Our guard had also slowed and was gawking over his shoulder. A scarlet tapestry emblazoned with a golden coat of arms swished dramatically open and two courtiers appeared, wearing rich liveries of cream and bronze, each carrying a gilded cage. There was a bird in one, and in the other . . . a *rat*? Then my attention switched to the solitary figure behind them. Like his attendants, he was dressed in cream silk, but the trimmings on his tunic were gold. His hands were protected to the elbows by heavy leather gauntlets, matching boots covering his legs to the knee. His face was hidden by an ornate mask, crafted to represent the head of a snarling predator.

In spite of everything I couldn't help staring over my shoulder. I was certain this must be the Mauler's Keeper, and the Mauler wouldn't be far behind.

But I was wrong. The Mauler was already there.

The Keeper paced slowly towards the throne. His hands were held at chest level, like a waiter in one of those expensive restaurants you see on television. On the palms of his hands, resting on the gauntlets like a tray, was a plump velvet cushion of purest gold.

And on the cushion, with her paws curled under her, wearing a golden collar studded with jewels and looking mighty pleased with herself, lay Tiger Lily.

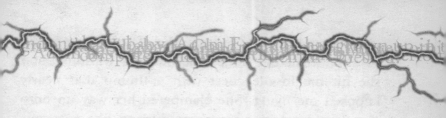

THE GRACE OF THE MAULER

'*IT'S THAT DARN CAT!*' Richard's voice, never soft at the best of times, rang out to every corner of the throne room.

'*Rich – pipe down!*' I hissed. Our guard had turned pale and was desperately hustling us through the door – I realised that if he was caught hanging back in hopes of a glimpse of the Mauler, his head would be on the block.

But it was too late. The second she heard Richard's voice, Tiger Lily was off the cushion and streaking down the scarlet carpet towards the doorway. The Keeper stood helplessly as if turned to stone. Shrill shrieks of terror came from the queens' gallery – out of the corner of my eye I saw one after the other fainting to the floor, like brightly coloured flower petals falling in the wind.

For the first time, King Karazeel was bolt upright, leaning forward avidly, an expression of greedy anticipation on his face as he watched the savage Mauler bounding towards the unprotected prisoners.

Just before she reached us, Tiger Lily sprang. She

191

was only a little cat, but months of soft living in the royal court hadn't done much for her waistline, and she hit me in the chest with a thump that nearly knocked me flying. She clambered her way up onto my shoulder and hung there purring like a steamroller, kneading my jerkin with her claws. Apart from the rumble of the Mauler's contented purring, there was absolute silence.

Then King Karazeel rose slowly to his feet. Gesturing to the Keeper to follow him, he walked slowly down the length of the throne room towards us, Evor hobbling after him like a shadow.

He stopped an arm's length away from me. When he spoke, it was to the sorcerer, though his eyes were on Tiger Lily. 'What is the meaning of this?'

'It may be . . . that the creature has in some way . . . evolved, my lord king.' The slimy voice had an undercurrent of uncertainty. 'We know it to be a sacred beast. It may be . . . that its wildness has for some reason deserted it.'

The king turned his head a fraction in the direction of the Keeper, standing motionless at his shoulder. 'Can this be so?'

The Keeper's reply was muffled behind his mask. He stepped forward and plucked Tiger Lily off me, though she dug her claws in and hung on as tight as she could.

His eyes glittering, King Karazeel gestured towards Kenta, Rich and Jamie, standing by with their mouths open. The Keeper held Tiger Lily out towards them one by one. She hung purring in his hands, placid

192

and relaxed, blinking sleepily at them with blissful golden eyes.

'You see, my lord king, it is as I supposed. I fear your Mauler has become tame. Observe . . .' Evor sidled forward, one hand outstretched towards the little cat. Instantly her ears flattened against her head, her mouth widened into a snarl, and a paw lashed out, claws extended.

Evor leapt back with astonishing speed and agility – but not fast enough. Four deep scratches appeared on his shrivelled hand, oozing purplish blood.

'Hmmm.' King Karazeel didn't seem too displeased by the turn of events. Slowly, very cautiously, he extended one hand in the direction of Tiger Lily himself. The Keeper, clearly alarmed for the king's safety and his own skin, took a rapid step back – but a glance from the king stopped him. Instead, the leather gauntlets tightened on Tiger Lily's sides. Her golden eyes, fixed on the king, narrowed dangerously, and she gave a low, warning growl. The king stepped back and smiled at Evor – but it was a smile without humour.

'So. It seems you know less than you would have me believe, Evor. I will think on this, and draw my own conclusions. Guard – take the prisoners below. Their skins have been saved – for the moment. Saved –' and again the cruel lips curved into a thin smile – 'by the grace of the Mauler.'

The guard bundled us back down the spiral staircase and into our cell. He removed our shackles and slammed the heavy gate, locking it securely. Then he replaced the key on its empty hook on the rack above the guards' table, made a mark on the slate, and disappeared the way we'd come, the portcullises rattling down behind him.

Absolute silence settled on the dungeon. I looked round at the faces of the others – only three of them now. They were grey in the gloom, and bleak with despair.

For what seemed a long time, no one spoke.

And then the silence was broken by a voice from the next cell, where a pale shadow like a ghost had crept up to the bars and was peeping through, unnoticed. 'Adam,' it said reproachfully, 'why did you take so long to rescue me?'

We were all huddled up to the bars between the cells, holding a whispered council of war. 'So you see, Hannah,' I was explaining, 'I haven't rescued you – not yet, anyway. It isn't that simple. I wish it was.' I was trying to put a positive spin on things for her, but there didn't seem to be one. 'You see, even though we've got the microcomputer, we can't leave without Gen.'

'But where *is* Gen?'

'That's the problem: we don't know. She could be anywhere. She's been taken away by King Karazeel's soldiers, to be made into a kind of servant.'

'Gen won't want to work for *him*,' Hannah said matter-of-factly. 'He pretends to be nice, but he's not. He looks young and handsome, like a prince in a fairy tale, but he smells like an old person. A *nasty* old person.' She was right. That was the smell I'd been battling to place – the musty, oniony odour of unhealthy old age. 'You'll have to rescue her as well, Adam.'

'Yeah, but Hannah, it's not that easy. Blue-bum, for goodness' sake stop doing that! You're making me feel dizzy!' Weevil was the only one who seemed remotely cheerful. He'd been hunkered down on his haunches listening intently to the discussion . . . and then at the first mention of Gen he'd started twirling round on his blue bum like a spinning-top. 'What the heck's the matter with you?'

'We had a dog that used to scoot along on the grass to scratch his bum,' Jamie said. 'It was *so* embarrassing. The vet said he had *impacted anal glands*, whatever they are. Maybe that's the problem with him.'

Weevil did a little capering dance of frustration, and chittered up at Jamie crossly. Then he sat down again, spun round three times, and looked up at us expectantly.

'*I* think he's trying to tell us something,' Hannah said thoughtfully.

'Shhhh!' hissed Rich. 'Someone's coming! Weevil – back in the bag! Quick, everybody – lie down and pretend to be asleep!'

There was the distant rattle of gates opening, and the sound of footsteps. A pause, then the squeal of a key in a lock, and the creak of hinges from the empty cell on the far side of ours. 'In with you!' It was the gruff growl of the Captain of the Guard. 'Here's food and water – and stay away from the vermin in the next cell if you know what's good for you.'

The footsteps moved to the guard station. A chair grated back on the stone floor and a heavy body settled itself with a creak and a grunt. Then there was silence, apart from the rustle of parchment and the scratching sound of a quill, and an occasional grumbling mutter.

I opened my eyes a crack. The Captain was at the table, the lantern beside him, writing laboriously in a thick leather-bound book. Who was the new prisoner? Could it be Gen? My heart thumping with wild hope, I turned my head a fraction and peered into the gloom of the neighbouring cell.

Unlike ours, it was furnished – if you could call a rickety table and chair and a narrow bed with a threadbare blanket folded at its foot 'furniture'. I squinted through my eyelashes – and then my eyes popped wide open with shock. The prisoner wasn't Gen. It was the Mauler's Keeper.

He was standing at the table with his back to us, still in his cream satin get-up, pulling off his gauntlets. And perched on the table beside him was Tiger Lily, daintily lapping something out of a richly engraved metal bowl. My head spinning, I battled to make sense of it.

Had he been thrown in prison because Tiger Lily had been so friendly to us? But then why all that stuff about 'saved by the grace of the Mauler?' Unless King Karazeel had *thought on it* like he'd said, and the conclusions were bad news for Tiger Lily and the

Keeper. But then surely he'd be wailing and flinging himself against the bars? But he wasn't. He was lifting off his heavy mask, cool as a cucumber, and putting it on the table . . . running both hands through his sweaty brown hair with the air of someone just home from a hard morning at the office . . . and settling calmly down to lunch.

Still with his back to us, he perched on the stool, gave Tiger Lily a scratch behind her ear, and tore a hunk off his loaf of bread. I watched, still totally bamboozled, my mouth watering. There was a wedge of cheese on the plate too; I could see it clearly. I could *smell* it. I couldn't take my eyes off it.

The Keeper fumbled at the gold-embroidered edge of his tunic pocket and dug inside. Pulled something out and fiddled with it for a moment. There was a bright flash of steel. He sliced neatly into the cheese, once . . . twice . . . three . . . four times. My stomach growled. Then he put the knife down on the edge of the table – and my heart turned a slow, sickening somersault.

It wasn't the rough, bone-handled dagger I'd imagined. It was a smooth, gleaming, bright red pocketknife . . . with a white cross clearly visible on the casing.

It was the Swiss army knife I'd given Kai.

Dimly aware of the sounds of the guard leaving, I stared at the knife in numb disbelief, my mind racing. Kai would never have parted with it. I remembered the look on his face when I'd given it to him as if it was yesterday – I'd never forget it.

Friends forever, we'd said.

Now, the Keeper had it. And that confirmed what I already knew. Kai was dead.

As the last echoes of the guard's departure died away, the Keeper skewered the tidy pile of cheese slices on the end of Kai's knife, stood, and stretched. Then he turned and ambled towards the partition between our cells, his thatch of brown hair sticking up in an untidy cow's-lick.

'Friends forever,' he said with a grin. 'Who's for some cheese?'

THE FEAST OF KARAZEEL

'I don't get it,' said Rich for what seemed like the zillionth time.

Kai grinned at him through the bars. 'A master of the Force-back fob you may be, Rich, but you sure ain't got a heavy head.' We were all clustered on the other side of our cell – the side adjoining Kai's. He'd shared his lunch between us, even giving a morsel of cheese and a crust of bread to Weevil, who was munching away at it so hungrily he'd completely forgotten about his spinning-top act.

Hannah was curled up on Kai's blanket in her cell with Tiger Lily snuggled under her chin, watching and listening.

'They came for me two sunsets after I met you,' Kai was telling us in a low voice. The dimple had disappeared. 'I woke to find them bending over me – the Faceless. I remember the stench of them . . . the chill of their shadows. Then nothing more, until the morn.

'I came to my senses in the back of a wagon, under guard, bound, gagged and blindfolded – headed for Shakesh, torture and certain death. I could not see or speak – but I could hear. And hear I did.

'I heard the guards tell of a mystical creature that had appeared by magic on the upper levels of the Temple, and used its powers to uncover and overcome a traitor to the king. I –'

'Do you mean *Tiger Lily*?' blurted Rich. 'It wasn't a traitor to the king we – I mean she – duffed up, it was one of those curator guys – the white one.' Then, remembering he wasn't supposed to know all this, he flushed.

Kai shot me the ghost of a wink that told me he knew – or suspected – a lot more than he was letting on. 'Aye, I do mean Fang – the Mauler – she you call Tiger Lily. It seems the Curator was selling the Potion of Invisibility in secret, for his own profit. It was to procure phials of potion to sell under cover of darkness that he crept to the upper level of the Temple – forbidden even to the Curators at that hour – just before the noon closing.

'The Curator was in the wagon with me, though I did not know it then. As was Fang – and she I *could* hear, hissing and growling at all who approached her makeshift cage. Then the jolting of the cart on the rutted road dislodged the fastening, the door sprang open, and Fang escaped. In seconds she was gone – into the upper branches of a tall tree, from whence even the bravest of the guards could not recover her. At last they hit upon a plan – to send the prisoner, who had no choice in the matter.' He grinned. 'I have always been good at climbing. All too soon I reached her and held out a trembling hand . . . and she gave a grumbling growl and rubbed her silken head against it. And I carried her down, tame as a glonk.

'We reached Shakesh, and I was cast into the dungeons. As for Fang – she became an instant favourite of the king. He kept her in a gilded cage beside his throne and tempted her with sweetmeats, hoping to make a pet of her. But they say she was as one possessed – pacing the confines of her cage with burning eyes, refusing to sleep or eat. Within days she had faded to a shadow of skin and bone, death staring from her sunken eyes. King Karazeel ordered his sorcerer to find a way to save her, or his own head would roll. And it was only then that Evor hearkened to the whispers of the guards: tales of the one who had gentled the Mauler . . . and now festered in the depths of the dungeons.

'And that is how I became the Keeper: part captive, part courtier . . . and one in whom the king's trust grows with every sun that rises.'

'But Kai – he's evil! Surely you aren't . . . *on his side*, now?'

'On the side of King Karazeel, Kenta?' Kai's face was grim, and though we knew the dungeon was deserted, he lowered his voice. 'Never. I am sworn to the Believers – the secret army that grows daily in the shadow of the evil reign of Karazeel, awaiting the return of the True King.'

'Zephyr?' breathed Jamie.

'Aye, Zephyr – the Lost Prince of the Wind. The time of the prophecy draws nigh . . . and Karazeel knows it. Even now, he is building a new fortress in the west, in the shadows of Dark Face: The Stronghold of Arraz. They say it will be mightier even than Shakesh, and that none – not even the True King – will be able to storm it.

'But if I can gain the trust of Karazeel, maybe I will be able to work towards his downfall from within those walls when the time comes.

'My friends, I believe it was not by chance that I was captured by the Faceless and brought to Shakesh. *There be patterns in the tapestries of destiny, yet those caught in the weave find the patterns hard to see.*'

I felt a strange thrill at Kai's words. I'd heard them somewhere before . . . but where?

'So you're planning to win the trust of King Karazeel, and kick him in the teeth if you get the chance? Wicked, Kai – way to go!' Rich's eyes gleamed.

'Yeah, that's great,' said Jamie bleakly. 'But, at the risk of sounding selfish, it doesn't help us much. We've found Hannah, but she's locked in a separate cell with bars as thick as my arm, too close together for anyone except Tiger Lily to squeeze through. We've found Tiger Lily, but if we took her home – not that there's any chance of that – your head would be on the block. One of us has been changed into a chatterbot, and it doesn't show any signs of wearing off. And Gen –' he gulped – 'Gen's going to have her tongue cut out and be made into a slave. As for the rest of us: we've been saved for now . . . but who knows how long it'll last?'

Right on cue came the echoing clang of the portcullis. We moved hurriedly away from the bars and huddled by the back wall, exchanging uneasy glances. But we needn't have worried. At the sight of the small procession entering the dim dungeon, every face broke into a broad grin of sheer disbelief.

At the head of the column strode the Captain of the Guard, and behind him marched three pageboys, each carrying a laden tray. I blinked and rubbed my eyes, wondering if I was dreaming . . . but the rich aromas escaping from the silver covers and tickling our nostrils were unmistakably real.

The Captain unlocked our door; the pages filed in and set the trays down on the floor. The four of us sat there gawking. Were we hallucinating . . . or had the king really decided to hand-deliver us a four-course gourmet banquet – courtesy of the Mauler?

The Captain gave us a rather nasty grin, slammed the cell door behind the retreating backs of the serving boys, and locked it. 'His Eternal Excellency High King Karazeel of Karazan has toyed with you enough,' he snarled. 'He bids you enjoy the Feast of Karazeel. I will return within the hour to collect –' that strange smile again – 'the remains.'

With that, he turned on his heel, hung the key on its hook and left.

Jamie and Rich were over at the trays in a flash. 'Hey, Adam, check this out!' squeaked Jamie, lifting one of the silver domes. 'A whole roast chicken – and roast potatoes! Real crunchy ones, too!'

'And this tray's full of desserts – steamed syrup pudding, and chocolate eclair-type things – raspberry buns – and what looks like pecan pie!'

After a second's hesitation Kenta had joined them, and was lifting the lids of the last two salvers. 'Fruit – fresh fruit! And crusty rolls, still warm – with butter and honey!'

Before I could stop him, Jamie reached out and grabbed one of the roast potatoes. He was right, it did look crispy . . . and it sounded crispy too, as he bit into it with a crunch that echoed round the walls of the dungeon.

'Hang on, Jamie!' I squawked. 'I don't think we should . . .'

I looked over at Kai for support. Their hands full of food, Jamie's cheeks bulging, the others followed my gaze.

We all froze.

Kai's face was grey, and he was clutching the bars as if he was about to fall.

'What is it?' I was first to speak. 'Kai – the food – is it . . .'

'Poisoned?' breathed Kenta.

Jamie spat out a huge glob of half-chewed potato.

But Kai shook his head wordlessly.

'What then?' Rich's voice was rough in the silence. '*What is it?*'

At last Kai spoke, with a terrible gentleness. 'The food is safe to eat, my friends. Enjoy it . . . if you can. For you have been sent the Feast of Karazeel – the Feast of the Damned.'

A SPINNING TOP

'How long do we have?' My voice sounded oddly calm and matter-of-fact.

'Not long. An hour at best.'

'So we have an hour to get out of here. Or else . . . there *is* no or else.'

Suddenly, the platters of food might not have existed. Instead, we stared hopelessly at the thick iron bars, the stout locks, the rack of keys that might as well have been on the moon. The seamless stone walls; the roof above us, invisible in the shadows. Two portcullises lay between us and the stairways to the rest of the castle. There was no escape. Except . . .

'The only missing piece is Gen. We've found Hannah and Tiger Lily. Even Kai. If Gen was here we'd be done and dusted and on our way home. Blue-bum, will you *stop* twirling and keep quiet!'

But Kai was staring at Weevil with a strange look on his face. 'Adam,' he said, 'have you used it yet?'

'Used what?'

Kenta's face lit up, and she clutched my arm so tightly it hurt. 'Of course – *of course!* How could I have been so stupid! It's been right under our noses — I should have realised!'

'Realised what?' growled Rich impatiently.

'Weevil's a chatterbot! And I actually *said* it in Chattering Wood . . .'

Suddenly I understood what Kenta was on about — and like her, I could have kicked myself. I could hear her words clearly in my mind: 'In the game, they were cute little furry things — *if you caught one, it could give you a wish.*'

We stood in a circle round Weevil, who was squatting on his bright blue haunches on the cold stone floor. 'I still think we should wish for a million more wishes . . .' said Jamie wistfully.

'Nay, Pinkie — magic don't work if you be greedy.'

'OK then.' Rich took a deep breath, frowning with concentration. 'Here goes. I hope I get this right. Weevil: we wish . . . we wish . . .'

'We wish Gen was here with us, in this cell, *NOW*!' Jamie blurted.

Instantly, Weevil started to spin. Round and round he spun, like a spinning top, faster and faster, till at last he was a blur in the middle of the floor. Suddenly there was a loud POP, like a cork coming out of a bottle . . . and Gen was standing next to Jamie.

Weevil collapsed on the floor in an exhausted heap like a bundle of rags, but all our eyes were on Gen. 'Gen . . .' said Jamie warily, 'are you . . . OK?'

It was clear she wasn't. Last time we'd seen her, she'd been dressed in a ragged brown tunic and cloak,

206

woollen hose and leather boots. Now, she wore a long gown of sky-blue satin girded with a skein of plaited silk, and flat leather sandals. She was cleaner than she had been for days, and her hair had been washed and hung in a tidy plait down her back.

But it wasn't her clothes that made us all stare at her as if she was a stranger. It was the look on her face: a dazed, unfocused look, almost as if she didn't recognise us.

'Is that . . . Gen?' Kai croaked in disbelief. For a second I didn't understand, but then I remembered that last time he'd seen her she had looked very different from the beautiful girl standing on the cold stone floor.

'Yeah – it's Gen all right. But . . .'

Then she spoke. 'Take me to my master. I await his bidding.' Her voice was flat and expressionless, like a robot – and totally unlike the Gen we knew.

'What are you talking about, Gen?' Kenta was beside her, peering into her face. 'Who do you want us to take you to?'

Gen looked through her as if she wasn't there. 'I await the bidding of King Karazeel,' she said in the same dreary monotone. 'His wish is my command.'

We gawked at her, dumbstruck. 'Have you gone crazy?' Richard stuck his face two centimetres from hers and scowled fiercely. 'Five minutes ago you were saying you'd rather be dead than serve him, and now listen to you!'

I looked into Gen's blank blue eyes, and suddenly I understood. 'You're wasting your breath, Rich,' I said grimly. 'It's not her fault. She's been brainwashed . . . or hypnotised, or something.'

'Aye. Evor has brewed potions for many things, and blind allegiance to the king be one of them. I have heard whispers that he works on others yet more powerful . . .' Kai's voice trailed away, and he shook his head.

'Does it . . . like . . . wear off?' croaked Jamie.

'Never mind!' I said urgently. 'The only thing that matters is, we've got Gen! We're all together and we can head on home!' I was digging in my bag as I spoke. Hannah was pressed against the bars of her cell, Tiger Lily in her arms, her eyes sparkling.

'Will I see Q again? And Bluebell?'

'You betcha, kiddo.' I held up the microcomputer. 'Here it is, guys. Kai . . .'

I turned to face him. He was standing very still, watching us.

'Kai,' I said awkwardly, 'what we told you before . . . about Winterton. It was true – it is a distant land. But it wasn't the whole truth.' I felt my face turn red. What I was about to say . . . well, it would sound real weird, and I doubted Kai would believe it. Still . . . friends forever. He deserved to know.

'Winterton is in . . . another world. And that's where we're from. It's called . . . I guess it's called . . . Earth.'

There was a long silence. Then Kai spoke, very softly. 'So. The legends be truth. The tales of a portal in the Cliffs of Stone . . .'

'Nope – we didn't come through a portal, whatever

that is,' said Rich cheerily. 'We came through a computer – and that's how we're going back. Come on, everyone: let's not waste any more time.' He grabbed Gen's wrist and dragged her to the bars between Hannah's cell and ours, the others hustling along behind. Weevil staggered to his feet and reeled up to me, clutching the leg of my breeches with one paw.

'Kai – we can take you with us, if you want to come.' He shook his head. I thought I could see a gleam of tears in his eyes, and knew that for his sake, I must keep it brief. 'Then there's just one last thing. Tiger Lily.' I met his gaze levelly.

'Aye.' The softest whisper. 'I know that Fang belongs with you – with the little princess.' He tried to smile. 'I knew in my heart that she be a creature from another world . . . and now, the time has come when she must go back there. Farewell, Fang . . . Tiger Lily. And . . . forever farewell, friends.'

He stroked Tiger Lily's silken head. One by one, we clasped wrists . . . and then I reached through and hugged him, the cold iron of the bars between us. 'Good luck, Kai,' I muttered. 'All that stuff with Zephyr and Karazeel – I hope it works out for you, and that us taking Tiger Lily won't get you in a whole heap of trouble. You can always say you tried to stop us, I guess. Anyway, thanks . . . for everything.'

And then we were standing in a circle, hands clasped. Tiger Lily and Weevil were stowed in backpacks, Richard's hand firm on the back of my neck.

The Feast of Karazeel lay forgotten on the floor. The screen of the microcomputer glowed ghostly green in the gloom. I gave the others a grin; rested my fingers gently on the three keys. Alt Control Q.

'So long, King Karazeel!' I said – and I don't think any words ever sounded so good. I pressed the keys.

And nothing happened.

A RAY OF LIGHT

We stood there holding hands, the silence stretching forever.

'Try again.' Jamie's voice wobbled.

I tried again. Nothing.

'Do you think it could be the battery?' There was something crazily out of place about Kenta's question – the kind of thing you'd ask if the car didn't start on a trip to the shops. In spite of the desperate situation we were in, I felt myself grin . . . and with the grin, my mind started working again.

'I don't think so. I think it's the dungeon – the rock all around us, metres deep. More. Remember what Q said that first time? About trying to make our re-entry from the same point we arrived at . . . the interface between the two worlds being stronger there? We're at least two days' journey from Arakesh – and under a mountain. I'm sure it'll work once we're out in the open.'

'Maybe,' said Jamie hollowly. 'Only problem is, we aren't likely to get a chance to find out.'

'So,' said Rich, 'what now?'

I was busy fishing Tiger Lily out of my backpack

and emptying the contents onto the floor. 'Plan A didn't work,' I said over my shoulder. 'So on to Plan B.'

'What's Plan B, Adam?' The confidence in Hannah's voice warmed me to the tips of my toes.

'I don't know.' I grinned at her. 'I haven't thought of it yet. But I will. We'll start by looking at what we've got available. There must be *something* we can use to get us out of here!'

I dug through our equipment, praying for inspiration. Tiger Lily was rubbing her head against my hand, getting in the way like cats do. Her heavy golden collar was studded with jewels – red, blue and green – and they scratched my skin as I shoved her gently away. Under the ornate collar, looking very shabby in contrast, I saw to my surprise that she was still wearing her old leather one, its square black cat-door magnet hanging down like a pendant.

Kai crouched by the bars watching as I fished more and more stuff out of the bag – everyday things to us, but strange and exotic to him.

'What be that, Adam?' he couldn't resist asking when I produced a disposable lighter. I flicked it on, the flame burning brightly in the gloom. 'Ah – a tinderbox! Now *that* be tempered and honed . . . and that, Adam? What be that?'

With an inward sigh, I flicked on the small, powerful torch, squiggling its beam in a figure of eight to demonstrate. Instantly, Tiger Lily hopped after it, pouncing on the circle of light as if it was a mouse.

Hannah laughed, the sound like music in the bleak

dungeon. 'Again, Adam – do it again!' I smiled back at her, wiggling the torch . . . and again, Tiger Lily scampered after it, trying to catch the beam with her paws, the jewels in her collar gleaming, the magnet swinging back and forth.

And then it came to me, like flicking a switch and seeing a ray of light where there was none moments before. Plan B. And it would work . . . because it had to.

We crouched at the front railing of our cells, peering through the bars. There was absolute silence except for the distant drip-drip-drip of water. I turned on the torch and Kenta lifted Tiger Lily out into the wide corridor that separated us from the guard station.

I played the beam of the torch on the far wall. It made a fuzzy, bright patch the size of a dinner plate. Would it be enough? I hoped so.

Tiger Lily sat down in the corridor and started washing her face. With my heart in my mouth, hardly daring to breathe, I shone the torch onto the floor beside her paw. She ignored it.

'Come on, Tiger Lily,' I muttered. 'If ever there was a time to play, it's now! Come on, Mauler – maul!'

But instead, she settled down on the floor with her paws tucked under her, too far away for us to reach. Time for a nap. Desperately, I dabbled the bright circle of light under her nose. She watched it haughtily . . . and then suddenly her eyes went triangular, and her whiskers bristled. 'She's the cleverest cat in the world, Adam,' Hannah whispered. 'And she's going to do it, you'll see!'

Utterly silent, we watched Tiger Lily rise slowly to her feet, crouch, wriggle her haunches from side to side . . . and pounce. Quick as lightning, I scooted the beam away, over to the leg of the table. Jiggled it, so it danced up and down the table leg.

Tiger Lily was after it in a flash. Up onto the table, chasing the light.

With my heart in my mouth, I shone the beam on the rack of keys . . . onto the rusty iron key second from the left . . . and then above it.

For a long moment, Tiger Lily seemed to consider. Then she stretched up, up, her paws patting at the circle of light . . . and her collar, with its dangling magnet, brushing against the key.

A centimetre more . . . she wasn't close enough . . . and then it happened. The key swung forward and connected with the magnet with a solid metallic *chink*.

Moments later Tiger Lily was purring smugly in Hannah's arms, and we'd unlocked our cell and were out in the corridor. Hannah pointed out the key to her cell, beside ours. I unlocked it, my hand shaking. Looked over at Kai, a question in my eyes. He shook his head.

It felt like freedom – but it wasn't.

'What now? Do you think one of the keys fits the portcullises?' Rich asked doubtfully.

'It's worth a try.' I scanned the long line of keys. They all looked the same, except one, alone on the bottom row . . . and it couldn't be that. It was covered

214

in cobwebs, and obviously hadn't been used for years.

'Nay, my friends.' Kai sounded grim. 'The guards take the portcullis keys with them. There be only one way out of the Dungeons of Shakesh, and that be the Way of the Dead.'

A chill trickled down my spine. 'What do you mean?'

'Sewers run under the castle. The bodies of prisoners be cast in among the waste and excrement.' He nodded towards the massive metal grid set into the floor. It must have been two metres square, thick, rusted bars intersecting every twenty centimetres or so to form a rigid network of iron. It would have taken a crane to lift it. Tiger Lily – and maybe Weevil – were small enough to fit through the gaps . . . but the stench rising up from it was sickening – especially now we knew what it came from.

'The sewers run out into the swamp,' Kai was saying. 'But it takes many grown men to lift the grating. And even if you could – even if you found your way through the sewers, and the shroud – they say the ford has been destroyed. There be no way to cross the River Ravven . . . for who knows if Rainbow Bridge – the Bridge of Sighs – be truth or legend? King Karazeel would loose the Faceless, and they would hunt you down. You have done bravely, my friends . . . but there are times when even the bravest must surrender to their fate.'

'Oh yeah?' Rich's face wore a crooked grin. 'I can tell you don't have much confidence in our computer, Kai,' he nodded down at it, lying on the guard table, 'but we've used it before, and we know it'll work once we're out of here. As for that: I don't much fancy what's under that manhole cover, but I like what's above it even less. If there is a way out, that's it. And I think I know how we can open it. There's something you've all forgotten. Look.'

He opened his hand. There in his palm lay a crystal phial, gleaming black as ink. Rich grinned. 'Yup – the Potion of Power. Worth a try, anyhow. Anyone for an arm wrestle?'

Richard took off his cloak with a flourish, hanging it on the horizontal bar of Kai's cell. He pulled out the stopper and downed the potion in a single gulp, upending the phial over his open mouth to make sure he didn't waste a drop. We watched warily, not at all sure what the effect would be. Kai hung through the bars staring, his eyes like saucers.

Rich licked his lips, and flexed one arm experimentally. Then he spat on each hand in turn, rubbed his palms together, and advanced purposefully on the grid.

PRISONER IN THE DARK

Rich looked the same as ever, but none of us had a moment's doubt that downing the potion had turned him into Superman – and neither did he. He swaggered up to the grid, bent and gripped the bars firmly in both hands, and flashed us a swashbuckling grin before heaving it effortlessly up.

Except it didn't budge.

Rich frowned. Shuffled his feet further apart, bent his knees, and crouched low over the stinking cesspit. The look on his face had changed from jaunty self-confidence to grim determination. He drew a deep, deep breath . . . held it. Then his thighs tensed and the muscles in his broad shoulders bunched and flexed. His face contorted with effort; sweat popped out of his skin and rolled down his face, leaving shiny tracks in the dirt. I could almost hear his muscles creaking with the huge strain of lifting.

And still, the grid didn't move so much as a millimetre.

At last he gave up, falling forward onto his knees exhausted, his breath harsh as a hacksaw. He knelt there for what seemed a long time, while his ragged breathing gradually eased. He didn't look up at us.

Then he clambered stiffly to his feet and crossed to where he'd left his cloak, still not meeting our eyes. He felt he'd failed us, I knew – but he hadn't. He'd given everything he had, and more. I didn't know what to say.

It was Kai who broke the silence, echoing my thoughts. 'You did as much as any man could, Rich. I salute you – you are a true hero.' A dark flush of pleasure spread over Rich's face. It was clear he didn't know how to respond. He shot Kai a sheepish glimmer of a glance, reached one hand through the bars, and gave his shoulder a friendly shove.

Kai flew backwards across the cell as if he'd been hit by a freight train, smacked into the far wall with a sickening thud, and crumpled to the floor.

We stared at Kai's limp form with our mouths open . . . and then at Rich. Then Kenta spoke urgently to Hannah. 'Which is the key to Kai's cell, Hannah – do you know?' Within seconds she was bending over him, the rest of us in an anxious semicircle behind her.

At last she glanced up. 'He'll be all right, I think. There's a lump the size of an egg on the back of his head, and he's unconscious – but he's breathing normally, as far as I can tell.'

Richard was green with guilt. 'Cheer up, Rich.' I was thinking aloud. 'Maybe it's not a bad thing. If the guards find Kai unconscious, they'll think we overpowered him and took Tiger Lily by force – there'll be no question of blaming him. And it'll be obvious he doesn't know how we escaped – so they won't try to make him tell.'

'Adam's right,' Jamie grinned. 'If Kai could, he'd be telling us everything happens for a reason. I vote we get moving while he's still out cold – and before the guards come back. Because one thing's for sure: we'll be able to now. It just took a moment to work – though not as long as Gen's beauty potion, thank goodness!'

Quickly, with gentle hands, Kenta put Kai into what she called the 'recovery position' and covered him with his rug. Then we re-locked his cell, hanging the key in its place.

Once again, Rich took up his place in front of the grid. He bent and grasped the bars, just as he had done before. He closed his eyes, almost as if he was praying . . . and lifted the huge grating up and out as easily as if it was made of polystyrene.

He set it down at an angle over the pit, leaving a wedge-shaped gap. The shaft below looked very dark, its sides glistening with black slime. The stink made me want to puke.

Jamie gave a tiny whimper. And then I was aware of another sound, from further away – a low, rhythmic lament. My heart skipped a beat – and then I realised what it was. The prisoner in the depths of the dungeon, down the stairway we'd passed on our way to the throne room. Suddenly I knew what I must do.

Quickly, I scanned the row of keys. Time was running out – the hour must be almost up. Which key would it be?

Then my hand was reaching out . . . reaching for the least likely key of all, the one covered in cobwebs, coated with dust. For a second I hesitated – surely it couldn't be? *Trust your instincts*, whispered a voice in my mind. Q.

I grabbed the key. The others stared. 'Get ready to leave. Put Tiger Lily in my bag for me – someone take Weevil. Jamie, pack some food – and whatever you do, don't forget the microcomputer! I'll be back in a sec.'

I spun and ran down the passage, the key clenched in one fist, my torch in the other. Reached the gaping mouth of the stairway; swung a left, and leapt down the crumbling stone steps two by two. Stumbled and almost fell – it was dark . . . too dark. I flicked on the torch and moved more cautiously. At the bottom I hesitated. The chanting was louder now, with a haunting note of despair that chilled my blood.

I crept quietly towards the sound, my heart thumping in my chest. The stone corridor stretched ahead into blackness . . . and then at last the dim circle of torchlight shone on metal bars: the door of a cell.

I fumbled for the keyhole, my hand shaking, praying the key would fit. Now the words of the chant had taken form: '*I am Meirion – Meirion the Prophet Mage. I am Meirion – Prophet Mage of Karazan.*' Understanding flashed through me. Alone in total darkness for who knew how long, the invisible prisoner was clinging to sanity by repeating his name over and over . . . holding on to who he was, because it was all he had.

The key grated into the lock – jammed. Cursing, I twisted it back and forth. It was stuck fast. I could feel the roughness of rust in the lock . . . desperately, I jerked, and it came free. I spat on the key – once, twice – rubbed it. Back into the lock – left . . . right . . . something gave, and the key turned.

I eased the door open. Silence filled the cell now, except for the drip – drip – drip of water. I edged towards the back wall, following the beam of light. Something squealed and skittered away. I could see something on the floor – a bundle of twigs. No – not twigs.

Toes, the flesh fallen away to leave bare bones under tents of skin. Above them, legs, shrunk to nothing, the knees obscene lumps. A filthy loincloth. Ribs as bare as a skeleton's. Arms cruelly stretched, shackled wrists bolted to the wall. A beard, matted with grime. A tangled mane of hair, dark with the filth of years. A face with no eyes, shrunken lids loose pouches of skin over empty sockets . . . a face tilted up at a strange angle as if it was staring sightlessly towards the invisible sky. An iron collar as wide as my hand circling the neck, forcing the chin up. The steady drip of water falling on the bare forehead, then trickling into the empty sockets and down into the beard like tears.

My hand shaking, terrified of touching him, I reached up, fumbling for a keyhole. Yes! There it was, I could feel it . . . but it was tiny, encrusted with rust. There was no way the key would ever fit . . .

A whisper of breath brushed my cheek like a

cobweb. I froze. The face was expressionless as a corpse – but I realised I could hear words – the faintest whisper, dry as dust in the darkness. '*The five are come, Man-child . . . the time is nigh . . .*'

There was the scrape of a boot behind me, and a heavy hand fell on my shoulder. My knees buckled . . . and Rich's voice came hoarsely out of the darkness: 'Hurry, Adam! They're coming back!'

'Rich – the shackles – the key won't –'

Rich pushed past me to the living skeleton hanging from the wall. Reached up and snapped the iron manacles and the collar like sticks of spaghetti. Hoisted the limp body in a fireman's lift and headed out of there at a run, with me behind him.

We raced back along the main passageway. The others were clustered round the open pit, Jamie stuffing a last handful of pastries into his pack. I could hear the rattle of the portcullis, and the echo of heavy footsteps marching towards us.

I stuffed the torch into my pack and shouldered it, Tiger Lily squirming inside. Vaulted down into the void. Felt myself falling, a metre, two metres – then landed thigh-deep in raw sewage, thick and stinking. Held up my arms to Rich. Took the prisoner from him, light as a feather . . . lowered him beside me. Jamie tumbled down with a splash and a moan. Rich lowered Gen, pale and bewildered-looking. Kenta hopped down, trying not to retch. I took Hannah gently from Rich's outstretched arms, and held her close. She clung to me like a little limpet. 'Yuck,' she whispered in my ear, and hugged tighter.

'Are we all here?' I breathed. 'Who's got Weevil?'

'Me – Kenta.'

The square of grey above us darkened, the stocky form of Rich blocking out the light. My heart lurched. The grid – how would he close the grid from inside? There was no way he could reach it once he'd dropped into the sewer. But Rich had thought of that. He swung by his hands from one rung to the next, monkey-bar style; then braced his feet against the wall of the shaft and heaved. The grille grated across the floor with a grinding squeal that almost drowned out the clatter of the second portcullis, close – so close.

The grid clunked into place and Rich plopped down beside me. 'Hard to tell whether we're in the shit, or out of it,' he muttered with a grin. 'And now – let's get out of here!'

THE WAY OF THE DEAD

A split second later all hell broke loose above us. There was a harsh cry of dismay and the rasp of swords being drawn from their scabbards. Shouts, the crash of cell doors being flung open, the drumming of running feet . . . then the hoarse fanfare of a trumpeted alarm.

We shrank back against the slimy wall where the shadows were deepest, hardly daring to breathe. We'd used precious seconds to re-lock the cell doors and replace the keys on their hooks in the hope that the guards would believe the mystical Mauler had somehow conjured us away – if we'd simply vanished into thin air, there'd be no point looking for us. But now the alarm had sounded, and the search was on. Kai's words echoed in my mind: *King Karazeel would loose the Faceless, and they would hunt you down* . . .

The crosshatch of shadow cast by the grid darkened and shifted as someone held a burning brand close to the bars. A rough voice boomed down the tunnel towards us, shockingly close: 'They cannot have taken the Way of the Dead, I tell you. They are children, fool – maggots, not flies. Use your wits, if you have them . . .'

Further away, another voice growled, 'We'll swing for this . . .'

A boot scraped against the grating, and heavy footsteps stamped away.

Rich gave me a shove – the sooner we got away from there, the better. I groped for the gaunt form of the old man beside me, and gently took his arm. It was like holding a broomstick. I was still carrying Hannah, her legs wound tightly round my waist, light as a feather. My eyes had adjusted to the gloom, and I could just make out the faint figures of the others. Without speaking, I motioned them on into the darkness.

As silently as we could, we crept forward through the stinking ooze. Soon we'd left the dim light filtering through the grid far behind us, and it was completely dark. After a whispered discussion, we dug in Richard's pack for his torch and turned it on, but it made the surrounding darkness even more oppressive.

The tunnels twisted and wound through the heart of the mountain like a labyrinth, branches leading away randomly to left and right. We ignored them, doing the best we could to keep heading in the same direction, trying to stick to what we hoped was the main tunnel. But it was like trying to navigate a maze in a nightmare . . . soon we had lost all sense of direction, and one way seemed as good as another.

We sloshed grimly on.

At some stage Hannah dropped off to sleep – her

head nestled itself in the angle of my shoulder, and her soft, regular breathing tickled my neck.

It felt like hours later that I realised the thick stench had lightened. The darkness was lifting, too ... at first the shaft of torchlight had cut through the blackness like a blade, but the beam had been fading steadily as we walked, and now I realised it had given out altogether. Without me noticing the pitch-dark had given way to translucent greyness, and the cess we'd been wading through had dwindled to a slimy sludge that made our booted feet slither and slide as we walked.

We rounded another bend and turned a corner ... it grew steadily lighter, and I could almost taste the fresh air.

I turned to the others with the beginnings of a grin – and then my feet scooted out from under me, and I found myself skidding helplessly forward. My boots kicked desperately for some kind of foothold, and I realised with a sickening lurch that the floor of the tunnel was sloping downwards. Far from slowing down, I was speeding up – I slithered round a bend, and saw the tunnel winding down in front of me more and more steeply.

My breath had huffed out when I'd fallen, and now I gasped out a warning to the others – way too late. I sensed rather than saw them skidding down the slope behind me, as if we were on a giant water slide ... and then the tunnel swooped round a final bend and straightened, and a bright square of light was rushing towards me with terrifying speed.

Legs kicking, my free arm flailing, I hurtled towards it, totally out of control, hanging onto Hannah like grim death and hearing her squealing in my ear: 'Isn't this *fun*, Adam? Faster – go *faster*!' With a sickening jolt I saw there were bars in the opening – metal uprights as thick as a man's thigh, encrusted with gooey red rust and dripping slime – we'd smash into them!

Then I was on top of the exit and saw it was huge – wider than a door – and the bars were far enough apart that if I twisted and turned and aimed myself . . .

I shot clean through them and down like a stone into nothingness, my eyes squeezed tight shut and my stomach somewhere back in the sewers of Shakesh.

And then there was an almighty *SPLASH* and I was sprawled waist-deep in water, scrabbling to get out of the way before the others landed on top of me.

The water was far from clean – there was an oily film on the surface, and it smelt like the toilets at Highgate on a bad day. But it was a huge improvement on the stuff we'd been in before, and Hannah and I splashed happily to the edge like kids at the beach.

We'd landed in a shallow, almost circular pool. A vertical cliff face, dark and menacing, stretched above us and away to either side. Squinting up I could see the aperture we'd fallen through five metres or so above us, a glistening crust of gunk dribbling down the rock wall below it like a festering scab. We were at the foot of the plateau the fortress of Shakesh was built on – I could see the buttresses of the castle far above, though from this angle most of it was hidden by the towering cliff. There was no entrance I could see, and no exit other than the one we'd come through – I guessed the main gate must be on a side where the ground sloped less steeply.

Turning, I saw that the pool narrowed into a shallow stream that wound away to meet the vast expanse of swamp . . . and at its edges, like a thick sea fog waiting to roll in and engulf us, loomed the edge of the shroud.

Jamie was beside me, fiddling importantly with something. 'According to my compass, we've come out on the western side of Shakesh – and I'm pretty sure the main entrance is to the south. Looking at the angle of the sun –' he pointed up to a hazy patch in the low cover of cloud – 'that must mean it's evening – and my stomach tells me it's time for dinner.'

'We should try the microcomputer again,' said Rich. 'Looking at where we've just been, it's no wonder it didn't work.'

Jamie's voice dropped to a whisper. 'What're we going to do with *him*?' He gestured across to the prisoner, sitting at the edge of the pool with his knees bent and his head resting on his arms. I stared at him, fascinated and full of horrified pity.

He was even thinner than I'd thought – and dirtier. His face was hidden, but I could count every one of his ribs and every bone in his back. The skin stretched over them was black with grime; it was impossible to tell the colour of his hair. The loincloth, soaking wet from its dousing in the pool, was a filthy, tattered rag that barely covered him.

'You brought him, Adam,' Jamie was hissing, 'but I reckon you should have asked us first. We don't know who he is – whether he's good, or . . . We can't just leave him. You should have thought it through.'

'He was in the dungeons of Shakesh, Jamie. That automatically puts him on our side. And I do know who he is,' I said. 'His name is Meirion, and he's a mage – a prophet mage.'

'What's a mage?' asked Richard. 'If you ask me, he's a crackpot. He's been locked up in the dark too long – I heard him burbling away back there, and he's totally lost it, poor guy.'

'He's starving, and he's probably been tortured,' said Kenta fiercely. 'I expect we're the first friendly people he's seen in years – and we're hanging back as if he's a leper, or an animal at the zoo. Shame on us!'

She was right. I felt myself flush as I watched her walk primly across to him, Hannah skipping along beside her with Tiger Lily in tow. Kenta bent and placed a gentle hand on the bowed and grimy back, then removed her own cloak – soaked as it was – and spread it over him. As if in slow motion, the tangled head lifted, the hollow sockets staring up at her. I should have warned her . . . but being Kenta, she smiled down at him without so much as flinching. Then she rummaged in her pack, brought out her water bottle, and held it to his lips.

'I guess we'll have to take him back with us,' Rich muttered reluctantly. 'Get him cleaned up, and give him a feed. Some medicine too, maybe. Then he can pop back again through the computer and carry on with his life in Karazan, just like before.' He grinned. 'Imagine old Q's face when he sees him!'

Imagine Q's face when he sees Hannah, I thought, watching her squat next to Kenta, solemnly unwrap a stick of gum and offer it to Meirion. 'Tiger Lily likes you,' she was chirping. 'And she hardly ever likes strangers . . .'

'You're right, Rich – he must come with us. And now, I've hung about here long enough. I'm for a hot shower and some serious food – wonder what's on the menu at Quested Court? Come on, Gen.' I took her hand. She was pale and dazed-looking – she hadn't spoken since we left the dungeon, following us through the sewers like someone sleepwalking. Now she trailed obediently across to the others.

'OK, Jamie – let's try it again.' I held out my hand. 'Well, come *on*!' I said impatiently. 'The microcomputer! Do you want to stay here forever? Dig it out!'

Jamie gulped. His eyes flicked to his bulging pack, then back to me again. He turned bright red, and his eyes filled with tears. He opened and closed his mouth like a fish, but no words came out.

You didn't have to be the Prophet Mage of Karazan to figure it out. Jamie had left the microcomputer on the guards' table back in the dungeon.

A SCIENTIFIC FACT

'OK, let's look at our options,' I said grimly.

'Not that we have any, thanks to *you*,' muttered Rich, giving Jamie a dark look.

We were sitting by the edge of the pool, sheltered from view of the castle by the cliff. The sun had come out from the clouds, its slanting evening rays reflecting off the swamp like a mirror of gold. The rock was warm against our backs, and a makeshift picnic of fruit and rolls was spread out on Richard's sleeping bag.

But the mood was dismal – and you only had to look at the others' tense faces and Jamie's swollen eyes to see why.

Far from wolfing down bread and honey like I'd have been doing in his place, Meirion had taken himself off a short distance and was standing with his back to us, his face turned up to the setting sun. He couldn't see it, I realised with a pang, but he could feel it – and maybe, after years of darkness, the warmth of sunlight on his skin was more important to him than food.

'Option one,' I went on, ignoring Rich. 'We go

back into Shakesh and find the microcomputer.'

'But it was on the table,' said Jamie in a small voice. 'The guards will have turned that whole dungeon inside out. There's no way in the world it'd still be there.'

He was right – by now the microcomputer would be in the hands of King Karazeel, Exhibit A . . . and trying to get it back from *him* wasn't even an option worth discussing.

'I won't go back in there,' said Hannah firmly.

So much for option one.

'Option two . . .' I hesitated. *Was* there an option two?

'We spend the rest of our lives in Karazan,' growled Rich. 'But cheer up, guys: with the Faceless after us, that won't be long.'

'We could ask Meirion for advice,' suggested Kenta doubtfully; 'though he hasn't spoken a single word. I wonder whether he's quite . . .'

Rich gave me an 'I told you so' glance.

Suddenly, abruptly, Gen spoke. I hadn't realised she'd been listening – and maybe she hadn't. There was a pretty, low-growing plant on the banks of the pool, with tiny white flowers like daisies. She'd made a little pile of them and was stringing them together into a chain. Now she looked up and across at Meirion, her eyes unfocused and dreamy. '*The legends be truth. The tales of a portal in the Cliffs of Stone . . .*'

We stared at her; then at each other.

'Huh?' said Rich. 'Say again, Gen?'

But Gen just smiled and sighed, and went back to her daisy chain.

'That's what Kai said when you told him where we came from, Adam!' announced Hannah.

'What's a portal?' asked Rich.

'It's a gate – or a doorway!' Jamie was on his feet, his face pink with excitement. 'Kai thought we'd come through it, but then you told him about the computer, Richard. So that means . . .'

Even Weevil had stopped gloomily nibbling his slice of apple and was capering about, chittering excitedly.

'It means there's a legend in Karazan about some kind of magical gateway to another world –'

'*Our* world –'

'But it's not just a legend –'

'It's the *truth*!'

'Maybe these are the Cliffs of Stone,' Jamie said hopefully, gazing up at the dark wall of rock above us. 'Maybe the portal's that hole . . . and if we go through in the other direction, we'll be home!'

Somehow I doubted it – it seemed impossible that the stinking, gunge-encrusted sewage outlet could be magical . . . and even if it was, there was no way we could ever climb back up to it. My mind was racing. Like the others, I hadn't heard about this 'portal' till today – so why did it sound so familiar? A memory hovered on the fringes of my mind, agonisingly close . . .

Kenta was stashing the leftovers away in Jamie's pack. Rich heaved himself to his feet, frowning. 'You know what I think of when I hear *cliffs of stone*? That real high cliff where we came into Karazan – remember?'

Jamie's eyes lit up. 'Yeah! If you think about it, it's logical that's where it would be – at what Q calls the 'entry point'! Remember what Kai once told us? *Magic be logic* . . .'

'That standing stone was a bit like a door,' said Kenta thoughtfully. 'Tall and narrow . . .'

'I'm sure we're right.' Jamie didn't sound too happy about it. 'There's just one problem – two, actually. To get to the entry point – and the portal – we'll have to find our way back through the shroud . . . without those weird snuffling things to guide us. Plus, as far as we know there's only one route – and you can bet King Karazeel's got a welcome committee just waiting for us to arrive.'

I thought of who – or what – the welcome committee might consist of – and suddenly realised how crazy we'd been to sit out in the open for so long. 'Come on, guys,' I said, glancing around uneasily. 'I think we should move somewhere less exposed, before –'

And it was then I noticed Hannah had wandered off, Tiger Lily padding along behind her. She was close to the edge of the shroud – too close. I almost called out – and then thought better of it. I jumped to my feet. 'Look where Hannah's got to! I'll run and stop her – follow me, and we'll use the shroud as cover while we decide what to do.'

I jogged towards her, shrugging on my backpack. Luckily the shroud shaded gradually into darkness on the Shakesh side ... but there was an anxious fluttering in my chest as I saw how close to the twilit fringe Hannah had drifted. I was a stone's-throw away, drawing a breath to call to her softly, when it happened.

There was a flash of movement at Hannah's feet – something small and swift, scurrying for the shelter of the swamp. Instantly, Tiger Lily was after it at a bounding run – straight as an arrow into the darkness. There was a squawk from Hannah – 'Tiggie – *no!*' – and she vanished into the shroud in hot pursuit, leaving me frozen in mid-stride with my mouth wide open in horrified disbelief.

Every instinct screamed at me to sprint in after her before she went too far. But logic told me it would be suicide – three of us lost instead of two. A balloon of panic bulged up through my throat, but I swallowed it down. Moved cautiously through the gathering gloom to the point where I could just see my hand in front of my face, then stopped. Cupped my hands round my mouth to channel the sound. 'Hannah!' I called softly. 'Hannah – can you hear me? Come back!' But even as the words left my mouth, I knew it was hopeless. They were gone.

And then a familiar voice came out of the darkness. 'You're a naughty cat,' it said severely. 'How many times have I told you not to hunt mouses?'

Relief flooded through me in a wonderful wave, like fizzy lemonade. 'Hannah! Stay still! Don't move a single step!'

'Why not? I'm coming back now – I've got Tiger Lily. She's caught a mouse.'

And Hannah materialised out of the shroud, a squirming Tiger Lily in her arms, complete with a mouthful of mouse. 'It's really dark in there, Adam! Lucky you called, or I wouldn't have found you!'

I goggled at her. 'Yeah, but . . .' Something just didn't add up . . . I needed a minute to figure it out – and get my heart-rate back to normal after the fright she'd given me.

But Jamie was onto it like a bloodhound. 'Hannah – *how did you find Tiger Lily in the shroud*?'

'What's shroud? Oh – the black-night stuff. I saw her, of course.' Hannah sounded surprised. 'She's pale, like a little light. It was easy.'

Jamie and I looked at each other. But it was Kenta who spoke, slowly and hesitantly, over the crunching sound of Tiger Lily devouring her mouse. 'But the mouse . . . how did Tiger Lily see the mouse to catch it?'

'Cats can see in the dark, Kenta,' Hannah explained kindly. 'Didn't you know that?'

We huddled at the edge of the shroud, battling to believe it was true – that Tiger Lily could not only see in the shroud, but be seen. Hannah was the only one to take it all in her stride. Even when Jamie tried to explain to her that shroud wasn't *ordinary* darkness, she came right back with, 'Well, Tiger Lily's not an *ordinary* cat. And anyway, cats seeing in the dark is a *scientific fact* – Q told me.'

Tiger Lily finished her dinner, washed it down with a drink of swamp water, and polished her whiskers. And then she decided it was time to head home.

She stood, gave a leisurely stretch, and padded purposefully away into the gloom. At the point where the grey deepened into blackness she paused, looked back over her shoulder, and gave a low, chirruping call. Hannah, who'd been sitting cross-legged while we talked in circles, hopped to her feet. 'Come on!' she said impatiently. 'It's time to go – Tiger Lily says so.'

I looked at the others, and they looked at me. Cats *could* see in the dark – even I knew that. And it looked as if the other part might be true too – Tiger Lily did stand out against the darkness with a pale, luminous brightness. Would she be able to find her way through the swamp? Time would tell.

I made up my mind with an almost audible click. Rummaged in my pack for the rope, hastily unravelling it and handing it down the line to the others. 'Come on, guys – we don't have a choice! Hang on tight – Rich, grab Weevil. Gen, Hannah – up here with me. Ready, Jamie? And Meirion –' I wound the very end of the rope round his hand, curling it into a fist and giving it a squeeze – 'hold this tightly! Your life depends on it. We're taking you out of here.'

I thought there'd be no reaction, but to my surprise he put his other hand over mine for a second. I'd have expected it to be brittle as a bunch of twigs and cold as ice, but it wasn't. It felt strangely warm and firm, and made my skin tingle slightly as if a very faint

237

electric current was passing between us. Startled, I looked up into his face . . . and for the first time it wore the shadow of a smile.

Tiger Lily had waited long enough. She moved away into the shroud like a pale beacon . . . and the rest of us straggled blindly after her.

As I walked, I found a song was playing through my mind – a song I'd never heard before, yet as familiar as my own heartbeat. It warmed me, comforted me . . . it was like a lullaby playing softly in my head . . . or in my heart. And then I realised it wasn't coming from inside me – someone was singing, close by. The softest, warmest, gentlest voice I'd ever heard, a voice that rocked me like the waves on the sea. I'd heard that voice somewhere before, a long, long time ago . . . but where?

Suddenly Jamie's voice interrupted my thoughts. 'Hey, guys – anyone got any money?'

'*Money?*' Rich sounded as surprised as I felt.

'Yeah – for the Captain Creamy van!'

'Have you gone crazy, Jamie? There's no Captain Creamy van. We're about to run on for the big game, you blockhead – can't you hear the crowd?'

Then Kenta's voice came urgently out of the darkness: 'I have to go! It's the bell – the bell above the shop door! There's a customer, and Father's left me in charge!' There was a tug on the rope.

Irritation flared through me. Why couldn't they all shut up? The song was fading, growing fainter – the singer was moving away from me through the

238

darkness, and once she was gone I'd never find her again. And then suddenly I knew who she was.

'Mother!' I heard myself cry, my voice as anguished as a little child's in the darkness. 'Mother – *come back!*' I took a step towards where I knew she was waiting for me in the darkness, feeling the tug of the rope, hearing the squish of water under my boot . . .

Then Kenta spoke, a raw edge of panic in her voice. 'We're all going crazy! It's not real. The sounds . . . the voices . . . it's the swamp, trying to lure us off track. We have to do something!'

'I'd give anything for a soft serve cone,' said Jamie wistfully. 'Please, guys – it's just round the corner!'

'You're wrong, Kenta – it *is* real!' The lullaby was fading, fading into the distance . . . 'I'm going – I have to! If I don't, I'll never find her again!'

Suddenly my shin exploded with agony, as if I'd been kicked by a mule. '*SCORED!*' yelled Rich triumphantly. 'Right between the posts! Come on guys, back to our positions . . .'

But the pain had brought me back to my senses. 'Kenta's right! That's why they blocked our ears on the way to Shakesh – not to stop us overhearing what they were saying, but to stop us being driven crazy by the voices in the swamp! We have to do something – but what?' Already the faint humming in my ears was growing in intensity, and I could make out snatches of the lullaby again, as if someone was trying to tune in a radio.

Hannah's voice spoke up beside me, sounding very chirpy: 'Just a minute, Q – I'm coming!'

I groped for her hand, holding it tight. 'What you're hearing, Hannah – it isn't real. Don't listen, OK?'

'But it's Q.' For the first time, she sounded close to tears. 'Please let me go to him, Adam – just for a quick cuddle?'

I had to do something – and fast. Already I was battling to keep my thoughts on track, the background soundtrack of that haunting lullaby filling my mind, drowning out reason and common sense . . .

Then I was groping in my bag, fumbling with desperate fingers till I found it. I put it to my lips, praying it would work. The pure, clear song of the penny whistle floated out into the darkness, unfurling and weaving around us in an invisible shield, as if we were cradled in a cocoon of silken sound. We walked on, and as we walked, I played.

At some point, the real darkness of night must have caught up with the darkness of the shroud . . . though for us, following the pale beacon of Tiger Lily as she picked her way delicately through the swamp, there was no way of telling when.

On and on we walked through the darkness, the notes of music falling around us like silvery starlight, until at last I realised that the starlight was real, and we had emerged from the shroud into the soft embrace of a clear and cloudless night.

THE BRIDGE OF SIGHS

Ahead of me I could make out the dark silhouette of the mountain range, the star-spangled sky above it. Suddenly I realised how tired I was – my fingers were stiff from playing, and my lips felt numb. But we were through the shroud – we'd made it! What's more, we must have been climbing gradually without realising it – when I stumbled round to face the others, I saw that the ground fell away behind us, the shroud like a bank of fog in the distance.

My face split into a weary grin. Behind me, Hannah was swaying on her feet, eyes half closed. One by one, the others plodded to a halt, Jamie sinking down onto the ground with a groan. But there was something niggling at the back of my dazed mind. Something was wrong – badly wrong. With a shock like a bucketful of ice water in my face, I knew what it was. Meirion was gone.

We dragged ourselves a little further in search of a sheltered place to rest, our hearts like lead. A short distance ahead the ground rose steeply into a rocky bluff; we found a deep overhang at its foot, and huddled under it.

Hannah, Jamie and Gen were instantly asleep, not even bothering to unroll their sleeping bags. Kenta covered them gently, her hands trembling with exhaustion. Tiger Lily curled up in the crook of Hannah's legs, too tired even to purr. Weevil was in high spirits, chittering cheerfully as he unfastened the pack containing the food with nimble fingers – he'd hitched a ride in Richard's pack the whole way, and slept most of it, I suspected.

Kenta passed round some fruit, but only Weevil seemed hungry. 'So,' said Rich, echoing our thoughts, 'what do we do about Meirion?'

There was a silence. 'We can't go back,' I muttered. 'He could be anywhere by now. He must have wandered off into the swamp – we'd never find him.'

'That's what's worrying me most,' whispered Kenta. 'The thought that he's out there somewhere, alone, afraid and starving . . .'

'Cheer up, Kenta,' said Rich bracingly. 'He's a mage, remember – according to Jamie, that's a kind of magician. He's probably tougher than you think. Maybe he went off for a reason.'

Kenta shook her head wordlessly. But I remembered that brief touch, the flicker of energy that had passed between us – almost as if he was saying goodbye, or trying to tell me something – and suddenly my spirits lifted. 'Rich's right,' I told her. 'Meirion *is* a mage – and this is his world. He's an adult, and we're kids. I'm certain he'd never expect us

242

to go back and look for him. Our job is to finish what we came here to do – take Hannah home safe to Quested Court and Q. And if we're going to stand any chance at all of doing that, we must have some food and get some rest.'

I woke hours later, stiff from the long walk and sleeping on the hard ground. Around me the others were grumbling reluctantly awake, stretching and yawning. Rich had obviously been up for a while and prowling around outside; now he ducked in under the overhang, reaching for a roll and looking cheerful. 'I've found a path,' he told us through a mouthful of bread. 'It's a narrow track – could have been made by sheep or something, I guess – if there are sheep in Karazan. But it heads in what I reckon is the right direction: uphill –' Kenta made a face – 'and south. I think Jamie was right: Karazeel will concentrate on the main route through the shroud. He thinks it's the only way we know – maybe he thinks it's the only way. Same applies to the ford – what's left of it.'

'Yeah – let's take the high road, and leave the low road to Karazeel's heavies,' I agreed. 'And as far as getting over the river is concerned – well, we'll cross that bridge when we come to it.'

'If there is one,' muttered Jamie.

I looked over at Hannah, sitting silently with Tiger Lily on her lap. She was very pale, and I was suddenly reminded of how sick she'd been such a short time ago. I smiled at her. 'Up you get, Hannah – we're on our way. Put your furry friend in my backpack, and the pack on your back.' Her eyes widened in surprise, and the others gawked at me. I grinned. 'Then hop up on my shoulders – it's piggy-back time.'

The path climbed steadily up the steep, rocky mountainside. 'At least we're getting the uphill part over with,' Jamie panted, and he was right – by what I guessed was mid-afternoon the ground had levelled out, and the going was easier. We were on a kind of contour path – the mountains rose steeply to our right, stretching away rank on rank to touch the clouds, and on the other side the land fell away to distant vistas of purplish plains and darker smudges of forest, with the occasional far-off flash of what I imagined must be the sea.

After a while the vegetation changed from scrubby grassland to the occasional tree and then to dense forest, and the view vanished. I was secretly relieved – I'd felt far too exposed out in the open. But the air in the forest was muggy and humid, and soon we were all sweating. The ground underfoot changed too – to a thick, dark loam that squished when we walked. Ferns covered the forest floor, and thick creepers like ropes dangled from the branches high above. Far down to the left I caught the occasional gleam of a stream running between the trees, and every now and then we came to a shallow trickle of water across the track, and had to pick our way carefully across.

Then Richard, striding along ahead of me with Hannah perched on his back, suddenly stopped. 'What's that? That . . . roaring sound?'

The moment he said the words, I realised I could hear it too – had been hearing it for a while. It was more a distant thunder than a roar – could it be thunder? Was there going to be a storm? Whatever it was, it seemed to be coming from up ahead. I shook my head, shrugging; one thing was for sure: walking towards it at the rate we were, we'd soon find out.

The roaring grew steadily louder, and soon there was no doubt what was making it. Water – huge volumes of it, falling fast and far. We trudged on; the ground was wetter by the minute, and there was a regular drip-drip-dripping of moisture from the leaves. The path was zigzagging back and forth now, up and down – one minute we'd be pulling ourselves up a steep rise, hanging onto handfuls of ferns; the next we were slithering down again, our feet slipping and sliding in squishy black mud.

Rich rounded a bend and stopped as abruptly as if he'd walked into a wall . . . and at the same time I felt a sudden breeze on my face and a mist of fine droplets on my skin. 'What is it? What's –' And then I saw what he had seen, and my jaw dropped.

The ground fell away in front of us, the path we were on vanishing into nothingness. On the far side I could see a steep, forested slope – fifty metres away, at least – and just make out the path again, winding away into the trees. But between us and the path was a void – a roaring chasm filled with a floating mist of spray. And to our right, frothing, foaming, plunging down in a rampant cataract: a waterfall. It was as wide as the gorge itself: a thundering wall of water falling hundreds of metres to crash into an invisible pool far below.

We'd reached the River Ravven – and a dead end.

Rich met my eyes through the swirling spray, his face grim. We both knew what this meant: back-tracking two hours at least the way we'd come, and then a wet, slippery scramble down the mountain through dense rainforest, with no trace of a path. And then what?

Suddenly Gen spoke up beside me, sounding so like her old self that I almost toppled over into the chasm. 'Look, Adam – over there.'

Leaning over at a crazy angle, half hidden by fern fronds and moss, was a signboard like the one there'd been at the ford downriver. I squinted at it through the swirling spray – and grinned. *Rainbow Bridge*.

'Well, we've come the right way.' Rich was battling to sound cheerful.

'And Gen's more like herself again.' Kenta was right: Gen's cheeks were pink and her eyes bright, but her gown was drenched and weighted down at the hem with mud, and she was shivering. 'The sun's come out,' she said, hugging herself and trying to smile, 'look at the rainbow!'

Sure enough, a rainbow had sprung out just above where we were standing, so close I felt I could almost reach out and touch it. The intensity of the after-noon sunlight slanting through the gully far above picked out the colours with picture-book brightness: a solid arc of red, orange, yellow, green, blue and violet spanning the gorge from one side to the other. The

246

girls gazed at it in wonder, but Rich gave it a single dismissive glance and moved on to more practical things. 'So there's the rainbow – but where's the bridge?'

He was right – there was no trace of a bridge anywhere. Cautiously, I leaned as far out as I dared and peered over the drop. Nothing. Scanned the banks: still no sign.

'I guess with all this water around, it must have rotted away,' said Jamie gloomily.

'Unless . . .' The dreamy look was back in Gen's eyes, and Rich watched her warily. 'Unless the rainbow . . .'

'Unless the rainbow what?'

She gave him an embarrassed smile. 'Nothing – sorry. I'm just being stupid.'

'Well,' piped up Hannah, 'do you want to know what *I* think? *I* think *that's* the bridge.'

'What? Where?' We all stared wildly around, hoping a swing-bridge had magically materialised out of nowhere.

'There.' Hannah pointed – and I realised with a lurch of horror what she meant . . . and that she was right. She was pointing at the rainbow.

'It can't be,' whispered Kenta. But we knew it was.

I felt as if my stomach was in vertical free-fall along with the water. 'If it is,' I croaked, 'if Hannah's right – we need to move fast. Look at the angle of the sun. It's not going to be around for long, and once it's gone . . .' I gulped.

Jamie was looking green. 'And then there are the clouds . . .'

Weevil made a soft chittering sound – or it could just have been his teeth chattering.

'Well,' I said, 'either Hannah's right, or she's not. And there's only one way to find out.' Cautiously I picked my way up the slippery bank towards the end of the rainbow. As I'd expected, it faded as I drew nearer, and by the time I'd scrambled up to where I remembered it being, it had vanished altogether. 'There's a platform here,' I called down to the others. 'A wooden platform, big enough for us all to stand on. It must be here for a reason.'

They clambered up to join me. Rich stood, arms folded, scowling across the chasm. 'So where's the rainbow now?' There was a definite note of relief in his voice.

'The sun's gone behind a cloud,' Jamie pointed out. And as he spoke, the sun beamed out again . . . and the bridge materialised in front of us.

From this angle it was colourless, like a bridge of translucent glass, or cloud. It started just in front of the platform, and arched up and away until it vanished in the spray. It was about a metre wide.

Suddenly my mouth felt very dry. 'Well, here goes.' I stretched out my left foot, and lowered it tentatively onto the bridge. It went right through as if it wasn't there. I lost my balance, teetering on the edge of the platform, my arms flailing like a wind-mill, the dizzying drop spinning sickeningly beneath me . . . and then a strong hand grabbed me by the scruff of my neck and hauled me back to safety.

'So much for that,' said Rich gruffly. 'Looks like you were wrong, Hannah.'

Hannah was gazing out over the gorge, her eyes very round and solemn. She didn't reply. Tiger Lily was snuggled in her arms . . . and then she wasn't. With a wriggle and a squirm she leapt down onto the platform, gave Richard a single haughty glance, stalked to the edge of the chasm . . . and over it.

Hannah let out a little shriek – and then we were all silent, gaping.

Tiger Lily was strolling up and over the rainbow bridge as if it was made of solid concrete. For a moment she was silhouetted at the highest point of the arch; then she had disappeared over the other side, leaving us all staring after her with our mouths open.

'Right,' said Rich, his jaw set. 'We know it's possible. So . . .' he stepped forward.

'Do be careful, Richard,' quavered Gen. 'Maybe it's only strong enough to take light weights . . .' Richard scowled at her. One foot reached out to the bridge, prodding experimentally – but I noticed he kept his weight well back. And just as well.

Gen sighed, the sound almost drowned by the thundering of the water. Kenta shot her a rueful smile. 'Maybe that's how it got its other name – the Bridge of Sighs.'

'Thanks, Kenta – that's real useful,' growled Rich sarcastically. 'And watch out, for goodness' sake, Weevil – if you jump about like that you'll fall over the edge – and I'm not going in after you.'

Blue-bum was hopping and skipping about as if he'd gone crazy, pointing at us each in turn and chattering away nineteen to the dozen. It made me feel giddy seeing him cavorting so close to the edge of the platform . . . and then suddenly I realised he wasn't *on* the edge, he was *over* it – leaping up and down on the bridge itself, solid as a rock.

'So – he can cross it, too,' said Rich thoughtfully, as Weevil disappeared onto the other side. 'Why can Tiger Lily cross, and Weevil, but not the rest of us? And what set him off like that, I wonder?'

'It was what Kenta said about the Bridge of Sighs,' Gen said.

'The Bridge of Sighs,' repeated Jamie. 'The Bridge of Sighs . . . do you have to *sigh* while you're crossing?' He rolled his eyes and breathed gustily through his mouth to demonstrate, then poked one toe at the bridge . . . and through it.

'No, silly!' chirped Hannah. '*I* know what it is – and Tiger Lily knew before *anyone*. It's not the Bridge of Sighs – it's the Bridge of *Size*!'

'Huh?' said Rich.

But before we could say anything else – before we could even begin to stop her – Hannah had scampered out across the roaring void and over it, laughing back at us over her shoulder.

GEN'S DREAM

Kenta crossed next, then Gen. 'It's you now, Jamie,' said Rich, grinning down at him, 'though I guess it depends what kind of *size* it goes on.'

Blushing, Jamie moved to the edge of the platform, then stopped. 'Well, hurry up,' said Rich. 'Don't stand there all afternoon admiring the view! The sun's moving fast, and there are two of us still to go!'

'It's just . . .' I could barely hear Jamie over the roar of the water, '. . . it doesn't look awfully . . . solid.'

He was right – it didn't. My guts were churning at the thought of crossing – and as Jamie had said, what if the sun went behind a cloud?

'Just do it!' growled Rich. 'The longer you hang about, the more danger there is of the sun disappearing when you're halfway over. Hurry *up*, for crying out loud!'

Jamie shuffled reluctantly forward, his arms outstretched like a tightrope walker. He took one tiny step . . . then another, and another. Then he stopped. From where we were standing, it looked almost as if he was suspended in mid-air.

We waited. But Jamie was frozen, immobile on the bridge.

I cupped my hands round my mouth and yelled across to him. 'Jamie – kneel down! Crawl – you'll feel safer!' For a moment I thought he hadn't heard me. Then he sagged at the knees, sinking down till he was on all fours and crawling forward with agonising slowness until he vanished over the top. Still we waited, Rich muttering impatiently, until we saw him arrive safely on the other side, the girls all over him.

Rich turned to me with a grin. 'So, Adam: you or me?'

We eyeballed each other, dead level. I had no idea who it would be – Rich looked heavier, but I was maybe a centimetre or so taller. 'I'll be last, I bet,' said Rich with a swagger. 'I'm bigger, and stronger too. Go on – and make it quick!'

Warily, I made as if to step out onto the bridge – but my foot went clean through it, just like before.

To my relief, Rich didn't waste time arguing – and once he was on the bridge, he crossed it at a trot. I glanced up at the sun slanting over the bluff. There wouldn't be more than a minute or two before it disappeared – already, it had a blinding intensity that meant I had only moments left.

I took a deep breath, readied myself . . . and the second Rich was over, tested the bridge with my foot. This time, instead of emptiness, I could feel it under my boot, slightly yielding, but solid. Arms out for balance, trying not to look down, I walked out over the abyss. I could hear the thumping of my heart over the roaring of the falls . . . but the surface of the bridge was firm underfoot, almost bouncy, like a trampoline strung extra tight.

I reached the top. The shimmering surface curved downwards now, and I felt a sickening lurch of vertigo, as if I was toppling forward. Then a desperate shout reached me over the thunder of the water: 'Adam – *run!*'

I looked up – and saw with a stab of horror that the last sliver of sun was disappearing behind the cliff. Where seconds before there'd been a glare of light, now there was a chilling pall of shadow, only the tiniest edge of dazzling brightness still visible above it.

Panic ripped through me. I flung myself desperately towards the bank with huge, driving strides, my feet sinking deeper with every step as the bridge dissolved with terrifying speed beneath me. The torrent roared in my ears like a ravenous beast – I was running on nothing, stepping on air – I gave one last frantic leap, feeling the faintest resistance as my foot shot downwards into space – then threw my body forwards like a long-jumper, hands outstretched in a desperate grab for the bank I knew was still far beyond reach.

Then I was falling, a last thought spinning crazily through my brain: *So this is how it feels to die.*

Time spooled into slow motion, every second stretching into an eternity, freeze-frame following freeze-frame. Then unbelievably – impossibly – my hands were closing on something as I fell, something coiling out like a rope flung into mid-air – I was gripping it with every atom of strength I possessed –

falling, falling – then a massive jerk almost wrenched my arms from their sockets and I smashed face-first into the fern-covered cliff below the path and hung there, my legs dangling over the void.

Real time snapped back into place, seconds thudding by with each beat of my heart. My hands were locked onto the rope like steel clamps – but it wasn't a rope, it was a creeper, wet with spray and slippery as soap. I realised with a surge of horror that my weight was pulling me gradually downwards, centimetre by slow centimetre.

Then the creeper gave a jerk and I was hoisted upwards, my face scraping through mud and foliage and my feet kicking against rock . . . I flopped forward onto the forest floor and hugged it as if I'd never let go.

We walked on, leaving the sound of the falls far behind us, the ground underfoot growing gradually drier. At last it was too dark to see the path, though the trees had thinned and we could see occasional patches of sky.

Rich, who was leading, slowed and stopped. 'I vote we set up camp here for the night. We can afford a rest – nobody's going to be crossing the bridge till morning, that's for sure. And I'm whacked.'

No one was about to argue, we were all too tired. We wolfed down the last of the bread and some fruit, unrolled our sleeping bags, and settled ourselves down for the night.

I fell instantly into a bottomless sleep – and then,

what felt like seconds later, jolted awake again, my heart hammering. What had woken me? I lay still, listening. I could hear the tiny sounds of the forest – rustles, a faint hooting, the gurgle of a stream far below in the valley. The clearing was bathed in a strange, coppery light; I could see the bright glow of a full moon like a lamp above me, shining through the shifting leaves.

Something – a stone or a twig – was digging into my hip. I turned over onto my side and wriggled to get comfortable. Closed my eyes and breathed deeply, trying to relax. But it was no use – every sense was on the alert.

And then it came again – and I knew instantly it was what had woken me. Laughter, coming from Gen's sleeping bag. Something about the sound chilled me to the bone. It was an odd sort of giggling, with a falseness about it . . . I propped myself up on one elbow, frowning. She was murmuring now – talking in her sleep. Snatches of words spilled out into the still air: 'Come . . . water . . .' a sigh, then another soft giggle, and, very clearly: 'rainbow!'

And suddenly Gen was sitting bolt upright, her hair a wild tangle and her eyes huge and frightened in a face as white as paper.

'Gen?' She whipped round to face me with a gasp. 'It's only me – Adam. What's the matter? Did you have a nightmare? You were babbling away to yourself . . .' I was trying to sound casual and comforting, but I couldn't shake a deep feeling of unease.

'I'm fine.' Her voice shook slightly. 'It's just . . .

I had the strangest dream . . .' She shuddered, pulling the sleeping bag closer round her shoulders.

'Tell me.' The feeling of dread was growing with every word.

She glanced round at the sleeping shapes of the others with an expression that looked almost like shame. 'It's silly, really.' She was whispering so softly I could hardly hear her. 'I dreamed I was doing the walk again, the whole way we've come . . . every step. And *he* was with me.' I didn't need to ask who she meant. 'At first, I thought it was my dad – he was so gentle and caring. And by the time I saw who it really was, it didn't seem to matter, because he was being really, really kind – helping me over the difficult places and laughing with me as if it was all a wonderful adventure. Having him there was lovely, soothing and safe, as if someone was sort of . . . *stroking my mind*.'

I felt the hairs on the back of my neck rise. 'Go on.'

'We crossed Rainbow Bridge . . . and then he asked how much further we had to go.'

'What did you tell him?' But I didn't want to hear the answer.

'I told him . . . all the way to the Cliffs of Stone.'

'And then?'

'Then he laughed – but it was a different laugh. It turned into black bats that flapped up to the sky and blotted out the stars . . . everything was darkness and echoing with his laughter . . . and . . . and . . .'

'Yes, Gen?' I asked as gently as I could.

'Then I woke up.' Her voice was as small and

lost-sounding as a little child, and her face was wet with tears. 'It was only a dream, wasn't it, Adam? Tell me it was . . . please?'

THE DOOR BETWEEN
TWO WORLDS

I shook the others roughly awake. 'Quick – Rich, Kenta. Up, Hannah – now! We have to get moving – and fast.' I was cramming my sleeping bag into my pack as I spoke.

Rich gawked at me, his hair rumpled and his eyes bleary with sleep. 'What –'

'Karazeel knows where we are – and where we're headed. He got into Gen's head while she was sleeping . . .' I didn't need to say more. Richard was out of his sleeping bag in a flash, ripping through the campsite like a whirlwind, stuffing things willy-nilly into his bag.

'I'm sorry,' said Gen in a tiny voice.

'It's not your fault,' said Jamie staunchly, pulling on his boots. 'You were vulnerable, after what happened in Shakesh.'

'I always wondered what it would be like to be beautiful,' Gen whispered. 'But if I hadn't looked like this, he'd never have noticed me – and this would never have happened. Oh, how I wish . . .'

'No point wishing,' growled Rich, slinging his pack over his shoulder. 'The one wish we had, we used up.'

He glared at her, no doubt remembering what we'd used the wish for.

Less than five minutes later we were hurrying along the path in tense silence. I had an almost irresistible urge to look back over my shoulder – an uncomfortable sense of being watched, or followed, even though I knew it couldn't be true. Rich must have felt the same. He slowed slightly and muttered over his shoulder: 'I've been thinking, Adam – they won't come this way. What we said last night holds true – the ravine's impassable till the sun rises. They'll cross at the ford – knocking together a new ferry won't take Karazeel's merry men two minutes. They'll come down the north road, and intercept us at the Cliffs of Stone. Our only chance is to get there before them.' Rich always seemed in his element with practical stuff – the more dangerous the better. I nodded agreement, not saying what was in my mind: that getting to the cliffs before our pursuers was one thing . . . but finding the doorway back to the safety of our own world might be another.

The twin moons of Arakesh were high in the sky and side by side when we set off, and full. The effect was spectacular – like two glowing lamps in the sky, one silvery-white, one bronze. The light they shed made it almost as bright as day, with a strange metallic lustre that paved the path with gold.

We hurried on, Jamie puffing and panting at the rear, the girls in the middle, and Hannah hanging onto my hand, stumbling with tiredness. I gave her a grin and hoisted her onto my back, and we made faster progress.

Soon we were out in the open. Far below, gleaming in the moonlight, I could see the coppery thread of the River Ravven winding away to the sea. The ground on either side of us was becoming steeper, rising almost vertically to the right and falling away on the left. The path had narrowed, and it would be easy to lose our footing. And if we did . . . I glanced down, and my stomach turned over at the sheer drop below. I wondered how visible we'd be from the ford, silhouetted against the cliff face in the moonlight.

At last the path started to descend, and I saw the welcome shadow of trees ahead. 'I'm betting that's the fringes of the forest outside Arakesh,' said Rich in a low voice. 'And if I'm right, it means we're nearly there.'

We hurried on, grateful for the shelter of the trees. The moonlight faded as the twin moons vanished over the horizon behind us, and I realised it must be almost dawn. As the sky slowly lightened, my sense of urgency grew stronger. It was as if I could sense an evil presence growing closer, grey shapes materialising like wraiths out of the misty light. 'Rich,' I muttered, 'we must hurry.'

We picked up the pace till we were almost running, stumbling along at a jog for as long as we could, then slowing to catch our breath before pushing on again. The forest had dwindled away to nothing now and we were in the open, feeling horribly exposed but making faster time. Some deep instinct was driving me on, urging the others to hurry. It was more than fear of the Faceless, or whatever might be hunting us – it was a feeling that we were facing some strange deadline I didn't even begin to understand . . . racing the sunrise . . . and if we were too late, everything would be lost.

Far away over the sea the sky turned grey, then the purplish colour of an old bruise. Purple shaded to pink, then gold, a pearly whiteness, and finally the clear blue of a new day. We could see the forest spread out below us now like a nubbly black carpet. Somewhere, hidden deep among the trees, was the road to the north; and somewhere on that road, growing closer, closer with every minute that passed, were the Faceless. I could feel them.

Though the sun hadn't yet risen, the tiny clouds over the sea were lit from beneath like bright slits in the sky. I realised the path had disappeared – we were moving through rough tussock along the foot of the sheer cliff that reared endlessly above us.

Without slowing his pace, Rich pointed. My heart lifted. Far away to our left, indistinct in the morning mist, but unmistakable, was the walled city of Arakesh. We broke into a run, Tiger Lily and Weevil bounding along beside us. Panting, staggering under Hannah's weight, I saw the clouds had turned crimson and the first brilliant rim of sun had crept over the horizon, turning the sea to blood.

Rich stopped so suddenly I almost cannoned into him. His face was rosy from the glow of the rising sun, but bleak with despair. 'Look,' he said in a hollow voice. 'There – to the left of the city. Between the edge of the forest and the city walls . . .'

I saw them, and my heart turned to ice. They were pouring from the shadows of the distant trees like ants, flowing towards us over the open ground in a tide as swift and unstoppable as the sea. They were almost too far away to see, too far away to count . . . and the forest still lay between us. But they were coming – and coming fast.

We stumbled on. The sun wrenched itself from the sea and leapt free into the sky. Birds began to sing.

And there it was at last. The standing stone. The low, moss-covered rock. The entry point to Karazan – and the gateway between the worlds. It was here somewhere. But *where*?

'It has to be the stone,' Rich panted; 'it's *got* to be!' The standing stone reared up in front of us, its pitted surface pink in the glow of the sun. It was the size and shape of a door, with a rounded top like an arch. If you imagined a magic portal, the standing stone was exactly how you'd expect it to be.

'You're right – it must be.' Jamie advanced on the stone with an enquiring, scientific air, and rapped on it with his knuckles. 'Ouch!' he said, sucking them. 'It's solid rock, that's for sure.'

I walked all round it, examining every millimetre. Looking for something – anything – any clue as to how it might open. 'A doorknob,' I muttered, 'a rune – a sign of some sort . . .'

'Maybe there's a password,' suggested Gen hesitantly. 'Like *open sesame*, or something?'

Jamie stood in front of the stone, his back to the sun. His shadow stretched tall on the surface of the rock, looking very imposing. He reached up both arms and said impressively: 'Open sesame!'

Nothing happened.

Weevil chattered anxiously and turned to face downhill, in the direction of the forest. It was too soon, no matter how fast they were moving, but I knew he was watching and listening for the first signs of the Faceless. He looked up at me, chittering; then hopped away to the edge of the forest and scampered up the trunk of the nearest tree. Hard, nut-like fruit pattered to the ground, autumn leaves drifting down like butterflies – and moments later there was a rustling in the upper branches, and his furry head popped out of the canopy. 'Looks like Weevil's on lookout,' I said to Rich. 'Good thinking, Blue-bum!'

'I know!' said Kenta excitedly. 'There'll be a clue on the map – or even on the old parchment, like before!' Her hands shaking with excitement, she hauled them out and we unrolled them, our hearts in our mouths.

The parchment was blank.

'The map . . .' More of the map had been revealed by our progress – much more. Rainbow Bridge was marked – and best of all, the Cliffs of Stone – there was even an oval for the standing stone, and a tiny circle for the mossy rock. There wasn't so much detail anywhere else – it must be significant! And it meant we were definitely in the right place.

But there was no mention of a portal, or how to open it.

'Think, everyone – *think!* We haven't got much time . . .'

My mind was racing – in circles. *Portal . . .* where had I heard that word before?

The others moved round the rock, pressing, tapping, muttering who knew what. Jamie was over at the mossy stone, trying to peer under it, his bum in the air. Tiger Lily was soaking up the morning sun, completely unconcerned.

It was something to do with last time . . . it must have been. Last time we'd been to Karazan . . . or that first time, on my own . . .

Yes! It was on the porch of Argos and Ronel's cottage! I'd overheard them talking – but what was it they'd said? I racked my brains. Something about the *fourth span*, whatever that was, and *the portal* – though I'd thought they just meant some dumb gate in Arakesh – and *sunbalance*. That was it: *You know as well as I that it is not until sunbalance that the portal opens, and that is eight moons hence . . .*

The others were standing in a semicircle round me, staring at me. I must have been talking aloud . . . and by the looks on their faces, they'd not only heard what I said, but understood what it meant. The end of the road.

Jamie spoke very slowly. 'So the portal only opens at one particular time of year: sunbalance, whatever that is. That was eight months away when we were last here – just over two months ago.'

Rich's face was very grim. 'You don't need maths extension to work that out. The portal will open in four months – and that's four months too late for us.'

'Five and a bit,' said Jamie automatically, looking sick.

'So we're trapped,' Gen whispered.

Suddenly there was a screeching alarm call from Weevil's tree – a shrill jibbering shriek. 'They're coming! Quick – hide!' hissed Rich. I looked wildly around for some kind of shelter – but we were pinned against the cliff face like animals at bay, with no hope of escape.

Branches were swaying wildly as Weevil swung through the canopy, downhill and away from us, towards our pursuers. Kenta and Gen were huddled in the deep shadow behind the standing stone, Hannah between them, trying to shield her with their bodies. Jamie was clearly visible behind the smaller rock, which didn't even begin to conceal him. Rich faced the forest, fists clenched, teeth bared in a snarl of defiance. He wasn't going down without a fight.

I saw the first grey shadow between the tree trunks; then another, and another. They must be running, but to me they seemed to be drifting towards us as silently and swiftly as dead leaves blowing in the wind. Nothing would stop them now.

There was a chittering shriek and a commotion in the forest canopy, as if the upper branches were being rocked and shaken. *Weevil* – but what was he doing?

And suddenly the grey figures were slowing, weaving, slipping, sliding – falling. Weevil was swinging through the trees ahead of them, shaking the branches so the hard nuts fell on the Faceless like hailstones, turning the forest floor into a sliding mass of rolling marbles. The cloaked figures hissed with rage, ducking away from the missiles firing down at them, their arms raised above their hooded heads to protect them. But still they came on. I turned blindly away, my only thought to join the girls and somehow protect them – even though I knew it was hopeless.

And then I saw Tiger Lily. She was walking daintily towards the rock where the girls were crouching . . . and past it, into the deep shade. There was something purposeful in the way she was moving . . . something that made me watch her.

She headed straight for the cliff face, to where the shadow of the standing stone cast a stark black rectangle on the rock's surface. Walked into it – and vanished.

I stared. And then, in a blinding second of clarity, I knew.

The portal wasn't the standing stone. It was its shadow – the shadow cast on the cliff by the rising sun, the size and shape of an arched doorway. Except it wasn't the size of a door any more – it was knee-high, and shrinking fast as the sun rose. Soon it would be gone.

'Kenta, Gen – to the cliff! Quick – *run!*'

I grabbed Hannah by the arm and dragged her to where Tiger Lily had disappeared. Threw her at the narrow opening, hearing Kenta's shocked gasp . . . but the portal swallowed Hannah without a trace. Gen and Kenta goggled at each other, then bent and squeezed through into the darkness.

'Jamie!' I yelled. 'Over here!' He crawled towards me from his hiding place on hands and knees like a pull-along toy, and scuttled straight into the opening at the speed of light.

Rich was still standing with his back to us, frozen like a boxer with fists raised, watching the Faceless advance. With every second the distance between them was closing – and so was the portal. '*Rich!*' I shouted. '*Come here! We've found it!*' He half turned, the grim determination on his face giving way to confusion, baffled disbelief – and the beginning of hope. I dropped onto my stomach and wriggled through the opening, feeling the weight of the warm rock above me, then squirmed round, peering through the gap, screaming '*Rich! Weevil! Run – before it's too late!*'

At last Rich's face cleared. With the first grey shapes almost on him, he wheeled and pelted for the cliff. But the portal was almost closed – he wasn't going to make it! He was at the standing stone, then past it into shadow, arms pumping, breath rasping, the Faceless on his heels. A hand reached out for him, clawing at his cloak –

He launched himself forward into the air in a desperate, skidding dive, arms outstretched, and slid halfway into the opening. I'd ducked away into the darkness to give him room, but now I saw he was stuck fast, the weight of the cliff pressing down

267

on him, inching lower, lower with every second . . .

Rich struggled and thrashed, his legs kicking frantically on the ground outside, his fingers tearing at the ground in front of him for grip . . . but he didn't budge. Then suddenly he lay still. He looked up at me, his face ashen: one desperate, pleading glance. 'Adam . . . my ankle . . . they've got me . . .' He buried his face in the ground with a moan of despair.

Then I was on my feet – bending to grab his wrists – flinging my entire weight backwards with strength I never knew I had. For an endless moment nothing happened; then Rich shot through the gap like a cork from a bottle. I landed flat on my back with my breath knocked out and Rich sprawled on top of me like a sack of potatoes.

Struggling for breath I shoved him off and was back at the opening in a flash. I squeezed my cheek against the cold earth floor and squinted out . . . into a confusion of swirling grey cloaks, as if a choking, stifling fog had descended on the world outside. A whisper of fabric flicked through the tiny gap, brushing my skin like the breath of a corpse, reeking of death and decay. Coughing and retching, I rolled away, my hands over my face.

Someone was shouting, over and over again, his voice hoarse and echoing: '*Blue-bum! Blue-bum!*' Someone was sobbing.

The last sliver of light vanished, and we were in total darkness.

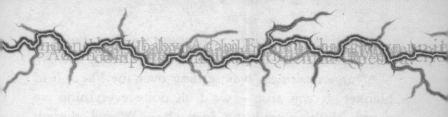

THROUGH THE PORTAL

'Where are we?' Gen's voice, small and frightened.

'At Quested Court?' suggested Rich.

'No.' Hannah was very definite. 'It doesn't smell like home.'

'Maybe we're in some sort of limbo.' Jamie was the only one who sounded remotely cheerful. 'A kind of world-between-the-worlds?'

'What about Weevil?' My voice sounded strangely flat.

There was silence before Jamie spoke: 'He was way up in the trees. They'll never catch him.'

'I expect he'll go back to Chattering Wood and join the others,' Gen said hopefully. 'It's probably all for the best. How would we ever have explained . . .'

A small hand snuggled itself into mine. 'Don't be sad, Adam. You did your best. It wasn't your fault.'

'Yeah – it was you who found the portal. *And* pulled me through.'

'No! Tiger Lily found it first . . . but Adam found it second.'

'Looks like you were wrong about it only opening at that sunbalance-whatsit time, Adam. Luckily for us.'

A huge weariness was settling over me like a lead blanket. It was true – we'd all done everything we could. Nothing could be done about Weevil, though the knowledge made me sick at heart.

For the time being at least, we were safe. I rummaged in my pack and found my torch; flicked the switch, and played the dim beam around the darkness. We were in some kind of a cavern. Apart from the torchlight, it was completely dark, and utterly silent.

Gen yawned. 'I don't know about the rest of you, but I'm exhausted. I feel as if I've lived a hundred lifetimes in the last two days – and we've hardly slept. Can't we rest for a while, and worry about where we are later?'

So we snuggled down together in a nest of sleeping bags, Tiger Lily's rhythmic purring a lullaby rocking us almost instantly to sleep.

I opened my eyes to the dim glow of daylight. It must have been night when we arrived . . . wherever we were. I untangled myself from the others, trying not to disturb them, and sat up, staring around.

We'd fallen asleep at the back of a cave the size of a small room. Behind us – where we'd come from – was a wall of rock, smooth and featureless. There was no sign of an opening anywhere. The floor was bare earth, cool and slightly damp to the touch. There was a faintly musty smell. At the far end of the cave was what looked like a narrow passageway, a fissure in the rock . . .

It was the source of the light. I clambered out of my sleeping bag and crept towards it, wondering whether to wake the others. I squeezed through and found myself in a larger chamber, with a huge boulder almost blocking the entrance. There was a gap at the top where a shaft of bright sunlight beamed through. If I jumped and grabbed the ledge with my hands, I could pull myself up onto the other side. Then I'd come back and report to the others.

I padded across the floor; readied myself; jumped, and grabbed. For a moment my hands slipped, then with a grunt and a heave I was up and through, rolling out into a tangle of thorn bushes. I struggled free, twigs catching in my ragged clothes; then staggered to my feet, squinting in the bright light.

My mouth dropped open. I knew where I was. I rubbed my eyes, certain I must be dreaming . . . then took a few uncertain steps forward to where the ground dropped away into the valley, knowing what I would see.

There below me was the familiar roof of Highgate, patched and peeling in the morning sun. There were the smudged windows with their ragged, threadbare curtains drawn untidily across; the shrubbery; the tall white gate; the concrete porch.

I could even smell breakfast – the stodgy smell of lumpy porridge and the tang of burnt toast. My head spun.

I heard the distant sound of a car engine, coming

closer. It roared up to the white gate and stopped. A figure climbed out and opened the gate, and the car drove through. The wheels crunched on the gravel drive. If it had been Q and Shaw, or even King Karazeel in a stretch limo, I'd hardly have been surprised. I felt like nothing would surprise me ever again. But it did.

Three figures – two policemen and a policewoman – got out and climbed the steps to the front door. Stood there for a moment, shuffling papers. Police – at *Highgate*? A hand reached out for the doorbell. I could hear the sound clearly in my mind, a sound I'd known all my life – the faint wheeze, then the off-key *boing* of the broken bell.

There was a long pause before the door opened a crack. I knew who it would be – Matron, her thin face tight with suspicion. She didn't like unexpected guests. Perched high on my rock, I felt myself grin. She'd like these ones even less. They'd be out on their ears in no time flat.

I was wrong. The door opened further, and they disappeared inside. I waited a few minutes, eaten up by curiosity. What could have happened? Who'd called the police? Could it have been Matron? And why? But time dragged by, and they didn't come out. I should go back and see if the others were awake – they'd panic if they woke and found one of us gone. I started to turn . . . then froze as the door opened again. Stared down with my mouth open as the police escorted Matron to the car and ushered her inside.

Then the doors slammed shut and the police car drove away down the hill, the growl of its engine dwindling into silence.

EPILOGUE

I walked slowly down the wide staircase of Quested Court. I knew the way.

My hair flopped into my eyes, soft and smelling of shampoo. My jeans felt stiff and tight after my loose leggings. My stomach was stiff and tight, too, from non-stop eating – but that felt great.

I stopped for a moment on the landing, looking down, remembering . . .

The reaction of the others when I told them where we were, one wild theory following another, till eventually Jamie's was pronounced the most likely: '*You* found the portal, Adam – so it took us to *your* home. Magic's logical, like Kai says – but who ever said it was convenient?'

Gen's wail: 'Never mind why we're here – how do we get back to Quested Court?'

Hannah's reply, matter-of-fact to her; unbelievable to me: 'In Q's helipocter, of course.'

Me, in a croak: 'But . . . who'll drive it?'

And Hannah, with the air of one stating the obvious: 'The helipocter pirate.'

Sneaking past the tall white gates of Highgate,

ducking low so no one would see us, fighting a crazy urge to giggle . . .

The curious looks of passers-by as we waited at the phone booth to make the reverse-charge call to Q; how they'd nudged each other and avoided our eyes . . . all except one little girl about Hannah's age, who skipped up to us and chirped, 'Can I play too?'

Hannah's withering reply: 'This is *not* a game!'

The taxi pulling up to take us to the airport . . . Q jumping down from the helicopter, hugging us as if we were all his children, not just Hannah . . .

The expression on Q's face, even more wonderful than the helicopter ride.

Now Q had asked to speak to me, on my own.

I knocked softly on the library door. Almost at once it opened and Hannah peeped round. Her eyes were sparkling, and her face had a strange, secretive expression that fizzed with excitement. I grinned to myself: she was up to something.

She skipped in ahead of me and scrambled up into the big leather armchair. At once, the little grey kitten hopped onto her lap and began to purr.

Q smiled at me, his eyes very warm behind the smeary specs. 'Ah – Adam. My boy.' Off came the glasses; a quick polish on the edge of his frayed jumper, and they were on his nose again, cloudier than ever. 'This visit hasn't turned out quite how I'd planned, what with . . . well . . . one thing and another. But now it's back on track.' He smiled. 'A special dinner for you all tonight – if you have room

275

for more food, that is. Specially chosen by Hannah: chicken nuggets and chips, with – what was the dessert, Chatterbot?'

'Marshmallow and jelly ice cream, chocolate sauce, and hundreds and thousands,' Hannah recited with great satisfaction.

'Precisely,' said Q. 'And afterwards . . .'

'*Fireworks!* A special b . . . I mean, a special firework display to celeb . . . I mean, fireworks.' I narrowed my eyes suspiciously at Hannah. She gazed innocently back.

'But first, I have something for you. There will be presents too, of course . . .' I blinked at Q. What was he on about? 'But this . . . well, this is something rather different.'

Q held out his hand. In it was a newspaper. 'Happy birthday, Adam.'

Hannah gave a little wiggle of excitement. Huh? Not beginning to know what to think, I took the paper from Q and stammered my thanks. *Was* it my birthday? And trust old Q – a newspaper for a birthday present!

I glanced down at it, pretending to be pleased. A mugshot of Matron stared back at me. Above it was the date: 22 September. Dazed, I read the headline: *Serious Fraud Squad Swoops.* Tried to read the small print below, but the letters mixed themselves up into a jumble that didn't even begin to make sense.

I realised Q was talking. 'It seems Miss Filcher was aptly named, Adam.'

'Pilcher,' corrected Hannah.

'*Filcher*,' repeated Q with a smile. 'It appears she has been stealing funds from Highgate for years. Amounts adding up to hundreds of thousands – maybe more.'

'Did you . . .' I croaked.

Q smiled. 'No, Adam. Investigations have been underway for some time, I believe. But my evidence will doubtless be called for in due course, to strengthen the case against her – and I will be delighted to assist. And there's an additional factor: a young lad has disappeared from Highgate, and the police will be looking to your Matron for answers.

'But as far as you are concerned, Adam, the important thing is this: you will start the next year of your life as a brand new chapter, in the certainty that she will never return.'

I felt a smile spreading slowly over my face. But before I could say anything, there was a rustle and a thud and Tiger Lily hopped in through the open window. Hannah's face lit up. 'I've been wondering where you were,' she said sternly. 'Catching mouses, I bet. Look, Bluebell! Here comes your new friend!'

Tiger Lily took one look at the kitten curled up asleep on Hannah's lap, and her back arched. Her tail puffed out into a bottlebrush. Her eyes went triangular, and she advanced on the chair with slow, menacing steps.

'I'm afraid not, Hannah,' I said with a grin. 'Here comes trouble!'